BLUES HARP GREEN

Nicole Schubert

Earnest Parc Press

For my dad

THAT SUMMER...

Sometimes you meet someone. And they look at you and it's a thing. Like, somewhere inside you that is touched. Like your soul. That poetic memory thing. And it's like you were always connected. You've always known each other. Now. And before. And forever in the future. And it's like you were always traveling together through the galaxy and different universes. And your souls are connected always without time. And you love that person. And they love you. And sometimes they just make you happy for a minute. And then they're gone. In this now, this life. But that knowing of the connection makes you know everything will be okay.

–FRANCIE MILLS
(aka FM on the Radio Dial, Scream Queen, etc.)

1

Francie stared at the TV, not really paying attention. All she could think about was her knee. And how she hated it right now. And how she was going to have to work super hard to get it back to normal so she could play that tennis tournament next month. And get ranked high enough so she could go to nationals next summer. She could totally do it. Even if the doctor said she had to wait to play. Even if she didn't start playing till she was fourteen and no one believed she would ever be any good. She didn't care. Tennis was the only thing that mattered. The only thing she had any control over. The only thing that gave her freedom. And if her knee hurt because of torn cartilage, she'd just have to deal with it.

She squeezed her quad muscle hoping her knee wouldn't hurt. It did. Maybe if she imagined it better, it would heal faster. She squeezed it again, harder. It hurt even more.

Why did this have to happen?

She looked back at the TV and heard her mom turn on the blow dryer in the bathroom. She couldn't wait for her parents to leave. Then she could do her leg workout without them asking her ten million questions or trying to tell her it was a bad idea. Thank god her dad upgraded to two rooms so she had her own space. Sort of. She heard her mom's muffled voice yelling to her over the blow dryer. Why did she do that?

"What?!" Francie yelled back.

Her mom poked her head out, "Aren't you getting ready?" Then disappeared back into the bathroom and continued yelling, "It's going to be a great dinner. And it might be our last one in Austin. I think that nice actor is throwing it for the whole crew."

That made no sense. They'd still be there another four days, and they'd gone out to dinner every single night for the past two weeks. So why would this be the last dinner? But Francie knew her mom just wanted the three of them to be together. It was a backhanded guilt trip if she ever saw one, and as usual, it worked.

She pulled herself off the bed. The thought of disappointing either one of her parents was worse than going. Her dad was so happy she was there. He always missed them when he went on location for a movie. She missed him too; but sometimes, she hated him. Especially when he drank and became possessed by aliens and turned into that obnoxious guy she didn't know, who was loud, sarcastic and the life of the party and who couldn't remember anything the next day anyway, so what was the use? Those were the times she missed her dad the most. And they seemed to be a lot lately.

She looked in the mirror and pulled her long brown hair into a ponytail and stared at her semi-flat chest hidden behind the letters P-U-N-K on her pink tie-dyed shirt. Would anyone notice they were growing? Hopefully not. Too embarrassing. She hated when anyone noticed anything about her at all. She wondered why she wore this stupid shirt and put on her beanie.

Better.

At least she liked Austin. And could get out of the hotel. She didn't really care about the actors and the party, although it was cool that her dad worked on these big movies. There was always something happening, and he had tons of good stories that he loved to tell.

Her mom came out. "You aren't gonna wear your new shoes?" she asked cheerfully.

"I like my sneakers," Francie replied.

"And no lip gloss?"

"No, I'm fine."

"I feel naked without my lipstick," her mom said, coming up behind Francie and looking in the mirror. Side-by-side they looked like mom and daughter. She kissed Francie's head.

Francie pulled away, pulling her beanie further down, "Okay, okay."

Unlike Francie, her mom was beautiful with or without lipstick, which was the only makeup she wore anyway, so why did she have to give Francie such a hard time about not wearing any? Besides, it shouldn't be that big of a deal because her dad seemed to love her mom no matter what, even when her mom thought she got too fat from stress and when their crazy relationship blew up and she made him feel guilty for drinking and then he'd say mean things, like telling her she was fat and making her feel stupid. Francie figured it was probably because her mom put up with him and would never leave. Although lately, her mom didn't seem happy, and last week, she yelled that she couldn't "go on like this." He yelled back that he couldn't either, even though he probably wasn't as serious as she was.

Francie suddenly felt like she couldn't breathe and just wanted to get out.

Her dad poked his head in from the next room. "And how are my two gorgeous ladies tonight?" he said, as he gave her his biggest, most charming smile. "Ready to go?"

Actually, charm was his middle name and it got him far, in spite of the fact that Francie could see that watery look in his eye and knew he'd had at least one drink already. He loved her and sometimes, for a second, that was all that mattered.

The dinner was okay but the restaurant was loud and Francie's dad was getting louder to match, now that he'd had a ton of drinks. Francie sat tense, holding her breath as she watched him toasting the crew. She didn't dare move, afraid he'd say something even more embarrassing, as if bracing herself would help. She wondered if anyone else noticed how loud he was. Surely, they must. And that's probably why they looked at her with that smile. They felt sorry for her or agreed he should shut up and stop hogging the stage. There were plenty of actors there to do that. Didn't he know they were supposed to be the center of attention, not him?

"And here's to Mac, our fearless leader," Francie's dad toasted his boss, the director of the movie and an old friend. "And to the amazing little '64 Mustang parked out back that we'll be using for Friday's shoot. If anyone wants to go for a spin, we'll be out there in five."

Francie pushed her earbuds back in and turned up the volume as the crew cheered and toasted. He loved to brag about the cars he brought in for the film. He did a good job and everyone seemed to love him for it, but did he have to announce it to the world? She couldn't stand it anymore. She had to get out.

She spotted her mom at the other end of the place with the director's wife, Libby. They always hung out on location, probably mostly because Mac and her dad liked to work together and used to know each other in high school because they were both in punk bands. She didn't see Abigail though, Mac and Libby's daughter. That was good. Francie liked Abigail, but Abigail was so stupidly perfect it always made Francie feel not good enough.

Francie made a beeline for her mom and Libby and interrupted her mom, lying, "Someone's going back to the hotel and said they'd give me a ride."

"Really? You don't want to stay a little longer?" her mom asked, glancing over at Francie's dad.

Francie shook her head. "I just want to go back. I'm tired."

"Well, okay then, I guess we'll see you back at the hotel."

"Yup."

Her mom was probably relieved Francie was leaving so she wouldn't have to feel guilty and worry about Francie seeing her dad like this, as if it didn't happen all the time. Then, later, at home, she could get mad at him for drinking too much *again*.

"Hey, we might go to the outlet mall tomorrow," Libby said. "Abigail too. You should come with us. She'd love it if you did. I would too."

"Yeah, maybe," Francie lied again and gave Libby a kiss on the cheek.

There was no way she was going with them. She was going by that tennis club to use that ball machine again. She could stand in one spot and work on her strokes without running.

She turned to go and twisted a little too much. A sharp pain shot through her knee. She clenched her teeth, trying to hide it from her mom, and walked around the side of the restaurant to avoid everyone else. She held back the tears. There was no way the doctor was right. He said two months, but she was playing that tournament in Ventura next month, no matter what.

She heard her dad across the room and picked up her pace until, finally, she was outside.

Total relief.

2

The night was warm, and there were a lot of people out. It might take a while, but if Francie just went over and down Sixth Street, she'd be at the hotel with only one semi-scary part to go through. The rest was packed with people listening to live music in bars, one after another, so she knew she'd be safe. And entertained. And it was going to be great to get some kind of a workout, even if it was just walking.

She glanced back into the restaurant and saw that cute chestnut-brown-haired guy heading outside. Probably to smoke again. She'd seen him doing it before. He was the one that was probably her age, like he might be a junior in the fall, like her, or a senior. And he seemed friendly, chatting to the other smokers outside. And artsy. Like he was wearing a formal blue plaid jacket-slash-blazer, but then a worn "God Save the Queen" t-shirt and jeans and lace-up Vans. So he was weird. But cool.

She'd watched him and his two friends that day by craft service smoking a gazillion cigarettes. The friends seemed older, like maybe in college. But all three were totally funny and kept making up these stupid songs about everyone on the crew and making the craft service lady laugh. Then they started singing about how good her food was and she'd laugh even more.

The guy waved at Francie and smiled as he stepped outside, his bright-green eyes sparkling. And then, it happened. Their eyes met, and it was this crazy, weird intense thing. Like, wow. Blam. *Who are you?*

Francie smiled back and said, "I'm going back to the hotel," and instantly felt stupid. She turned quickly and walked away. Why the heck did she say that? *I'm going back to the hotel?* How dumb was that? She didn't even know him. But also, he was so...*something.*

He yelled after her, "Hey."

She waved again as if to say good-bye and just kept walking, picking up her pace. She couldn't talk to him. What would she say? He may be amazingly gorgeous and she'd promised herself to be less shy, especially around guys, but he was probably just being polite. But how would she know if she didn't talk to him?

Lame. That's what she was. Lame. And all because of the stupid all-girl school her parents sent her to. Total social death. She had no idea what to do around guys and hated her parents for it. Couldn't they see she felt weird enough already and cutting her off from normal people made it worse?

She wondered if the guy was in the band that was playing in the rodeo scene in the movie. Her dad called them the "teeny-bopper brigade" and said Mac knew their uncle from his days as a punk rocker. Her dad thought they actually had talent but that it meant nothing because it was impossible to make it in music and they were "lucky to be in the movie."

Anyway, who cared? And who cared if she just said the most stupid thing ever? She was going to find the perfect guy for her and hold out until she did. Someone cool and smart and funny, that she could totally be in love with, like Jimmy from that Bakersfield tournament who winked at her, even if he lived an hour away in Studio City and she never got to see him and told herself to forget him. At least, he gave her hope that there was someone out there.

And what were the chances that Green Eyes back there was that someone?

But that thing. When he looked at me. It was different. And weird.

Whatever. She wasn't going find out. Instead, she turned on her music, turned off the noise in her head and picked up her pace. Finally she was alone. And safe. Her knee hurt but she didn't care. It would stop soon, the more she walked.

She made her way towards the busy part of Sixth Street and could swear someone was behind her. She turned up the volume more. If she didn't look back, she'd be fine. Anyone could see she wanted to be left alone.

Finally, she reached the main area and started passing one live music bar after the next. She loved that there were so many people out. And loved walking through them, being a total stranger. Slowly that feeling that she didn't belong anywhere or that she'd never be a pro tennis player faded and in came the feeling that anything could happen and life was exciting. No one was judging her and she could be herself and soak up the happy electricity in the air.

She laughed at the people wearing cowboy hats—real cowboy hats! And was amazed to see them doing the Texas two-step in a corner saloon. For real!

She kept going, turning down the volume on her music to see if there was some band that she liked in one of the bars. Finally, she heard a grungy rock band and stopped. Her dad always listened to old-school rock and some of it had rubbed off on her, even though she'd never admit that to anyone. She listened for a few minutes. Not bad.

"It's gotta be pretty hard to hear with these on," said a slightly Aussie-accented voice in her ear.

Francie jumped back, and there was the cute guy—charm, green eyes and all, his smile beaming.

Francie's stomach flipped. "Yeah, I mean, no, I have the volume down," she said as she fumbled to get the earbuds out.

He took them playfully and put them to his ear, "Green Day?"

"Good ear."

"Good choice. Just the right amount of old school. I like it."

God, was he flirting? His smile said he was. He was flirting! Her heart raced. She took her earbuds back. "So, do you always follow strange girls?"

"Only when they blow me off when I'm trying to say hi," he teased.

"I didn't blow you off, I just...I didn't hear you," she lied.

"Aha, can't hear, listens to music on low. Hmmm, doesn't quite add up."

"Okay, okay, I just, I didn't want to bother you. I mean, I didn't want you to think I needed someone to walk me back." *Oh my god. Could it get any worse?*

"Oh, no, why would I do that? Mystery girl. Out adventuring. Amazing music. Warm summer night. Mmm. Not me."

She started to turn red. *God, why?* Every time she talked to a guy her emotions flared and her palms sweat and she turned *red.*

"I'm Chet, by the way," he said, holding out his hand.

"Francie, Francie Mills," she said, quickly wiping her hand and shaking firmly. Somewhere she'd heard that was a good thing to do.

"Yeah, you're Hank's daughter, right? The transportation coordinator."

How'd he know? Did he ask about her? No, he probably just remembered the last name. "Yup, that's me."

"He's a cool one. That old Thunderbird is totally sweet."

"Yeah, he finds some great cars," she nodded, not sure what else to say. "How about you? You someone's kid too?"

He laughed, "Well, I am someone's kid, but they're not exactly here."

"Oh, right," she said, embarrassed again.

"Actually, I'm um, kind of *in* the movie," he said, looking embarrassed now too. "I'm in this band with my brother Billy. Billy Jones?"

"Oh, yeah, I think I saw him at the dinner." So she was right! It was them!

"Yeah, the loud, obnoxious one who thinks he can tell me what to do cuz he's eighteen, which he does, which is why I'm here. Our uncle got us this gig during the rodeo scene. Actually, he's our godfather. And my brother thinks it's a big deal. Like it's gonna help us be famous or something." He laughed. And was so adorable.

"Oh, yeah, I heard about that scene. Cool!"

"Actually, it's quite lucky, and my brother is delusional," he said and then whispered, "because we're not so good. Somewhat scrappy actually. Don't tell anyone."

She laughed, "So no overnight rock star sensation for you?"

"Exactly."

Their eyes met. Her stomach shot all the way to her throat.

"So, hey, the real reason I was *stalking* you was because I was gonna go down by the river where the bats are."

"Bats?"

"Yeah, apparently, they live there for the summer. Completely harmless. Like to join me?"

"Me?"

"Yes, *you*. C'mon, I'm curious."

She glanced down Sixth Street towards the hotel wondering if she should go with him. Of course, she should! Why not? Her parents would never know, and more importantly, finally something good was happening! "Well,

I don't know if I can trust someone who follows strange girls," she teased.

"What can I say?"

No, what can I say? Francie Mills being followed by probably the cutest guy ever. With the cutest accent. From Australia! Or was it England? Or South Africa?! It didn't matter. It was so cute. *And exciting!* "Sure, yeah, why not? As long as the bats don't bite."

"I can vouch for the bats, on my honor," he said, holding up his hand. "But as for me?" He shrugged. She laughed, and he took her arm and led her back up Sixth Street, through the crowds milling about, drinking, listening to music, having a good time.

She felt like a kid at a carnival, all excited, but totally nervous and awkward too. Like she didn't even want to breathe. But he kept making silly comments about everything, which completely put her at ease.

How was this happening?

They rounded the corner off the main drag, and it quieted down quickly. There were mostly businesses and warehouses at first, and then, they came to a neighborhood with small houses, some with charming, colorful little porches and others run down. It was quiet, but she could see people inside watching TV and going about their usual Saturday nights.

"Hey, there's the river," Chet said and led them out of the neighborhood and down to the water. Thank god she wore her Chucks and not those flashy rhinestone sandals her mom bought her.

The river wasn't huge but seemed wide enough for freight boats to go down. Chet took her hand and led her under the bridge. His hand was warm and held hers tightly.

It was musty under the bridge, and she could definitely hear fluttering above.

"There they are. Our little fanged friends," he said with a devious smile. "Mwahahaaaaa."

She laughed. The bats fluttered. "You sure about this?" she asked.

"Don't worry. It's fine. Have a seat." He gestured to the ground as if it were a fancy couch, and they sat down.

He opened his jacket and pulled out a lone beer and a harmonica. "Another reason to come down here," he said and played a few bars. "It's quiet. So you don't have to worry about anything."

She got that. It was exactly how she'd felt in that crowd of strangers before. Not having to worry about other people and their judge-y eyes. She could be herself.

He played a song, kind of bluesy rock. And was good, and she wondered why he'd said they were scrappy. He sang a few bars every once in a while. Trying to get it right. Messing up. Laughing. Eyes meeting. Flirting. *Oh my god.* He was so cute.

And funny. And nice.

After the song, he did a little bow, and she applauded.

"That was great. I really liked it," she said, glad she didn't have to lie.

"Thanks. Hopefully our friends up there liked it, too."

"I'm sure they do."

He opened the beer and toasted, "To the bats!" And took a sip and offered her some.

She toasted, "To the bats!" She'd never drank before but took a sip. It was gross, but she didn't care. For once, she felt cool. And present. All at once. "So, what are you called?" she asked. "The band."

He smiled, looking slightly embarrassed, "Blues Harp Jones. For our surname. And harmonica, which is blues harp. I hate it."

"Aw, I like it. It's cool. And weird. So you remember."

He laughed, "Well good. Maybe it'll get us some fans. Or bats." He yelled up at the bats, "Hey, bats! We're Blues Harp Jones! Please love us!" He looked back at her, eyes laughing, sparkling, "It's true, we have no fans. Anywhere. Not even in The Valley. Or Encino, which is where we're from. Ever heard of The Valley?"

She nodded, "Conejo Valley, here," and raised her hand.

"Ah, a valley girl but not a *real* Valley Girl. More like a *rabbit* valley girl? But it's close."

She laughed, "Half an hour."

"Perfect." He smiled and looked happy they lived so close.

He also checked out her hair.

Her heart started to race. What did that mean?

"Yeah, Big in The Valley," he said. "Maybe someday. But right now, we're just kind of big in our carport." He toasted playfully and took another sip.

"But you're good. I mean, not that I know, but still. Right? That harmonica thing was awesome."

"Still needs work, I'd say."

It was also awesome how he got all shy about his music and wasn't at all stuck up. And then there was his adorable accent.

"So how long have you lived here?" she asked. "I mean, in the states. With your accent. In The Valley. I mean, how long have you lived in the states? You're English right?" *Oh, god. Awkward!*

He laughed, amused by her, thank god. "Half Australian. On our mom's side, though she moved here in high school. To Indiana. Still, I guess it rubs off a bit. Especially when we visit the relatives. Which we just did."

So cute!

"But enough about me. Let's talk about you, Miss Francis."

"Francine."

"Francine," he sang.

She blushed, "It's from this silly book my dad likes. Well, he likes the author."

"Salinger?"

She nodded, surprised he knew.

"So a literary transportation coordinator, huh? That's unique."

You're unique, she thought. "I guess."

She never met guys that talked about books. Or anything. Maybe it was the all-girl school. Or the tennis.

"He used to be a journalist," she said. "And in a band, too. Well, in high school. And college. Which is how he knows Mac. And he used to have a radio show."

"Nice."

"Yeah. But then he kind of just gave up on stuff, and now, he just kind of, I don't know, works a lot and gets bummed out and parties."

Wow. That was weird. She never talked about her dad. Ever.

Chet toasted, "To partying." He took an exaggerated swig and handed her the bottle. She did the same, laughing and spilling some of it. It felt good. A warm sensation ran down her arms and up into her neck. And it just felt amazing to do whatever and not think about it.

"You're funny," she said, handing him back the beer.

"Gots to be funny about serious things." He toasted again and took another swig.

"Yeah." Not that she ever did that but it sounded good.

"Besides, I can relate. My parents are always on the outs too. Breaking up. Getting back together. Breaking up. Saving the world. Not saving the world. Trying to save the world. Trying to save us. Dad moving to London to save the world. Mom making him feel guilty for leaving us to save the world. Then she does it herself. Like a competition. Billy bossing me around, hating Dad, trying to save Mom. Everybody miserable. Woohoo." He laughed and shook his head.

Wow, he wasn't at all relaxed talking about his own parents but he still managed to be funny about it, and she was just so relieved someone understood.

"And I noticed, about your dad," he said and got this weird concerned look.

Noticed what? That he was loud. And embarrassing. And a loser? No kidding.

"Yeah, whatever. It is what it is," she said. Shame. Stabbing in the heart.

"I mean, I noticed *you.*"

What?

"Like. You were done. Back there at the party."

"Oh, right," she said, suddenly confused. He noticed *her?*

Wow. Like her feelings were naked. He saw she was embarrassed about her dad.

This is why he followed her.

He understood.

The knife came out of her heart. And her heart swelled, in a good way.

"So what do *you* do, Miss Francine?" he asked, smiling, crinkly happy eyes, like he was trying to make her feel better.

The blood rushed to her cheeks and she shrugged, "Nothing?" She hated to talk about herself.

"No one does nothing."

"Well, I do stuff, but it's not very interesting," she said. *Not like you.*

"Like what?"

"Homework," she said, blurting out the first thing that came to mind.

"Homework, huh? Well, that's studious. And?"

And nothing. Except tennis. But she didn't want to tell him about tennis. Or how much she cared. And how it was the only thing that was all hers. That her dad couldn't ruin. Or take away. And how she wasn't that good yet. But she was going to be ranked. And play in college and be a professional. And then she'd feel good about herself and could tell him. But now, she'd just be embarrassed about how much she cared. Unless he could tell.

What if he can tell?

"And I sleep," she said.

"Sleep is excellent."

"And I eat and go to school. And that's it."

"That's it? A smart, Chucks-wearing girl like you? I don't believe it."

Oh my god, why was she trying to convince this amazing guy how lame she was?

"Ukelele player? Actress? Dolphin wrangler?" he said.

"Dolphin wrangler?" she laughed.

"I don't know. You gotta gimme somethin' here."

"Okay, tennis. I play tennis. And sometimes I make collages."

"Wait, what? Collages? Tennis?"

She hid her face.

"I knew you had something going on."

She shook her head and kept hiding her face.

"Well, I think tennis is pretty cool. In fact, I've been known to dabble. Me and my brother. And collages. To die for." He played a note on the harmonica and sang, "To die for."

She laughed and took her hands down.

"I'm serious," he said. "There's nothing like a good collage. In fact, in some cultures, the collage is a highly regarded art form."

She laughed. He was totally freestyling, but she was grateful he embraced her lameness.

"Anything else? Any other hidden talents?"

She shook her head.

"You sure?"

"Yes."

"Alright then, I guess that's it." He finished the beer and stood up, holding out his hand, "C'mon, I have a surprise for you."

"Surprise?" She let him pull her up and kiss her hand.

"Yup. And I think you'll like it."

"Okay."

"It's a club our uncle took us to last night. The guy's pretty cool so there shouldn't be an issue getting in. And this incredible guitar player is there. Junior Brown. You'll love him. *Very* old school."

"Well, I guess I'll have to trust you on that."

"I guess so. Bye vampires!"

"Bye," she chimed in, waving as they climbed back up to the street and took off along the river.

They walked and he told a funny story and smoked until they came to another, quieter part of town and the saloon filled with loud people and music.

Chet's eyes lit up as they approached, and he ushered Francie in with his hand on her back, proud. And Francie felt so grown up. And special. Like they were together.

The owner came over immediately and was so happy to see Chet and introduced them to everyone. He bragged about how Chet and his brother were the next big thing. And Chet told Francie that the guy was just being nice because of Uncle Pete. But still, they got to sit at an awesome table, with free sodas and whatever they wanted off the menu.

Still special.

Junior Brown came on right as they got their fries and was amazing. Chet was so excited, like enthralled and wanting her to experience every bit of it, too. And Francie couldn't remember being so happy or seeing such a great show, except maybe when her dad took her to see Jack White.

She also couldn't stop thinking about how Chet knew how she felt about her dad.

After Junior Brown finished, the owner chatted some more then called them a cab, his treat, and they walked outside to wait.

It was quiet on the street and Francie felt awkward. So she just started talking about how much she liked Junior Brown. And Chet said he liked her. And she smiled. And blushed. And he laughed. And she shook her head and got in the cab. Because luckily, it came right then.

And then, Chet looked at her hair again and said, "Yeah, I like that Junior Brown, too."

And then, he told the driver where to go. And talked more about Junior Brown and what inspired him. Which was basically music. He was so excited about music. And how it influenced his own thing. Like right now, it was ska and reggae and The Clash and Buzzcocks and Sex Pistols. And this punk thing. But also the Beatles and Robert Johnson and Clapton and Oasis, oddly. And Etta James.

And Francie watched Chet move and talk. With his happy eyes. And dash of freckles. And perfect hands. And straight shaggy cut hair that looked so cool and moved when he talked. And sometimes, she wasn't even sure what he said. She was just utterly entranced.

When they got to the hotel, he insisted on walking her in, and her stomach got all nervous as they reached the elevators in the lobby.

"Well, I guess this is it," he said.

"Yeah, I had a great time. Thanks for stalking me."

"My pleasure," he said, doing a little bow. "Anything for a damsel not in distress."

She curtsied.

He laughed, charmed. By her! *How was this even happening?*

"So," he said. "Keep in touch?"

"Uh...yeah. Awesome," she said, somehow remaining totally calm and cool.

"Oh, hold on," he said, patting his pockets. "No phone. Oh! But there's this." He pulled out a notepad and pen before she could even mention her phone. "Cuz I'm old school like that and forget my phone all the time," he said, making fun of himself again. He wrote down his email and gave it to her.

"Leon Chillday?"

He shrugged, "Cuz I'm so chill."

"And *email*?" she laughed.

"Like I said, old school. For deep connections and vibes, Mate."

She laughed again, "Wow."

And then everything went into slow motion as he leaned in and kissed her. Lightly. Like a cheek kiss. But on the lips. She felt nothing. Because her lips were in shock. But her stomach did a back dive.

The elevator dinged, and a man got off. Chet held the door and smiled, "We're leaving tomorrow, but I'll look out for your email." His eyes were sweet and genuine.

"Okay," she croaked and got on. The elevator doors started to close.

"Long, gushing emails," he winked through the last bit of space, like he didn't want to go.

"Okaaay," she yelled as the doors shut in front of her. She stared at them in a trance. *Oh my god, did that really happen? It did!* She screamed to herself and jumped and totally wrenched her knee. *Ow!*

The doors opened on the next floor, and she hobbled to her room. And jumped again and did a handstand because she had so much energy and flopped on the bed which also hurt her knee like crazy. But she didn't care! Finally, she had something to be excited about.

He was so amazing. And not just some fantasy.

And his eyes. What was it when he first looked at her? Like they were connected by a beam of something. Something magical. She didn't know what. And she tingled. And her heart swelled. And she knew she needed to see him again. She had to. Her heart said so.

3

Francie stared at the blank email on her screen to "Leon-Chillday."

She'd been almost writing him for one week, exactly. Since they met. But she kept getting too nervous. First, she worried he didn't really like her that much, or not as much as she liked him. Like maybe the whole kiss thing was just a stupid fantasy, like it was a European cheek kiss but on the lips. Like some people did with relatives and friends, like that director her dad worked with who lip-kissed everyone at parties. *Gross.* That would make Chet more like a brother.

Francie also kept doing stupid stuff like stalking Chet online and embarrassing herself, which just made it worse.

Like the first night in the hotel when she googled him immediately and found the band's website and Facebook page but nothing for Chet except as LeonChillday, like everywhere, like Facebook, Instagram, Twitter, Snapchat, whatever. All LeonChillday and a photo of John Cleese and nothing else. Apparently, John Cleese was from Monty Python. She had to look that up.

So, like an idiot, she followed LeonChillday on everything. Then she unfollowed him immediately because she didn't want to be stalk-y. Then she refollowed him because she realized he might see that she followed and unfollowed him and didn't want to hurt his feelings. Or maybe he couldn't see that she unfollowed him, but what if he looked at his followers and suddenly didn't see her anymore? That'd be weird. And rude.

And probably none of it mattered because he didn't do any of that stuff anyway. At all. And wouldn't notice.

Oh my god! She was so stupid.

So, she watched Monty Python to find out what that was about. "The Ministry of Silly Walks" sketch was her favorite. And it made her like Chet even more.

She also looked at the band website a gazillion times. Like Chet said, they'd only ever played in their "carport" and at one backyard party and in the movie, which Billy was making a big deal out of. Probably in hopes of getting popular or something. She wasn't sure how that worked. But apparently, their Uncle Pete, the one that was in the punk band with director Mac and that her dad knew, was a real-live music agent, so maybe they had a chance. She only knew this because she googled Uncle Pete, too. Pete Sheffland. Different last name. And he wasn't from Australia, so probably just their godfather, like Chet said, and not a real uncle.

She also found out that Chet was seventeen, while the drummer, Stu, and the new bass player, Memphis, were both eighteen, like Billy.

And most importantly, she found Chet's song, "Louisa, Hey." And fell in love. And listened to it *ten* gazillion times. And got the chills. Especially when she watched the video, that looked like it was shot in their "carport," which made her laugh. And it was so good. And funny. And kind of rock but with this punkish ska thing, too. And a tiny bit of blues with the harmonica. And it was clever. And catchy. All at once. Because it was totally original. And she saw how amazingly talented Chet was. And she started to feel intimidated, like why would he ever like her? Even if he was just a normal person in a carport band and seventeen. He wrote this amazing song!

She also felt intimidated by the band's Facebook page. She kept reading comments and Google-stalking everyone to see who they were. They all seemed amazing too and like they knew each other in real life. Not that there were that many people, like twenty-five, but still.

Like CocomoBear. You couldn't see her face in her picture, but you could tell she was super pretty and popular and not embarrassed about anything. Puke-worthy. And of course, everything she said was confident and sounded like she was from England. Like "hey lads, mighty fine video u boys put up" or "lurved singing w/u at the party, xox," even though it said she lived in Reseda. So, she was probably just a regular friend from school or something.

Then, there was this quirky chick, YoYoMatilda, who wrote hysterical stuff and had green and purple hair and obviously was friends with the band IRL too. She lived in Burbank. And there was JustJez, also from Burbank, who was in a band called Shout! Shout! that was no big deal either but had a gazillion followers on everything and played parties in The Valley.

Still, it intimidated Francie, as did the dorky guys because they were all funny or cool looking, and she decided if she ever commented or liked any Blues Harp Jones thing, she'd seem like a weird groupie.

Whatever. Chet was never on there anyway and that was the whole point!

She had to get a grip here.

And write to him. *Now! Pronto! Tonight!* Because her excuses didn't hold up anymore. First, she'd told herself not to email until she was home from Austin so she didn't seem too eager after the whole follow/no-follow debacle. Then, she decided to wait until after the house was painted and she was back in her room because it was comfortable and private. Which she was now. In her room.

But still, writing just seemed so scary. *Why? He's so nice!*

She grabbed her phone, snapped a photo of her room and texted Katie: *Hey. New lime green paint! Of course. What u think? How's Scotland? Miss you.*

Francie scrolled through Katie's photos of her family and some sheep. It was pretty hilarious, and Francie wished she was in Scotland, too. She loved her best friend, and it would be so awesome to hang with her and not have to think about anything and see sheep and "lochs." Like, what was up with those amazing castles in Scotland anyway?!

But no, she was here and psyching herself up to write Chet. She wanted to tell Katie about Chet and her first-ever kiss. Sort of kiss. But still, between them, it was the first kiss of any kind. But Katie would just say it was totally stupid and any type of further connection with Chet was unrealistic because he lived so far away. And then Katie would tell Francie to forget about him and the kiss and not write at all. Katie was practical and difficult and not dreamy like that, like how she totally hated that Francie played tennis and thought it was useless and dumb.

Francie really wished Katie didn't feel that way. In fact, it knotted her stomach and made her sad. She loved being best friends with Katie, and they'd been totally inseparable since they moved in across the street from each other in fifth grade. Then, Francie got obsessed with tennis in ninth grade and Katie hated her for it. They were still best friends, but it was like there was this thing between them, and Francie felt guilty, like it was all her fault Katie was mad and hurt or whatever she was, which it kind of was, because up until then, they'd done everything together.

Yeah, it was better she didn't tell Katie about Chet until she was sure what it meant.

She took a deep breath and went back to the email for Chet.

To her, it meant a lot. Chet meant a lot. Even if she didn't know exactly why.

And she had to just start typing. So she did.

Subject: letter from Francie, your Austin stalkee
Dear Chet,
I can't believe it's been a week since Austin! I missed you. A lot. Already. But we drove back from Austin to

boring suburbia and I was so busy and I'm really sorry because I've been thinking about you a lot...non-stop actually...and the bats too...and how it was so weird that I felt so comfortable with you, like more than anyone I've ever met, and how you noticed about my dad, and how I talked the whole time and didn't give you a chance until we were in the cab and how you wrote that amazing song and who is Louisa in the song and exactly what's up with your parents? Like does your dad live with you? And I hope they're gonna be okay. Your parents, I mean. And that you're okay. And I hope I'm not asking too many questions.

Francie stopped. Okay. That was lame. She deleted everything and started again. This time, she'd pretend to be one of their cool band friends. Maybe it'd be easier if she was "honestly" someone else. At least to get started.

Subject: Francie from Austin
Hey Chet,
It was really cool to meet u. Sorry I haven't written yet. Lots going on here. We drove back from Austin so it took a couple days to get back to boring suburbia, Thousand Oaks to be exact, and the Conejo Valley, which you know about! I love that!

Anyway, we also had our house painted while we were gone but when we got back my dad wasn't happy so we couldn't move back in right away. And then he kept having the painter redo stuff and was being a total jerk about it and critical and worried it wasn't good enough and would cost too much. And then my mom tried to make it better.

Like smooth it over with the painter. Which was a mess. So there was a lot of fighting. Level ten, twenty-four/seven. And stress. I try to block it out but somehow can't get away. Like my parents have a vice grip on me or something.

The good news is I got my room painted. Lime green. Which is my favorite color. So that's awesome.

And there's no school for 2 more months! Hooray! I guess that's obvious. But I go to this wretched school (all girls) which I hate even though my best friend Katie goes there. So there's that. And hopefully I'll get 2 the beach at some point. Zuma. If I can find a way. I just got my license a month ago but my dad won't let me drive all the time. Only for tennis practice and tournaments. (Yeah, I'm just 16, so I'm slightly younger than u—I saw on your site ur 17.)

I really like your song btw. Louisa, Hey. Now that's a weird name! Is Louisa a real person? Either way U lads r really fab!

She stopped. Yeah, way too CocomoBear. She deleted the "lads" part.

I really like your song btw. It's great!
Let me know what's up. U were really fun to hang with.
Francie (aka the stalkee)

Francie reread the email. Changed the part about her dad being "a total jerk" to say "totally bossy," then hit send. And reread it at least ten times before deeming it corny but acceptable.

Now what?

Hot chocolate! Thank god for chocolate. She wondered if the box was back on the shelf or still packed because of the painting.

She wrapped herself in a blanket and trudged downstairs to see. Her dad was sprawled out on the sofa in front of the TV, asleep and snoring, mouth open, salsa stains all over his shirt. Empty beer bottles and half-eaten nachos across the coffee table. God, if anyone knew they had the near equivalent of a drunk homeless man in their living room every night, she'd have yet another reason to die of embarrassment.

Her mom wasn't around. Must be upstairs reading or chatting or whatever it was she did.

Francie was relieved that her parents didn't fight that evening when her mom came home from work because that morning had been a disaster. Her parents were totally at it about her mom's new costume assistant job that she was so excited about because she was doing something new and creative and Libby had recommended her for it. Francie's dad was being a jerk and complaining that the job was nonunion and didn't pay much, even though her mom thought it was something she'd really like to do. Her mom said she didn't want to go back to marketing and this might be fun. Then her dad went on and on about how marketing was at least a respectable job. She was a manager and not some assistant getting people coffee for sixteen hours a day.

Her mom got so discouraged and was almost in tears and stormed out. Francie hoped her mom wouldn't give in to her dad and stop doing the job. If he'd gotten her the job and not Libby, he would've thought it was the best idea in the world for her to go back to work.

Whatever. Francie wasn't going to think about it. Really, she was just happy to be alone and not being bugged by either of them right now. She definitely preferred to be alone. Especially around her parents.

Francie headed into the kitchen, and there was the hot chocolate on the counter. Her mom must've put it out for her.

She put on the kettle and leaned against the counter, staring straight past her snoring dad, past her snoring dog, Max, and out to the yard with the impeccably manicured lawn, tuning it all out and disappearing into her own world, replaying the email in her mind.

She imagined Chet liking it and writing back. And them writing more and more. And him inviting her to come see his band play in someone's backyard. And his smile when he saw her. And sitting on the curb talking about serious things, like life. And real things and ideas and really connecting. And it being obvious to everyone that they were good together. And Chet asking her to keep writing because he loved her emails and could relate.

Everything Francie imagined seemed so real in that moment, like she could actually see it and feel this deep connection, from right there in her kitchen.

Then she imagined being Chet's girlfriend and watching him rehearse in their carport after she got to the finals of Sectionals, beating the fifth seed, which meant she got to go to nationals. And them celebrating, and her playing satellite tournaments in Europe. And Chet totally getting how cool that was.

Suddenly, Max's ears pricked up, and he started to bark. Francie's dad stirred, wiping drool off his face and peering up through squinted eyes. "What are you doing?" he mumbled.

Francie immediately tensed up as he stumbled up and turned on the kitchen light.

"It's dark in here," he said. "You're gonna ruin your eyes."

"I'm just boiling water. It's not like I'm looking at anything."

He glanced at the hot chocolate box and pulled some leftover pot roast and herring out of the fridge. He doused them in ketchup and took a disgusting bite, clearly still drunk. "I like that," he said and started eating, standing at the counter, swaying.

"What?"

"You drinking your hot chocolate," he said with a smile and dug in more, swaying more.

Oh my god, it was awful when he got like this. Totally gross. She grabbed a mug and shook in a packet of hot chocolate, wishing the water would just hurry up and boil.

"How are the prospects looking?" he asked, mouth still full.

"Prospects?"

"For the summer, what are you doing with all your free time?"

Immediately, she got nervous. What was he getting at? He knew she didn't have any plans besides practicing and getting her knee back in shape and trying out some tournaments. "I don't know," she said, hesitantly.

"Mmm." He took another bite then "mm, mm'd" like he was on a BBQ commercial.

She could feel her stomach getting more and more tense and just wanted to bolt. He was definitely gearing up to something, and it probably wasn't anything good.

He belched loudly and took another bite, "So, no summer job on the horizon?"

Job? Oh my god. Was he serious? "No," she said, immediately starting to panic.

"Mmm," he nodded.

She tried to stay calm but it was impossible. She couldn't get a job. What about tennis? When would she practice? She shook the kettle again.

He belched. "You know when I was your age, I was already working for two years."

Oh my god, here we go.

"Two long years. Cleaning race cars, changing tires, hosing down the garage." He took another bite.

"I know, Dad."

"And it was a damn good experience," he said and grabbed another beer out of the fridge. "Paid for car insurance, clothes, food, everything. And I didn't have to rely on anyone."

"I know, Dad. I've heard it a million times!" She stopped. Why was she getting so angry?

He looked at her like she was out of line then popped the top of his beer. "Well good," he said and took a long swig and went back to his pot roast.

Oh my god, what did this mean? Did she have to get a job? Again, she panicked. Of course, it did. Because he could care less about tennis. He thought it was ridiculous that she cared so much about it and started too late and was never going to be any good, so why bother? Even though all he ever did was brag about her and couldn't wait for her to get a tennis scholarship so he could tell everyone.

"What about your friends?" he asked, taking another bite of pot roast.

"My friends?"

"What are they doing for the summer?"

"I don't know."

"You don't know what your friends are doing?" he asked, as if this was impossible.

"Katie's in Scotland, and Amy's working at her dad's office," she said, finally just grabbing the kettle off and pouring the water.

"Aha, working. I like that. And your tennis friends?"

"They're playing tennis! And Cecelia's in Michigan."

"No jobs?"

"No."

"And Mallory?"

"Mallory's too young to get a job!" she yelled in total exasperation.

"I know that. I was just wondering how she's doing," he said with a condescending look, like Francie was out of line again and he was on perfect behavior and better than her.

"She's fine."

"And she's going to nationals?"

"Yes, she's going to nationals."

"I like that," he said with a pleased smile.

Here we go! This was when he made her feel like a big, fat, worthless, useless, nothing loser. Because everyone else was better than she was and made better choices and had more talent and brains, including him.

"And I like her attitude about her career," he said, taking another bite and looking all proud, as if Mallory's success were his doing.

"She doesn't have an attitude about her career; she's twelve! She just likes to play tennis."

"But she does have some career ahead of her. Good thing she started so young." He took another bite and let out a long, loud belch.

The anger rose inside her again. She grabbed her hot chocolate and stormed off, spilling everywhere. She didn't care and just kept going.

"Francie?" he yelled when she was half way up the stairs.

She stopped, "What?"

"Turn off the light in the hall, would you? It was on all night last night."

She watched him belch again and continue eating, totally oblivious to her, and she felt so angry. She continued upstairs, slamming off the light and shutting the door to her room.

She took a deep breath and leaned back against the door. It didn't matter. She was going to have a tennis career too, like Mallory. And then he'd see. And tomorrow, she was going to hit on the ball machine and practice her serves and practice with Ricky. Even if it killed her knee. And she was going to practice every minute she could, no matter what.

She sat down at her laptop and took a deep breath. She looked at her collage on the wall. And Chet was going to write to her. Because he liked her. Her! And then it would all be okay.

She checked her email. Nothing. Then reread her email to Chet and immediately started to doubt herself. She had no idea anymore if it was okay or not. She closed it out. *Shit!*

Then she went to the Blues Harp Jones site and looked at Chet's smile. He was so cute and positive and funny all at once. And he laughed at serious things. And she imagined him laughing at her right now and understanding how angry she was at her dad. And it totally helped.

Then she crawled into bed and let herself listen to Chet's song over and over, trying not to think about anything else. Just the upbeat rhythm. Lifting her. Soaring. Drawing her in. She couldn't get enough. Not just because it was a great song, but because she felt like it was hers. A part of her.

With the "Back beat girl." In her "denim jeans." With her "Violet hair, like she's going somewhere. And calling me." And it was about a girl he loved. That he was pining for. But in this good way. Like he totally adored her. Because she was like no one else. Like him. And the girl totally owned it. At least, that's what it seemed. But who was that girl, Louisa? Was it *her*? Did he somehow know her before they even met? Like some cosmic thing? So she could hear it? Like it was her destiny to hear his song and connect with him?

The guitar coursed through her veins. And slowly, she started to feel better. And hoped that somehow she would get to see him again. Soon. She had to.

4

The alarm rang and Francie hit snooze for the third time. She didn't want to get up. She kept thinking about this job thing and it was too awful. She rolled over to get away from it.

And there was her room and the collage and the laptop and her phone. And the email. What if Chet didn't write back? That thought was larger than she could stand. She pulled herself up. She had to go to the club and practice. That'd get her out of her head.

But there it was.

Subject: Francie from Austin

Oh my god. He wrote back. At 2 a.m.! How late was that?

Gorgeous Francie!

Oh my god! Gorgeous! Chills.

I can't believe you actually wrote me. You're amazing and called my bluff because I am terrible at writing. Just like I am terrible at remembering my phone. But will do my best for fab Francine.

Austin! The pleasure is all mine. Bats and you. Genuine +kind and u have a cute limp. A rarity. (insert knave bowing)

Knave???? Hilarious!

I'm sorry about the level 10. I know all about it from my parents before the big split. Now it's just my brother level-10ing on me with the band thing. Do-wop, do-wop. Or on our dad. He's angry that brother of mine. Which is a pain and does nothing but make our mum upset. And sad. And makes me wish it'd go back to the way it was. But then we'd have the level 10 again. So what can I say? I digress. Vicious circle.

And onward to greener pastures...

Like Fraaaancine...You make my heart...bling!

Let's see, if I were to write a song about you...shy at first glance. On the outside. Hmm, what is it about Francine? Shy on the outside with a knockout smile. And when she walks away is when it begins. Something in her step. A limp. Yes. But something more. A purpose? Freedom? That comes out when she's away. And is so enchanting. But away from what? Tell me Francine. Or would that be Walk-away Franny? Tell me what gives you freedom?

Oh my god. Her heart turned into a lump in her throat.

Glad you like Louisa. It's my favorite too...and only. But we're working on more. Becuz...get this, thanks to my brother obsessively harping on him, and not in the har-monica sense, our Uncle Pete got us a show in two weeks at The West! aka Lyric Poet West. Do u know it? It's a big deal. Well, it used to be. Doors Dylan Tom Waits Elton John Miles GNR...crazy back in the day. Tho our gig not so much. To give u perspective, we're opening for three bands no one ever heard of so no one will be there for them or us because no one's heard of us either and the only reason we're there is cuz Uncle Pete knows some-one and Billy's a pain in his ass. Quite embarrassing.

Anyway, I hope you can come! Now that I've made it sound so terrific. I'm actually quite honored to play there. And I want to see more of that rabbit-Val smile. And hear more about Fraaaancine. Settled in with green. Happy to hear. Green is a fantastic color.

Keep me posted. Tell me what's up with tennis. And collages. Send photos!

Peace
Chet

Oh my god. Francie had to sit down. She couldn't be-lieve it. He wrote so much! And he was flirting. And asked about tennis. And who she was, like he really cared! And he wanted her to come see him! At The West! Oh my god. It was too good to be true.

And he was so normal. And nice.

She wanted to write back immediately but decided to be chill. Like CocomoBear.

She closed the email. Then reread it a gazillion times. He called her "gorgeous"! *Ahhhh!* She let it sink in and finally started to get ready.

She checked herself in the mirror as she brushed her teeth. Her hair miraculously looked less flat and gross today. She imagined talking to Chet, smiling, laughing. Now *that* was gross.

She spit out the toothpaste and decided he must like her for her personality or something. Her mom always said she wasn't beautiful but interesting. She hated that. It made her feel like crap. But maybe there was truth to it. Maybe, finally, someone saw the real her. Like how she felt free when she was away. From her family. And her house. And her room. And being lonely. It was so depressing.

Should she tell him? Because he asked. Would he get it? Or was it too weird?

She looked at her reflection dead-on and tried to be objective. No, she wasn't beautiful, but she was okay. Okay enough for Chet to like her. More than okay enough, because he did!

She put on her favorite tennis skirt. The one she only wore to tournaments. Purple with lavender lace. It made her feel good. And lucky. Then she pulled on her P.U.N.K. t-shirt so she wouldn't look too dressed up and because that's what she was wearing when she met Chet.

She reread the email one more time and headed downstairs.

Her mom was puttering in the kitchen, and her dad was watching the news and reading the paper and drinking coffee, all at the same time. She saw him notice her tennis clothes but ignored it. She wasn't going to let him get to her.

"I made your favorite, oatmeal," her mom said cheerfully from the kitchen bar.

"Francie, can I talk to you for a minute?" her dad asked.

Francie tensed up. Her mom did, too.

"Yeah?" Francie replied.

"I wanted to check in about the job situation, but now, I'm curious about this tennis gear."

"I'm just gonna go out and hit some serves," Francie said, immediately defensive.

"Really?"

"And maybe use the ball machine." There was no way she was telling him that she was hitting with Ricky.

"I thought the doctor said no tennis for two months," he said.

"*Maybe* two months. And it's been six weeks. And I feel fine."

"And you won't twist your knee at all?"

"No. I'm just gonna stand there. It doesn't hurt. At all," she lied.

He looked over his glasses all judge-y, then went back to his paper.

"What?" she said.

"Don't mind me. You obviously know exactly what you're doing," he said with tons of sarcasm and without looking up.

Jerk. She scooped oatmeal into the bowl her mom set out. Heart racing.

"So, no more thoughts about that summer job? I mean, if you can't play, it's the perfect time," he said.

"What are you talking about summer job?" her mom asked.

Francie tensed up again. "I haven't thought about it. Okay? And I'm playing Ventura. I don't care what anyone says. My knee is fine!"

"Ventura?" he asked.

"What summer job?" her mom asked.

"Francie's thinking about getting a summer job. And apparently playing a tournament."

"I'm not thinking about a job," Francie said. "You're thinking about me getting a job."

"Why does she need a job?" her mom asked.

"I quite liked that teaching idea," he said to Francie, ignoring her mom's question.

"What teaching idea?" Francie asked.

"With that woman with the visor," he said. "You told me she had a camp and your friends helped her. Or worked for her."

How did he even remember that? This was exactly why she never told him anything. He always brought it back in some distorted way, like ammunition.

"Annie," Francie said. "Her name's Annie. And you've talked to her a million times."

"Why does Francie need a job?!" her mom asked again.

"To keep her busy," her dad said, finally.

"She's already busy," her mom replied.

"With what? She hurt her knee. She's supposed to be resting. And I don't know where this Ventura thing is coming from." He shook his head as if it was insanity and looked back at the paper.

Her mom stared in exasperation. He was clearly trying to rile her up or pick a fight with either one of them, and Francie could tell her mom was trying as hard as she could not to let him.

"Physical therapy," her mom said, with her best angry-calm voice. "And practice. That's what she's busy with."

"I'm sure she'll be able to work this in, too. And it couldn't hurt if she brought in a little something."

"Excuse me?" her mom said, in total disbelief.

"Learn the value of the dollar. You know, Francie, we both work pretty darn hard to give you everything you need and send you to that school."

"I don't want to go to that school!"

"And I definitely think you should get a summer job to pay for your extras. In fact, I insist," he said and smiled obnoxiously.

"Hank, for chrissakes, she doesn't need to work," her mom said.

"I think she does."

"You don't even want *me* to work!" her mom yelled, finally losing her cool.

"It's final," he said with a smile.

Francie couldn't stand it. "It's fine! I'll work!" She slammed her oatmeal in the sink. "I'll find a job and make tons of money and have zero time for tennis. I'm sure that'll make you happy. And then, you'll totally get your way. Like always!" She grabbed her rackets.

"Now, hold on; don't be upset. I just think it's an excellent idea, and I'm sure you can find time for tennis, too. You know when I was your age, your grampa had me tuning up cars and…"

"I know, Dad, you told me. A million times! Like last night you told me!" She looked at him for effect then stormed out, slamming the door behind her.

Ahhh! Total frustration! Why did he do this?! And why did she let it get to her?! Every time! And why couldn't she just have a normal family?!

She grabbed her bike and rode away from the house, pedaling mostly with her right leg since her left knee still didn't bend enough when the pedal was at the top.

She had no control of her life. And she was going to have to get a job. But she'd find a way to play, too. And go to tournaments. Because she wasn't going to let this happen. He wasn't going to win. In fact, she was going to get an amazing job and have her own money and become an amazing player and make tons of money and then she'd never need her parents or anyone for anything ever again.

5

The sun was getting really hot on the court, but Francie didn't care. She was getting tired, and it just felt so good to be out there and focused on playing and not be so amped up as before. She loved that it was just about hitting the ball and working out and nothing else. Black and white. And she loved that she had something to do, with a purpose and a goal.

She pulled her racket back as the next ball shot out of the ball machine to her forehand. She tried to stay low, even though her left knee was already killing her, and hit up as hard as she could, pulling up and over the outside of the ball. It spun up and crosscourt, over the net perfectly and then came down just inside the line.

Yes!

She got back into position and kept going until the basket was done. She was definitely getting back to normal even if her knee really hurt.

She did a couple more baskets of forehands then switched to backhands. That was much better because she could keep all her weight on her right leg and it felt like she was actually getting some good practice in. Maybe it wouldn't be that hard to come back after all.

At 2:00 p.m. exactly, Ricky and Jeff came on the court. She felt embarrassed that she was still there. She'd already hit with Ricky, like an hour before, and wasn't even supposed to be hitting at all. But they didn't know that or seem to care. They just said hi and started hitting.

She felt jealous that they could practice all they wanted. But whatever. She'd done okay with Ricky in spite of being out for six weeks. He'd beaten her pretty badly because of his serve but they had some great rallies and she knew if she kept practicing she'd nail the return. She was getting good at cutting it off on the rise and her knee probably wouldn't keep her from doing that. Except on the forehand.

She got up to go and felt a sharp pain in her knee again. For a second, she worried she'd done too much but told herself to ignore it and squeezed her quad muscle just in case.

Then she started out to the front of the club, trying to hide her limp as much as possible. It was time for her to focus on this job thing. She didn't have a choice. She was going to see about working at the snack shop there at the club. Or in the front office. There were always kids from the club working there, usually people she didn't know that weren't that into tennis but were there because their parents belonged to the club. Kids that had tons of time because they didn't care about anything. Maybe that would bum her out too much. Maybe she had to find something at the mall or a coffee shop so she didn't have to work while her friends played and have it be in her face.

She decided to talk to Mrs. Sullivan in the front office on her way out. And get something from the snack shop to see what it was like to work there.

She passed the side court where Coach Annie was teaching the younger kids. Annie waved and smiled from under her giant visor. She was definitely really nice, even if she wasn't as good a coach as her coach, Coach Hawkins, aka "Hawk." Annie even took some of the kids from the club skiing. Cecelia, who she was sort of friends with and hit with sometimes, had invited her because she knew Annie better, and it was a blast.

Francie waved back. Yeah, she liked Annie, but she'd be way too frustrated teaching tennis at her camp. Even if it was just beginners. Francie wanted to be the one out there playing, not watching. She'd already lost so much time. Why was her dad doing this to her? Wasn't it bad enough she hurt her knee?

She saw Coach Hawkins on his court drilling Mallory on her forehand. Mallory was amazing, even if she was just twelve. Again, instant jealousy.

"Well if it isn't our favorite gimp!" yelled Hawk.

"Hi," she said, totally embarrassed. She knew this was coming.

"Francie!" yelled Mallory, as she pounded back another forehand.

"What are you doing out here?" Hawk asked, as he hit Mallory a drop shot.

"Just hitting some serves," she lied.

They watched Mallory hustle forward and return the ball with an amazing drop shot. She was so fast!

"You've gotta put some ice on that knee and stay off it till it's ready," Hawk said, as he hit Mallory a lob. Mallory raced back and got it, placing it perfectly in the back court. He hit another drop shot, and she raced forward, stumbling over her feet to get it, and tumbled into the net.

"And that's why she's gonna kick some butt at nationals," Hawk said, banging his racket on the ball basket for emphasis.

Mallory laughed.

"Now talk some sense into your buddy here and tell her to stay off that knee," Hawk said.

Francie's heart sank.

"She's just hitting serves," Mallory said, playfully defending Francie, "right?" Mallory beamed at Francie, totally happy to see her.

Francie loved Mallory, even if she was totally jealous that she was ranked top-ten in the country and was only twelve. It didn't matter. Probably because Mallory was Francie's friend and biggest fan. At least somebody thought she was good!

"Alright, you get out of here," Hawk said to Francie, pointing his racket towards the front of the club. "And you get back there and hit your own serves," he said to Mallory.

Mallory ran back, amused, and waved to Francie. Francie waved back and continued on. At least Hawk said something to her. Like he cared or something, even though she knew he didn't believe in her either as far as being good at tennis went. She wished he did but the only way that'd happen is if she proved it to him, like by going to nationals.

Francie shook it off and got back to focusing on the job.

Axe, Tanner and Liam were up ahead just hanging out. Typical. They were older. Like, Tanner had just graduated and was going to Cal Poly in the fall, even though he acted like he was five. Together, they spent all their time off the court doing nothing but giving her and anyone younger or less cocky a hard time.

Francie tried to veer by the pool to avoid them, holding her breath as she passed, but sure enough, out of Axe's mouth came, "Hey Mills, did you kick some ball-machine butt today?"

Francie mouthed "ha, ha" and continued. What a pain. The teasing wouldn't be so bad except she'd always had a crush on Axe, ever since she joined the club, like a year before. She liked that Axe was funny and serious about tennis at the same time. He was really good and played nationals and was hoping to go to ASU on a full-ride. But he never liked her back. He was in love with Mallory's older sister, Piper, who didn't like *him* back.

Whatever. Compared to Chet, Axe suddenly seemed like a totally stupid person to like. He would never in a million years have any idea how she felt about anything. Take, for example, how he always asked her what she was doing "later" or on the weekend, and she'd say "nothing," hoping he'd ask her out, but then he wouldn't. Like he had zero idea about her. Or was torturing her on purpose.

Like when he gave her a ride home so she wouldn't have to ride her bike in the dark. But then it meant nothing to him. Totally lame.

She thought about Chet following her in Austin because he knew exactly how she felt about her dad. Her heart swelled.

Better.

She took a deep breath and continued toward the club house and snack shop.

That weird, pink-and-black-haired goth chick Stella was standing behind the snack shop counter window. She was one of those kids whose parents belonged to the club and who worked there even though she didn't play tennis. She also lived in one of the ginormous "Club Villas" on the lake, so she could just walk over.

Francie had never really talked to Stella before. Maybe they'd said hi like ten times because Stella was good friends with Cecelia, the one that invited Francie to Ski Day. Actually, Cee always asked Francie to do stuff with them outside of tennis, which Francie never did. Maybe she should. She liked Cee because she was funny and got excited about mundane stuff. Even though Francie didn't know why Cee liked her. Maybe because of tennis. Cee seemed to think it was cool that Francie was so into it.

But Cee and Stella together seemed way too party-ish, like they just drove around and went crazy, which seemed pointless. And Francie knew she wouldn't have anything to say to them because she was so serious and they weren't. And maybe she was worried something bad would happen. Like it'd be too reckless. And she wouldn't be able to focus on tennis. She had to stay focused on tennis at all times, even when she wasn't playing, like think about it and keep it in her mind always or something bad would happen.

Was that weird? Probably.

She took a deep breath. She was getting super nervous about talking to Stella and tried to tell herself it didn't matter because she was just ordering a drink.

Then, she started thinking about Stella's brother, Eddie, because she sort of knew him. But that didn't help either. Maybe because Eddie was slackerish. High-energy slackerish, but still. Like he seemed busy and thoughtful but without purpose. Or goals. So she couldn't relate or feel comfortable around him either.

Eddie hung out with Axe, Tanner and Liam and played tennis but wasn't serious. Like he used to play for Westlake High and had this brown, curly, crazy hair and seemed kind of stoner-ish. And he was older, like seventeen or eighteen, and apparently, even though he'd graduated a year early, which meant he was super smart, he was going to a JC instead of a regular college next year. Or so she heard.

But Eddie was nice. Not mean and tease-y like his friends, and you could actually have a conversation with him. Like the time he asked her how a tournament went. And then there was the time Hawk made her play with him in the club mixed doubles tourney and she'd gotten mad and thrown her racket at the fence and Hawk almost pulled her out and Eddie made a joke and told her they were fine even if she tanked, which she did, and then she felt better thanks to him, even though she was super embarrassed, too. Which made it so she never ever wanted to talk to him again, so why was she even thinking about him now when she had to focus and just go up to Stella and order a friggin' drink?!!

Shit!

She took a deep breath. Her mind was out of control and she had to just do this.

You don't even have to talk to her or anything!

Francie continued up to the snack shop where Stella was listening to music, reading Vogue and biting her black-painted fingernails that matched the jet black in her hair. It was cut drastically shaggy and Francie wondered how she got it to stay frozen in juxtaposed angles all over her head. She admired the little red pins positioned strategically throughout. Clearly, just decorative.

Stella looked up. Her eyes were big and black and super round. And curious and playful behind her funky red cat glasses and smirky lips that curved up with dimples. "Hi," Stella said and forced a smile, like it was part of her job.

Oh, god.

"Hi," Francie replied and quickly looked at the menu. She could feel Stella's eyes judgingly checking her out.

"I'll have a mixed berry smoothie, small," Francie said, trying to appear nonchalant, like she could totally care less about anything, especially working there or what Stella thought of her.

"Sure," Stella replied and got up to make the drink. "You talk to Cee?"

"No."

"Me neither. Not in person at least." She laughed, as if it was some kind of inside joke or Francie should know what it meant.

Francie just smiled and then tried to watch closely, without seeming obvious and weird, as Stella made the smoothie: berries out of the freezer, into blender, ice, a few more berries, yogurt. Go! The blender whirred loudly. Yeah, she could do that.

"This *okay* for you?" Stella said, as if Francie's staring was totally annoying her.

"Huh?" Francie said, not sure if Stella was serious or teasing. "I mean, yeah, totally, I was just watching. I'm thinking of getting a job here."

"Why?"

"To make money?"

"It pays minimum you know," Stella said and turned up the blender.

"Oh."

"Yeah, it kind of sucks. Although, you do have a lot of down time and can do other stuff." She turned the blender off and poured the drink into a cup. There was extra, and she poured herself some. "You mind?"

Francie shook her head.

Stella took a sip, "Mmmm. What do you think?"

Francie tried it, "Good."

"Excellent," Stella said and sat down to drink hers. "Yeah, I only do it because my dad thinks we should learn a good work ethic. I guess because he likes to work so much."

Francie laughed. "Yeah, my dad all of sudden thinks I should get a job, too."

"Bummer. So why don't you teach at that summer camp here? I mean, you're good, aren't you? They've gotta need people."

Weird that Stella and her dad both came up with that.

"I was kind of thinking of doing something new, besides tennis," Francie said, and as soon as it came out, she knew it sounded stupid.

"Yeah, well, think again 'cuz you'd get paid way more and have a lot less to do. More free time. Unless you've got nothing better to do," Stella joked and tossed the rest of her drink.

"Yeah, I guess so." Somehow that made her feel bad about herself, like she had nothing better to do, even though she did. She had tennis. But a job made it seem like a big, fat nothing.

Loser. Wishes she was good at tennis. No one cares. Big waste of time.

"Well, it sure as heck can't hurt to ask," Stella said. "Heck, I'd do it if I could. Much better than this. Although, check it out, this is what I did before you got here." Stella's eyes lit up as she pulled a sketch from under her magazine. "It's for my friend's band's video shoot."

It seemed pretty standard garage band wear with goth-ish chains and metal thrown in. Totally not Francie's style. "Who's the band?" Francie asked.

"RatBat," said Stella proudly and showed Francie a video on her phone. Totally metal and punkish with no melody. "I met 'em online and they want me to do costumes for their next video. Which is supposed to happen if one of the guys gets the money."

Didn't sound promising. Francie sifted through the sketches till she came to one in color. It was totally awesome, kind of *Game of Thrones* meets Tim Burton. "This one's great!"

"Oh yeah, I did that one for fun. It's a set. Who knows, maybe I'll be a professional set designer and blow this popsicle stand."

Francie laughed.

Stella put the sketches away and sat back down. "They play parties around here and in Agoura. Like house parties. If you ever want to go. I mean, with me, since you probably don't know them 'cuz you go to that all-girl school. Right?"

God, Stella knew everything about her! "Uh, yeah, no, but sure. I mean, it's not totally my kind of music, but that'd be fun," Francie said, even though she knew she'd never go. They seemed totally party-ish and she probably wouldn't have anything to say to anyone.

Still, she never got invited to parties. She just hung out with Katie, and they were total geeks with no life. And no one at school ever had parties, at least not that she knew of. And if they did, it'd probably be all girls and they wouldn't want to go anyway. Maybe she should force herself to go with Stella. At least, it'd be interesting. Even if she hated it.

"Well, cool," Stella said and put her stuff away. "Anyway, the point is, I work here because my parents are a bore and want me to, but really, I'd rather be doing nothing. Or designing. Or eating my boogers."

Francie laughed. It was amazing how weird and funny and confident Stella was all at once.

Stella checked her phone, chuckled at something then threw it down. "How's the knee?"

"Better?"

"How about the movie set?"

"What?!"

Stella laughed. "Cee's got a big mouth. Meet any stars?"

"A few," Francie said and felt her cheeks get hot as she thought about Chet.

"Oooo! What? Who'd you meet?"

"No one. Really. Just some actors."

"I don't believe it. Who is it? Is he famous?"

"No! No one. I just, there was a guy in a band. In the movie. But it's no big deal. We're just friends."

"What band?!"

"Blues Harp Jones?" Francie said, feeling her cheeks get hot again.

"Blues. Harp. Jones." Stella YouTubed them on her iPad.

"They're *not* famous!" Francie laughed.

The "Louisa, Hey" video came up. "Oh, yeah. Sounds okay," Stella said. "Weird name though. So did you meet 'em in *Texas*?"

"Oh my god, she told you everything!"

"And you totally like him," Stella grinned.

"No! We're just in contact. Sort of. And writing."

"Yeah, you totally like him. Which one is he?" Stella poked Francie with the iPad.

Francie pointed to Chet, and Stella checked him out, "Nice name, kinda artsy-surfer-grungy cute. Yeah, I can see that." Then Stella went to Facebook and liked the

Blues Harp Jones page. "Oh, and look, they're playing The West!"

"Really? It's up now?" Francie saw the announcement. It was happening!

"You going?"

"I want to," Francie said, getting super excited at the thought. It'd be so amazing.

But then Stella went to the Lyric Poet West page, and they looked at the photos of the club and some of the bands and West Hollywood, and Francie knew it would be impossible. Her dad would never let her go. Or drive. "I can't imagine it actually happening though."

"You have to go. For Loverboy." Stella smirked.

"Ha ha."

"Seriously. You gotta do it."

"I don't know. It seems really far. And my parents probably would never let me go anyway. Or drive. Ever."

"Me and Eddie went to the Whiskey once. We figured it out."

"Really?" Francie said, impressed they went all the way to Sunset Boulevard to see a show.

"Yeah. Let's do it. And get Eddie to drive," Stella said, smiling.

"What?"

"Yeah. And maybe Chet can get us tickets. Or on the list. Right?"

"You wanna go?"

"Yeah. Why not? It sounds awesome."

Francie tried to hide her joy. How was this possible? Scary Stella was standing in front of her beaming and wanting to go *with her* to Lyric Poet West. And for a split second, Francie imagined them there. Standing in front of the stage, just like in the photo. Watching Chet play. Him smiling at her. "And you think Eddie could drive?" she asked.

"Yeah. I'm sure one of us could convince him. Or wait!" Stella's eyes lit up. "What about Scott?! Scott would love to go! And he could totally drive us."

"Who's Scott?"

"From school. Me and Cee go with him to Westwood all the time and just cruise around. What's a little further? Although, he can't always get the car. I'll have to work on that." Stella stopped as she noticed Tanner, Axe and Liam walking up. "And here comes the Butt-Head Pack."

Stella shoved her phone at Francie. "Put your number in. We'll totally figure this out. It's awesome!" Stella stood up and hid her iPad under her jacket.

Francie's heart started to race. Wow, this could actually happen. Unless Stella was insane. Or a total flake. But she didn't seem to be. And she'd done this before. Francie put her number in Stella's phone.

The only thing that could get in the way would be Francie's parents saying no. Which was possible. Probable, in fact. But maybe there was a way to convince them. There had to be. And she was going to figure it out. Because she couldn't miss this.

She handed Stella back the phone. "Thanks for the smoothie."

"Next time, it'll be the Stella Special. Way better. And on the house," she winked. "And if you see my brother, ask him about The West. He might do it. I think he likes you."

"What?" This was completely out of left field. And definitely untrue.

But the "Butt-Head Pack" arrived, and Stella didn't answer. She was super cool with them, with comebacks for everything. Maybe they gave Stella a break because of Eddie. Or maybe she was just used to them. Whatever it was, Stella was awesome and Francie felt so lucky. Like there was a crack in her universe and she just had to grab the light and hold on.

On her way out, Francie stopped at the front office and talked to Mrs. Sullivan about the jobs. Mrs. Sullivan said they didn't have any openings but she'd keep Francie in mind. Francie knew that meant it wasn't happening and tennis camp or something else lame was her reality for the very near future. But it almost didn't matter. This Stella thing was so amazing. Like it was part of her reality now too. For the very near future.

6

Francie snuck in the front door, hoping to get to her room unnoticed. Something was cooking in the kitchen so her mom had to be back from her job and in her room. Her dad was asleep on the couch in front of the TV. Again! Head back, mouth open, snoring. More empty beer bottles and half-eaten nachos. He started talking in his sleep, like he was distressed, or scared, yelling, and then he calmed down and just started muttering incoherently.

Francie felt that clutching in her stomach. He seemed to be getting worse. It just kept happening more and more and earlier and earlier. Like now, it wasn't even five o'clock.

The only good thing was that she didn't have to talk to him and he couldn't hassle her about the job. She really didn't want him to know about the club not hiring and that the nightmarish tennis job may be an option. To-morrow. She'd deal with it tomorrow.

"Hi, honey," her mom said cheerfully, walking to the kitchen from the bedroom, as if her husband wasn't sleeping like a homeless person on the couch. "Come have something to eat."

"I'm not really hungry. I had something at the club."

"Oh, good. I'm glad you did that."

"I'll just take something up to my room or come back later."

They never sat down to eat together any more, thank god, even though her mom still cooked and wished they would eat together, like a regular family, and seemed sad about it. But her mom never pushed it. Her mom never pushed anything, actually.

Francie grabbed a green juice from the fridge and poured it in a glass as her mom smoothed out her hair and told her not to worry. *Who said anything about worrying?!*

"I'm gonna take the Prius tomorrow if that's okay. To go look for a job."

"Of course," her mom said and kissed her cheek. "Daddy'll be proud."

Francie nodded and their eyes met. Again, that clutching, but this time it was in her heart and went up into her throat. Sometimes she thought her mom felt sadder than her dad, even though her mom always smiled and pretended everything was okay. Francie knew her mom did the cheerful thing for her sake but that just made it worse. Too much pressure.

Francie put her imaginary wall up between them, forced a smile and nodded. She could sense her mom's relief and started off with her plate.

"He got that job in Vancouver, by the way," her mom said to Francie's back. "Starting in a couple weeks."

Francie stopped and turned, "Great." She could see a glimmer of hope in her mom. It always came when her dad got a new job. Her mom hoped it would make him happy. And that he wouldn't drink.

Francie looked at her dad muttering in his sleep and knew the job would make it worse. He hated that job but her mom didn't want to see it. Francie could feel all the pain from her mom again and couldn't stand it. She hurried up to her room and shut the door. Relief.

She flipped open her laptop and opened the email from Chet. At least there was this one good thing. She wondered if Chet would understand how she felt about her mom. Even though she didn't even understand. At least with her dad, she knew she loved him and hated him and was embarrassed by him. But with her mom, it was just this total blah and pain that made no sense and made her want to run. Like her mom was a *ball* of pain.

No one would understand that.

And no one would understand how lucky she felt right now. That she met Chet. And Stella. And that Stella actually wanted to go to the show! How was this even possible? It was like magic.

She reread Chet's email and started to write. This time it came easy.

Subject: Another day in the life
Hey Chet,
Got your note. Thanks. Congrats on Lyric Poet West!
And yeah, it'd be cool if I could come see you play. Not

totally sure how to get there yet or how to convince my parents but I might be able to get a ride with this new friend Stella if they let me go. I met her at the tennis club today. She's this really odd goth chick. But actually, kind of cool. You'd like her. She's a costume designer for a band. Well, she's gonna be, and she's designing costumes and a set for her friend's video shoot. I don't particularly like the costumes but the set is amazing. And she's just totally relaxed and free and sure of herself (unlike yours truly). I'm kind of jealous actually. I guess because she knows who she is and doesn't care if she has to work at the stupid snack shop that pays minimum wage, and I just DON'T know what I'm doing. Besides tennis. I didn't really tell you how much I'm into tennis. And bummed that I hurt my knee. Hence the limp. Torn cartilage. Getting better though. And now I digress. But anyway, she's totally cool and I think she can find us a ride to see you.

And if I have to come on my own, I'll just have to steal the car! ;)

In other news, my dad decided he wants me to get a job. I'm hoping it doesn't interfere with tennis, but I don't think I have a choice. Unless he changes his mind. Which he does. Often. I hate it. Because I don't know what to expect. Ever. But never mind. The good news is that if I have a job I'll have money to come see u play. Yay!

Anyway, that's it. Sorry to rant. Just happy u get it :)
Francie
ps. To answer your question, I guess I feel most free when walking away from them. My parents, I mean.

She wondered if that was true. She didn't feel very free at the moment and she'd just walked away from them. Up the stairs. Into her room. And shut the door. And the only thing that'd set her free now would be curling up into a tight tiny ball and thinking about tennis, front and center in her mind so she couldn't think about anything else.

But that wasn't very free.

So what was different in Austin? The music? The hotel? Seeing something new? Maybe. Maybe the hope of something new kept her from being stuck alone in this prison of her mind.

ps. To answer your question, I think I feel most free when I'm walking away from my parents but only if it's towards something good and new that distracts me. In a good way.

Like you, she thought and hit send.

7

"Francie, honey," Francie's dad whispered.

Francie opened her eyes. He was sitting on the edge of her bed.

What?

"Hi, what's going on?" She came up onto her elbows, totally groggy, and looked at the time: 5:30 a.m. *Weird.* He never did this. And his eyes looked glassy. Did he drink already? No, he wouldn't drink before work. *Would he?*

"Hey, I just wanted to tell you how proud I am of you," he whispered. "I heard you're taking the car to look for a job. Which is an excellent idea. And if you don't find the right thing, that's okay, too. You need time for practice. Okay?" He smiled. Honest eyes. Gentle. Kind. "And I got a new show this week. Then Vancouver. So we're fine. And I'm so proud of you." He said it again. And kissed her forehead.

He means it.

His eyes say he means it. For sure. Her heart swelled. And then he hugged her. And left.

Francie stared at the door. The panic came back. What did this mean? And why were his arms shaking?

Confusion.

What if she did nothing, like he said, and then he changed his mind back again?

She pulled the covers over her head, trying to banish it from her mind. But she couldn't. She was trapped. Because this is what he did: He flip-flopped. And then it came back again. The craziness. Again. And again. And again!

She sat up. Heart racing. Chet. She had to think about Chet. And how amazing it was that she met him. And Stella. She had to keep these thoughts front and center. Together with tennis.

And how she was going to get to The West.

She exhaled.

And checked her email. Nothing from Chet. She opened the email she'd sent the night before. Maybe it was too much. Too long. Too much about Stella. Too much about her dad. Too much complaining. Too much truth. Just too much. She shut it. Why did she write so much?

She checked the band's Facebook page to see if he'd posted anything the night before, as if he would. *Idiot!* And, of course, nothing. Except about five people talking about a party at some guy named Tonga's house and how Shout! Shout! jammed and how it was fun. *Jealous. These people have normal lives. With friends.* And they were happy. And they didn't have to worry about their crazy, glassy-eyed, shaky dad.

She got up to get dressed. Today, she didn't look so hot. Her hair looked boring. Her face boring. Everything about her boring. Whatever. She put on her lavender t-shirt and purple shorts that were just loose and long enough to make her look passable no matter how bad she felt.

Ech. That didn't look so hot either. She tried the green t-shirt and then the "PINK" one and the Vans one, and finally, she put the lavender one back on and walked out. She was just getting applications, so why did it matter anyway?

She grabbed a bagel and orange juice without saying much to her mom.

"Your dad is so happy you're looking for a job," her mom said, pushing Francie's hair out of her eyes. "And I think if you don't find the right one, that'd be okay with him, too."

Francie nodded and forced a smile. She didn't tell her mom about her dad waking her up. She didn't want to tell her mom anything ever again. Her mom would just worry. About everything, even if there was nothing to worry about. And Francie couldn't stand it. Her dad was starting a new show and probably on his usual new-job high. Which lasted about three days and then he'd just complain because he was working fifteen-hour days. And he'd pick on them and come up with over-the-top decrees.

But that morning was different, and it made her anx-ious. He was trying so hard. Like he wanted them all to be happy and okay and normal, just like she did. But that'd never happen in Vancouver. He hated location.

"I know I shouldn't say anything," her mom said. "I mean, I don't want to say anything, but are you sure this outfit is okay for a job? And shouldn't you comb your hair?"

Ugh! Her mom had no clue. "It's fine," Francie said, trying to ignore the criticism. "I'm just getting applications. And it's not like it's some super serious job. Don't worry, Mom."

Francie forced a smile, grabbed the Prius keys and walked out the door.

It felt great to be out driving again. She hadn't driven since before Austin and she loved it. But she couldn't stop thinking about her dad. And how sad he was. And how sad that made her.

And how he used to be so fun and happy and funny. Like, get excited about things, like movies and music and politics and history. But now, he didn't. Sometimes he talked about getting a new kind of job and doing something cool. That gave her a little hope. But then he just went back to what was easy and paid a lot and was safe and made her mom happy. A job that he could brag about, like how good he was.

Which made him drink and be critical and mean. That's when he criticized everything she ever did to make himself feel better. Or made fun of her, like when she tried so hard at tennis and he'd just talk about all her friends who were amazing. Or when she was in the school play and he told her it wasn't nearly as good as the shows on Broadway, how it was kind of amateurish. Or how he called Chet's band teeny boppers because he gave up on his own band because someone said music wasn't a good job in the long run. And he was too scared to try. Or do what he loved.

Again, she felt that clutching in her stomach. She tried to think about tennis. If she could just get really good, maybe it would go away forever. She could work really hard, and if she worked really hard, she could do anything. And be a professional. That was her goal. Win the U.S. Open. Travel the world. Meet super interesting people.

And be really good at something.

And be ranked in the 16s. And beat more ranked players. Like she already had. People that'd been playing since they were little. It was perfect. Until her knee.

Fear. Heart racing. Deep breath. *Loser.*

Come on! Pull it together!

She focused back on the road. She was going to get job applications. And a job meant money. And freedom. And one day, she could get her own car! Like a Jeep Wrangler.

And she'd go to Chet's show in her Jeep. And he'd see her and smile with those green eyes. Her favorite color. And she'd have tons of money. To buy stuff. Like gas. Tickets. Jeans. Food at a diner after Chet's show. And more lessons with Hawk!

And he'd love her. Chet would love her. *And daddy would be okay.*

Francie pulled in to the club to talk to Annie about the tennis camp. Annie was super sweet and said she had Liam already, but maybe she could use Francie, too. She'd been thinking of adding someone and told Francie to come by in the morning to try it out.

Next, Francie went to two department stores and one clothing shop to fill out applications. In one department store, the people were overly friendly and said they were definitely hiring and that they would call. *Ech.* The guy in the other department store was fake-friendly and said they were hiring too but was in too much of a rush to tell her more.

The girl in the clothing shop was snobby and fake and made her feel like a freak in her tennis shorts. Next, she tried three restaurants. They all said maybe and asked if she had experience, which she didn't. Starbucks was nice but said she should apply online, and they probably didn't need anyone in that location.

Then she went to a sporting goods shop. There was a stupid guy who could care less about her and seemed like he'd be happy to give her his job. Maybe selling tennis rackets and shoes would be worse than teaching tennis. This was a drag.

She checked her phone as she walked back to her car. Still nothing from Chet. She drove back to the club in total silence and then sat there staring out the window at nothing.

She was exhausted and hot but her muscles felt relaxed. She was hitting with Ricky later and then she'd hit serves. Maybe she'd do stairs. Or just sit there. Or do stairs. She should do stairs. It'd be awkward with her knee. And more awkward if anyone saw her. Like Hawk, who'd tell her it was too early for her knee and think she was crazy for trying so hard when she'd never be that good anyway, so why bother?

But Hawk wouldn't see her. And stairs would help her footwork. And strengthen her quads and get her knee to bend and break up scar tissue. Usually, she did stairs three times a week.

She got out. Eddie and Tanner were sitting on the front steps of the club. *Oh god*, she'd have to pass them. And they'd ask her what she was doing. And tease her.

She moved back behind the car so they wouldn't see her. Maybe they'd just ignore her. Or maybe she should start a conversation with Eddie and mention The West. No. She'd chicken out. Especially in front of Tanner. He'd make fun of her. And she hadn't actually talked to Eddie since the doubles fiasco. Even though she'd seen him a lot. Like from a distance.

She heard Eddie laugh. Then Tanner made weird sounds. Then they both laughed. What if they were laughing at her? No. They hadn't even seen her. *Right?*

She got back in the car. She was insane!

She crouched low and peeked back. Eddie was wearing the same exact thing he always wore: faded blue and orange board shorts and a grungy t-shirt and Stan Smith sneakers with weird white socks that went half way up his calves. She couldn't actually see the shoes but she could see the socks so it had to be so.

She thought about how angry and out of control she was the day Hawk made them play in that stupid mixed doubles tournament, banging her racket and yelling, and suddenly, she felt totally insecure. Oh my god. It was so embarrassing.

She slouched down further. She thought about how Hawk had made her agree to play in the first place, to show that juniors supported the club, and how she had literally just come back from losing to stupid Gina Groshen in that tournament in Studio City. And how she was totally mad at herself. And how the next thing she knew she was paired up with Eddie, which would've been fine if she didn't feel like crap about losing to Gina and didn't feel ugly and like she was the only junior that was such a loser that she had to be out there playing stupid mixed doubles instead of still being in the *real* tournament.

She remembered the team they were playing, Mr. Halsten and Ms. Thomas, and how awful they were, totally chipping and slicing the ball because they could hardly move, which just made it worse when she kept missing everything and hated herself for being such a loser and kept getting madder and madder.

And Eddie kept trying to have a good time and was making sound effects whenever he hit the ball to make her laugh and kept cracking jokes and telling her to relax. But she couldn't help it. *It was impossible to relax!* And it got worse, and she started hitting literally everything out or in the net and yelling and banging her racket and throwing it.

And then Hawk gave her a warning and Eddie hit her in the head with his serve and she started crying and just tanked the last few games and was crying when they went to shake hands and everyone was really quiet and she just ran off the court.

Oh my god, there was no way she could talk to Eddie now. Or maybe ever. Even if he was a possible ride to The West.

She looked again. A woman in a white tennis skirt was walking up to the club. Eddie stood to let her pass. Francie saw his shoes: Stan Smith. And his duck feet that pointed out like he was in first position.

Did he have to be so polite and make her so uncomfortable at the same time?

She grabbed her earbuds and jammed them in. Found her favorite Green Day song and blasted it. Finally. That helped.

And took her into the music. And back to Austin and Chet whispering in her ear.

And she saw his green eyes. And him laughing. *With* her. Which made her feel sure of herself and excited about Chet. And tennis.

That's it! She just had to do the stairs *with* music! And blast it when she passed Eddie and Tanner and just wave and not even hear them if they said anything.

Go! Be impulsive! Do it!

Which totally worked until she stupidly looked right at Eddie and their eyes met and he was obviously talking to her and she obviously saw it and if she didn't acknowledge it, it would be super rude, which she didn't want to be.

Francie took one earbud out. "What?" she said, trying to sound polite.

"I said, hey, what's up?" Eddie replied. And he smiled. A genuine smile. Like Chet. Genuine.

She took a deep breath.

"Or not," he added.

"Just um, gonna run stairs before I hit," she said, trying to sound nonchalant.

"That's what we should be doing," Eddie said to Tanner.

Tanner laughed, "Yeah, no chance."

"But that's why you're good," Eddie said to Francie. "You're committed."

She felt the blood fill her cheeks. At least he wasn't saying anything about her knee.

"How many do you do?" he asked.

She shrugged, "Usually like twenty minutes, but now, I don't know. I haven't done it with the knee thing yet. It might be like once." She laughed at how lame she was. Literally.

"Wow," he said and looked at Tanner again. "You hear that? Twenty minutes."

"I'm out," Tanner said and disappeared into the club.

"Well, *I* should do this," Eddie said, getting up. "You mind?"

No, I mean, yes! I totally just want to be by myself.

"Sure," she said instead.

He looked down at his shorts and shoes, then shrugged, "Yeah, okay, let's do this," and gestured to the sidewalk leading to the stairs.

Oh my god.

She took a breath, wishing he'd change his mind, then started walking, totally dreading that now she'd have to have a conversation.

"I've seen you do this, like a thousand times, right?"

She nodded. Ever since she heard how good stairs were for footwork, she'd done them as often as possible.

"Cool," he said.

And then they just walked in silence and she felt totally awkward. Like what if she had nothing to say the whole time? And why was he watching her? And why was he doing this? And what if he *did* like her? That made it even more awkward. In fact, not liking someone back was worse than liking someone and not having them like you back. It made her feel weird and terrible all at once. Like she didn't know how to act to make sure he didn't think she liked him, while still being polite and friendly, and she also felt bad that she could possibly hurt his feelings.

"So what's going on with the knee and tennis?" he asked.

Oh, god. "Um, well, I guess it's coming along." She shrugged.

"Yeah?"

She looked at him. His eyes said he actually wanted to know.

"What?" he said.

"Nothing! Nothing, I mean, yeah, I'm hitting again. And it's awesome. And it hurts a little." She shrugged and couldn't help smiling. "And a lot."

He laughed, "Cool."

Not so bad.

Confidence. No weirdness. Just being herself.

He feels comfortable. And safe. She could talk to him like normal.

"So yeah, it's okay," she nodded. "And better. And hitting totally helps. Which is weird. Because the doctor and everyone say to take it easy. Although the PT guy also says to keep it moving and strong. So hopefully, this'll help. And…" She hesitated. "I'm gonna play Ventura in a couple weeks."

She held her breath, hoping he didn't think that was weird. So she didn't have to defend it.

"Wow, cool, you're totally on it," he said instead.

Oh my god. His eyes said he was being honest. *Weird.*

Also weird was that she spewed all that about tennis without hesitation.

"Thanks," she said.

"Yeah. I guess we just all want to get good. And you're doing it."

She smiled and nodded and had no idea what to more say. But that seemed okay, too. Like no pressure to say something amazing. Like he just liked her. Even if she was silent.

Bizarre.

Maybe he could be her friend.

Or maybe she could just shut up in her mind. Because maybe she was driving herself crazy.

Luckily, they got to the stairs so she didn't have to do anything.

The stairs were made of concrete and old railroad ties and led up to the houses on the hill, like some kind of shortcut.

"Alright," he said, looking up the long column of stairs.

Good. He could go first. But then he didn't. So she stretched and he joined her and said it was a good idea, as if everyone didn't already know you were supposed to stretch!

Then he narrated the stretching and made jokes about how stiff he was. And she tried to focus. *Adductors then hams then calves.* Then she tried to bend her knee but it was tight. *Whatever.* The stairs would help. She shook out her leg. "Okay, let's do this."

He gestured for her to go first, so she did. Her knee hurt immediately, and she was slow and awkward and embarrassed that he could see her, but she pushed it. Like when she hit. And halfway up, the pain eased up. Or numbed out.

"You doin' okay?" Eddie yelled.

"Yeah!"

At the top, he finally went ahead, thank god, because going down was super hard. Her left leg was weak, and she had to walk-limp down. And then she sat at the bottom and watched him do a few more rounds.

At the end, he flopped down, totally out of breath. "You're my hero."

"What?!" she laughed.

"And you have to promise to make me do this again."

She shook her head, totally amused. "Oh my god," she said and wondered why he couldn't just push himself. It felt so good to push. And made her feel strong. And in control.

Of something.

Was that weird?

No. It gave her purpose.

"So, I heard you're going to The West with Stella," he said, pulling himself up.

Really?! That was great news! It meant Stella was still in. "Uh, yeah, hopefully it works out," Francie said, sounding way more relaxed than she felt.

"Yeah," he said, and they started back. And she wondered if he was going too, but was too scared to ask. Like she'd ruin or jinx it. Pushing other people wasn't her thing. Only herself.

So, she talked about the weather, which was stupid, and then he told her how he had to go do his office-building cleaning job with his cousin, which was his cousin's business, who was like twenty-eight, and it paid okay so he liked it. And then they reached the front of the club and he said, "Thanks" and "Let's do it again."

She really wanted to ask about The West.

Instead, she smiled and bolted to her car.

8

The rest of Francie's day was uneventful except when she hit on the ball machine and played with Ricky and her leg felt tired. Maybe running stairs wasn't such a good thing. Or maybe she'd be stronger the next day for it. She decided to think positive.

She also told Annie she'd be there in the morning. And Annie seemed super happy and made her feel wanted and kind of excited, like this could be a good thing after all and everything was falling into place.

She'd hoped Stella would be at the snack shop, but no such luck. And no luck with Chet. She kept checking her phone every five seconds and still nothing.

She tried to avoid Eddie when she walked to the front, but he waved, so she waved back and felt her cheeks get hot. He was with Axe and Tanner and she knew they were talking about her. *Whatever.*

When she got home, her mom was out and her dad was still working, and she just stayed in her room and drank four cups of hot chocolate even though it was the middle of the afternoon and really hot outside and then she felt totally sick from it, like barf sick.

Was it all in her head that Chet wasn't writing back? She felt that slow heaviness creep in. Like she was trapped and couldn't breathe. And was...*a loser.*

And then her mom came home and looked sad when Francie didn't want to eat downstairs with her. And then her dad came home and started drinking without saying hi or asking about the job thing and was sleeping on the couch by 10:00 p.m. And she felt worse.

Then she sat in her room and imagined what it would be like if the tennis camp didn't work out and she had to get one of those jobs where she had to smile all day and make coffee and people complained if you got their name wrong. She remembered the time at Starbucks with her dad when this man got mad at the Barista for writing "Brat" on his cup instead of Brett and her dad made a joke to try to make the Barista feel better and the man stormed out and they all laughed. That was the good side of her dad. He could make people laugh and feel better if he wanted. But only if he wanted.

Then Francie imagined the job at the department store, standing in junior clothing, moving hangers to look busy and helping cute, skinny girls with boyfriends spend their allowances on all the coolest things. Nightmare.

Chet had to write her.

Or she would disappear into a black, hopeless abyss.

At midnight, Francie couldn't stand it anymore. Her head was killing her from thinking so much about Chet and the job and her dad and she couldn't sleep and decided there was no way to know if she'd written too much if she didn't ask him or at least apologize or do something.

Anything was better than this feeling that Chet didn't like what she'd said.

She got up, opened a new email and started to write.

Subject: bla bla bla
Dear Chet,
Sorry about the rant last night. Hope it didn't go on forever.
Job hunt was grim today. Will probably end up in tennis camp hell. Drag. Tho it may be okay if not too many hours. Also got renewed access to car thanks to potential job, which was fun. And ran stairs to help knee get back in shape. Still have hope Stella will get us a ride! So coming 2 see u play is a decent possibility.
Later,
Francie

She reread it quickly. The minimal amount of pronouns and articles made it perfect, short and nonchalant. She hit send and whispered, "Please let that be okay," to any beings out there, be they gods, goddesses, fairies, snowmen or whatever. And she felt better. There was definitely something to speaking your mind.

Suddenly, a new email came in.

Subject: bla bla bla

From him! Oh my god, he was on too. Right then. At the same time as her! It was a sign! She could write back! And they could chat! *No!* She had to slow down. That was the point. She took a deep breath and opened the email.

Hey sweetie,

Sweetie!

Forget the apologies. I enjoy your rants. And walking towards something good, huh? I can see that. I think mine is similar. Walking towards something good which would be music. Always music. Freedom in music. Like it saves me. Literally. You know that song "Wonderwall"...it's like that personified, where "you" is the music. My wonderwall is music!
And once again, I digress. Bor-ing. Do-wop, do-wop.
Great for The West! Lemme know. Will put you on guest list so you don't have to spend your hard earned job $s! Tennis gig sounds sweet. What's the issue?
CJ

Francie's heart swelled. He *got* her! He got what made her free! And of course, she knew "Wonderwall." Oasis. Her dad used to listen to it. A lot. She forced herself to wait a minute then hit reply:

The issue is I'd rather be playing tennis than teaching and it's going to be torture, but still probably better than *any retail torture. But you're right, it's a sweet gig as far as jobs go. Will have to look at it as more $ for little time. Will keep you posted.*

I'm glad music gives you freedom. I like that song too.

And cool on the show!!! Can friend Stella come 2? And her friend Scott as he may be our ride. And maybe her brother Eddie.

F

She hit send without a second thought. She had no idea if Eddie would go but wanted to cover all her bases. And this was so fun!

Two seconds later, another email appeared from Chet:

Yes, the more the merrier and be sure to bring the adorable limp along too. As long as you don't walk away from me again.

Oh god, now he was flirting!

She wrote: *The limp is a little self-conscious. But will be there.*

He wrote: *The limp shouldn't be. Although its demureness is charming.*

Demureness? What the heck was that? She had to look it up: shy, modest, reserved.

She wrote: *Well, I'll let it know. Maybe it'll break out of its shell for the show.*

Maybe she was breaking out of her shell. Maybe that's what was happening here. Maybe that was why all these good things were happening. She was getting out. She was free. And she had something, someone to walk toward.

He wrote: *Excellent. It'd mean a lot to me for you to see our show. I've been writing a lot. Would love for you to hear. And tell me what you think. Honesty inspires me. So does the limp. Good nite to both of you.*

She wrote: *Would luv to hear your songs! Good nite.*

He wrote: *Cool. Will send. Sweet dreams. To you and the limp.*

Oh my god, it was just like in that movie when the puffy English girl was talking to her boss about her skirt. *Bridget Jones!* Chet must've seen it. Like maybe his mom made him watch it.

And she inspired him! *She* did. Francie Mills. And he was sending songs! And flirting. With her. Now.

Francie grabbed her phone. She had to text Stella. And find out about Eddie and The West. And what about Scott with the car? And could Eddie drive if Scott couldn't?

She suddenly felt nervous. What if something went wrong? And what if she sounded desperate to Stella? Or what if Stella got bugged by her asking and pushing? And what if Stella didn't want to go in the end?

Panic. Stella had to go.

And Francie had to stay cool. And not bug Stella. And let it lie. Or maybe be tactful and just ask a little. Or what?! Finally Francie just texted: *Hey Stella. We're all on The West list. Any luck with Scott driving?*

Stella texted back instantly: *Awesome! Haven't talked to Scott yet.*

Wow! She was up, too. But she hadn't talked to Scott. What if she never talked to Scott? What if Stella waited too long to ask and then he couldn't drive? And Eddie made other plans? Or worse, what if it came together too late and her parents said no because of it?!

Stop! You're insane.

Francie exhaled. And let it lie. She texted: *Cool. Lemme know. Just have to tell parents so they say yes. Mom will be ok but dad is the issue. Ideas???* And then Francie didn't let it lie and texted: *If Scott can't drive, can Eddie?*

Her gut told her it was too much but she did it anyway. Her gut was right. She detected annoyance in Stella's reply: *Don't worry. I got it.*

Francie was worried.

And wished she hadn't sent that overzealous and paranoid text. This is why she didn't push people.

But she needed to know that Stella would follow through.

She reread the emails with Chet and reminded herself again how lucky it was that any of this was happening at all. Like total magic. Meeting Chet. Talking to Stella. Stella *wanting* to go. None of this would be happening if she wasn't meant to see Chet again.

Another text came from Stella: *Just come here for sleepover. Parents are out of town. Or say we're having a teen game night. Parents love that shit! Like it's educational or something.*

Oh my god, *see!* Stella just gave her the perfect solution. And wasn't mad. She was showing up. Over and over. And Francie had to just chill out.

A flash of her dad sprawled on the couch appeared in her mind. Beer bottles. Chili on shirt. Fly open. Why? Humiliation. Panic. That's what would happen if it didn't come together and she didn't get to go. If Stella flaked. Or her parents said no.

A flash of her room. Her in it. Trapped. Alone. Hopeless. Boring. Bored. *Loser.* Stabbing in her heart. This is what would happen if she missed Chet's show and had to stay home.

She had to get her dad out of her head.

She texted back: *K. Awesome plan. Thank you. Am going to do exactly what you said :)*

9

Francie hit a ball crosscourt to Margot Kenner and watched the nine year old run over and swing at it. Wiff! A complete miss. Francie groaned. Week two on the job and already she wanted to bolt. How on earth was she going to make it until 1:00 p.m.? It was almost impossible to stand still out there and hit balls at the kids.

At least she knew what to do and didn't have to think much. And at least it was part-time and not retail and Annie would let her off when she had a tournament. And at least she was hitting with Jeff later. And she beat him last time and felt ready to play Ventura next week.

How much longer was there anyway?

"That's okay, Margot," she yelled. "Try it again, but this time keep your feet moving."

Margot started bouncing around.

"There you go," Francie continued. "Now watch the ball closely, hit up on it and follow through. Just like we practiced."

Margot did a practice swing. Close enough. Francie hit the next ball gently and Margot miraculously returned it over the net.

"That's it," Francie cheered. "Now go."

Francie gestured with her racket as Margot took off on her mandatory sprint around the court and eight-year-old Harvey McAdams bounded out of the shade and up to the baseline, ready to go. Francie ran over to the bench and pretended to towel off and glanced at her phone. Fifteen more minutes. Was time even moving?!

"Okay, everybody gets a few more ups and then that's it for today," Francie yelled.

She could totally power through this. Because in four hours and fifteen minutes, at 5:00 p.m. that very afternoon, she was going to Stella's and they were going to The West.

"Forehand, backhand, drop shot, volley, then you run!" she yelled as they started the drill.

Francie could barely contain herself. She was going to see Chet. And it was going to be amazing. The whole past week had been amazing.

First, she'd emailed Chet and told him about her Ventura tournament next week. It was perfect because she'd gotten a bye and didn't play until Tuesday so she could practice all weekend. And he was excited for her.

And she was excited for him for his show and told him she couldn't wait to hear his new songs. And then he'd emailed her a video of him playing a song. In his room. With different versions. And asked her opinion. And then he Facetimed. With more songs. And she kept giving her opinion. And he was so logical and measured and caring about his songs. Even though his songs were kind of punk-ish and wild. But they were amazing. And he wrote all of them. And in between, he kept singing little snippets of "Wonderwall" with his own funny lyrics about her, as if she were "saving" him. And she was having so much fun and was so into him that she almost couldn't stand it.

And now she was going to see him. For real. Which made her nervous. Probably because she was so happy. And couldn't believe it.

Stella had gotten Scott to agree to drive to The West which was also amazing. And nerve wracking. Probably because Francie knew Scott could still change his mind. Or something could happen to his car. Or he and Stella could get stoned and not want to go or not be able to drive. She'd heard Stella talk about getting stoned, which made Francie uncomfortable.

Stella was also impulsive, and she imagined Scott was like that too. Francie still hadn't met Scott, but she'd found him online and everything about him was super dramatic. Like the photo of him in a cape in front of a David Bowie mural. And at *Rocky Horror.*

Her stomach tightened. Impulsive. Like her dad. That was why she was worried about Stella and Scott. Unpredictable. Unreliable. Like they weren't safe.

No. Stella's fine!

She took a deep breath and thought of Chet. The only reason she got to know him was because she'd been impulsive. For once.

Bats!

Francie hit the next ball and tried to focus on Chet again. And being positive. And how nice and normal he was. And how he took his time with things. Deliberate. But with a flow. That seemed relaxed. And hopeful.

And then her dad popped into her head. Not relaxed or hopeful. Just drunk, swaying at the counter. Irrational. Hurtful. Weak. He was the only thing that could get in the way of going. But right now, miraculously, it didn't seem like that would happen.

He had the day off and had seemed irritated when she left that morning. But as far as she could tell, her mom hadn't said anything about Stella's "game night," and if all went according to plan, she'd get home by 4:00 p.m., change and ride her bike to Stella's without him ever knowing.

At first, Francie had felt guilty about not telling her mom and dad about The West. Which is why she'd tested the waters by simply mentioning Chet's show.

Disaster.

She'd just kind of thrown it out there that she'd heard the teeny-bopper band from the movie had a show at The West and that it would be fun to go, like her dad used to go to shows.

Her dad immediately jumped on it, saying it'd be ridiculous to go all the way out there for a little club gig for a little unknown band. And then he launched into a forty-five-minute monologue about all the great shows he'd seen at the Greek and Hollywood Bowl and how the *real* bands had already come through The West ages ago, and when he and his brothers were kids, they'd seen a few amazing shows there. Nothing "these boys" did would be worth it; they "couldn't compare." And The West wasn't what it used to be. Only "low-caliber bands" played there now.

Francie kept waiting for him to use the word "losers," but he didn't.

Her mom thought Francie was too young to get in and asked if any of her friends were going. Her dad chimed in that it was an all-ages place but that Francie and her friends were way too young even for that, which made zero sense and just made Francie super angry at her dad for being so mean about Chet's band and completely dissing something that she totally loved. He wasn't even the one going, so who cared if he saw better bands?

Francie did everything she could to not let her anger show and just said "fine" and moved on. Her dad smiled smugly. Apparently, to him that meant he'd won and that he was right. And better. At whatever. So infuriating!

Then, she waited until the next morning after her dad left for work to tell her mom about game night. Her mom was incredibly happy that Francie had made new friends at the club and hugged her. Francie could feel her mom's relief. Her mom said her dad wouldn't be thrilled if Francie was gone that night since he was leaving for Vancouver a few days later. But they both knew he'd just be drunk and asleep after dinner anyway and not hanging out, so it didn't matter.

Francie didn't mention anything about the sleepover to her mom. She let that lie. And her mom didn't say it but Francie figured her mom wouldn't tell her dad about the game night since being open and telling the truth in their family never ended well. So, she was set.

When the rotation was done, Francie shuffled the kids off, rehashed the day with Annie and got her things together. And then, finally, she was free to go hit with Jeff.

That's when she saw the text from her dad: *Call me when you get a chance.*

Oh my god. She instantly felt her stomach tighten. This could be anything. She took a deep breath. Should she ignore it? Call? She had to get it over with. So she dialed. No response. *Ahhh!* She'd try later. Or wait till she got home. At least she'd called. And it was going to be okay. She took a deep breath and went to hit with Jeff.

It was a great day for playing. Francie felt loose and her knee didn't hurt, and she beat Jeff 6–4, which made her feel great and meant she'd have an even better time at the show.

There was nothing more from her dad so she made her way to the snack shop. Stella was there with two friends Francie didn't know and about forty silver "Happy Anniversary!" helium balloons crammed behind the snack shop counter. All three were opening balloons and inhaling helium, eating fries and listening to an old-school dance-y song, surprisingly, on Stella's iPad that sounded vaguely familiar.

"Well, if it isn't the tennis pro," Stella said with a cartoon-high helium voice. "This is Benny and Tulip. From school."

"Hi," Benny and Tulip said in unison with helium voices.

"This is Serena Williams. I mean Francie Mills," teased Stella.

"Hi, Francie," Benny and Tulip giggled.

"You want one?" Stella asked Francie, handing her a balloon.

Francie didn't but took it anyway.

"Francie finally decided to take the easy, high-paying job," Stella said to Benny and Tulip. "The job that finishes at two while I'm still here slaving away."

"Finishes at one and pays twice the hourly wage," Francie boasted in her helium voice. It was crazy how high it was.

Stella laughed and high-fived her. "Francie's coming with us to the show. You guys'll have to come next time," she said to Benny and Tulip, then turned to Francie, "Billy said they're having another show in Santa Barbara."

"Really?"

"Yeah."

Amazing. In one week, Stella had laid her claim to Billy Jones, because he was "hot," and had totally become friends with him online and was all over Blues Harp Jones everything, commenting and chatting with everyone. She was like a fire, blazing forward, getting everyone excited. Francie was slightly jealous but also glad because it meant Stella really wanted to go. And she could relax. A little.

"We'll let you know when," Stella said to Benny and Tulip and breathed in more helium.

They breathed in more too and replied, "Okay," in unison and cracked up.

Then Stella started singing to the song on the iPad in her helium voice and dancing a twist, kind of going nuts. And Benny and Tulip joined in too. So weird.

Francie wondered if you could get high from the helium. They all seemed high. And she started to worry again. But didn't say anything. "I can't believe they let you play music here," she said instead. "What is this?"

Stella turned her iPad to face Francie: John Travolta and Uma Thurman dancing the twist in *Pulp Fiction*. She'd seen it a thousand times with her mom and dad. They loved it. "Chuck Berry," Stella said. "It balances things out *at the country club*."

"Bye Francie!" Margot spurted from the walkway.

Francie immediately hid the balloon and waved.

"You're basically making a killing for standing in the sun with little brats at your beck and call, aren't you?" Stella said, then breathed in a whole bunch of helium. "Thank you very much. I mean, I accept *your* thank you for insisting you take the job."

Francie laughed.

"And insisting you come with us to the show. Though Eddie will be sad you love Chet."

"What?" Francie laughed.

"But we're happy that you're into Chet, right guys?"

Benny and Tulip sucked in helium and replied, "Yeeeeeessss." Kind of eerie.

"And you should definitely spend the night," Stella said to Francie. "So I can show you my costumes for the RatBat shoot. And we'll *parrrrtay*! And if your parents have an issue, we'll get Eddie to call and fake being my dad."

Wow, really?

That made Francie kind of nervous. She had to practice in the morning. And it seemed unpredictable. They seemed unpredictable. And reckless. What if something happened?

Nothing's gonna happen!

But before Francie could even reply or figure out what she wanted, Stella started the Chuck Berry song over and began dancing again, like kind of going nuts with the twist. And Benny and Tulip did too. And Francie just watched them dancing away, right there at the tennis club, like they didn't care about anything and weren't embarrassed at all, like they were totally free.

10

Francie made it home by 4:00 p.m. as planned, but when she walked in the front door, the tension was already at level ten.

Her dad was yelling and slurring something about the sprinklers and how if her mom didn't park far enough over in the driveway, she might step on one and either hurt herself or break it. Her mom was nodding and cooking. Why was she cooking now?!

"Do you even hear me?" he continued.

"Yes, I'll move the car as soon as I'm done," her mom said.

"And what if someone comes up the driveway and doesn't have enough room before you're done?

"No one's gonna come up the driveway! At three o'clock on a Friday afternoon!"

"Are you sure?"

Her mom threw down the dish towel. "Fine, I'll move it now," she said through clenched teeth and grabbed her keys and stormed out.

Why did she give in like that? His argument was ridiculous. Francie could feel her own anger building but knew she had to get out of there. She made a beeline for the kitchen as her dad took his beer and sat down on the couch to stare at the TV. She was going to avoid eye contact at all costs and quickly started to make a peanut butter sandwich.

Her mom came back in, smiling as if that whole thing never happened. "What are you doing? I made goulash," she said and grabbed a plate for Francie. "I think it's ready."

Francie eyed the goulash. It looked fair, like the usual. "Okay," she said.

Her mom seemed relieved, "So how was your day?"

"Fine," Francie replied.

"Fine? That's it?" her dad bellowed from the couch.

"Yup."

"And how's the job going?"

"Fine."

"Fine," he laughed and shook his head, mocking, as if her answer wasn't up to his standards.

She watched her mom prepare the plate. Why was it taking so long?

"So, nothing exciting? No new kids?" he asked.

"No, I told you, I just stand out there and hit them balls and show them what to do."

"So, nothing interesting at all to talk about?" her dad continued with a condescending tone, making her feel like she was boring for having nothing to say.

"No," she said, grabbing a spoon.

"No, of course, not," he said, as if he'd have a million things to say about the boring day making him better than her. She watched him get up with his smug smile and walk over.

He swayed a little, clearly drunk. He stuck a spoon in the goulash and took a huge bite, spilling as he chewed with his eyes half closed as if he was about to fall asleep, annoying her mom, who cleaned it up but said nothing.

"Now, what about this woman with the visor?" he said, opening his glassy eyes and smiling.

"Annie?" Francie said, instantly feeling the panic.

"I had a nice little chat with her this afternoon."

"What?"

"Very nice, I must admit, but Coach Hawkins is quite superior when it comes to tennis instruction. He really is supremely knowledgeable."

Oh my god, what was happening?

"Wouldn't you agree?" he asked.

Francie hesitated, afraid to answer. "I, I don't know what you're talking about."

"You don't know if Coach Hawkins is a knowledgeable instructor?"

"Yes, but it's not like that," she said, getting flustered.

"Well, I'd say he's definitely superior to the other instructor," he said and looked at her for effect then took another bite of goulash.

"She's fine; Annie's fine," Francie said, defensively. "They're just different. Why do you have to compare them?!" And why was he so mean and critical?!! Annie was so nice!

"I'm just looking out for your interests. So I let her know I thought it was too much for you working on the court while you're rehabilitating your knee."

Oh my god. "What?" she said.

"I just had a little chat with her," he said, smiling and trying to rile her up.

And it was working. "You're the one who wanted me to do it!"

"Well, if you were working with Hawkins, now that would be a different story," he said smugly.

"Oh my god! You told her I'm not working there anymore?"

He took another bite of goulash and belched. "Something to that effect."

"That's totally unfair! You can't do that!"

"Well, I did."

"But she made it work for me! She gave me extra hours! And now she needs me!"

"Now don't raise your voice. I'm sure, she can find someone else."

"And I can totally do it!" she exploded. "My knee is fine!"

He smiled again as if he'd won. He'd gotten her to that place where she was out of control, and he loved it. He could feel superior.

"I'm only raising my voice because you're being completely unfair!" she yelled, holding back the tears. "I didn't even want to get a job and now I did and it's not that bad and I can make some money." She looked at him pleading. "Please, just let me handle this."

"Now, tell me about this teen game night."

Francie stopped. Oh my god. She felt the floor drop out from under her, and her heart start racing instantly. Panic.

"Hmm?"

She couldn't breathe. She looked at her mom who diverted her eyes. Clearly, she told him.

"Your mom even came home early to make you dinner before you go."

Francie was frozen, too terrified to say anything. Did that mean she could still go? Or not?

He waited patiently, taking another bite. He knew he had her.

"Stella Plumb and her brother Eddie," Francie said, voice quivering. "They go to the club, and they're having friends over."

"How come we've never heard of this Stella before?"

"Actually, I think Libby plays doubles with the mom or golf or something," her mom said, also looking nervous.

He looked up from his food at Francie and belched again. Then he smiled and looked back down, his eyes starting to droop as if he would fall asleep then and there.

"She belongs to the club," Francie said, realizing this was the moment to get out of there. "Her brother plays tennis. They're totally fine." She turned and walked off. Hoping she could just get out of there before he stopped her.

She made it to her room and quickly started packing. She hated him so much. He was *insane*. How could he possibly have told Annie she couldn't do the job? Hopefully, he hadn't insulted her. Or hurt her feelings. She'd have to go by the club on the way to Stella's to see.

She grabbed her cute flower blouse and jeans and Chuck Taylors and shoved them in her backpack. As planned. Then she grabbed PJs and shampoo and a brush and mascara. She'd just take her stuff and shower at the club.

There was a knock on the door. Francie froze. Her mom poked her head in and smiled, that terrible apologetic smile. "I'm sorry honey."

Francie felt her anger rising and just shook her head, trying to keep it in.

"Are you crying?" her mom asked.

"No! Please just go away." Francie turned so her mom couldn't see her face. "I'm fine!"

"I brought you the goulash so you can have it before you go." She put it on the desk.

"I'm taking the car and I'm spending the night there," Francie said without looking at her mom. She felt her mom's hesitation. "And I don't care what either of you thinks." She didn't. If her mom said no, she'd just sneak out and take the bike.

"Okay, then," her mom said quietly. "Just be safe."

Francie closed her bag. Why wouldn't she just leave?!

"I'm proud of you for standing up to your father. It's so much more than I could ever do."

The iron hands clutched her heart and throat all at once and burning anger seared through her.

Then why did you marry him??????

This was why she hated her mom the most. She forced a smile, hoping her mom would go before she fell apart. Inside she was on fire and the tears were forcing themselves up.

Her mom came in and kissed Francie's head. "Be sure to eat before it gets cold. And wear your new sandals. They look so pretty on you." Francie nodded and her mom smiled and left.

Francie punched the bed in anger. Over and over and over.

Francie pulled into the club and went in and found Annie. She didn't know what to say, but somehow, Annie understood immediately when she explained that her dad was crazy and then started to cry and tried to explain that he had no right to say she couldn't work if her knee was okay and it wasn't too much for her. Then Annie hugged her and told her that her dad had been very nice and just seemed concerned about his daughter, like any good dad. And then Francie really started to cry. And Annie hugged her tighter and smoothed her hair and let her cry and said that her dad said he trusted Annie's "expertise" and would leave it up to her to decide if Francie was pushing herself too hard or not.

How was this possible?

"So he didn't say I couldn't work here?"

"No," Annie said, with her warm comforting smile. "And it looks to me like we've got ourselves a great new camp counselor on our hands."

Francie couldn't believe it. Annie gave her a tissue and another hug. And then went back to teaching, and Francie went to take a shower and get ready.

She felt totally beat up and just sat down on the bench in the locker room. She looked at the last email to Chet from the night before:

Subject: Show
Hey Chet,
Can't wait. Good luck!
FM

She'd been so excited. And now she felt completely rattled. Like, why would he ever like her? Why would anyone like her? Her family was insane.

Then she watched the first video Chet sent her. When he was singing. And trying different things. Because he cared. And was happy. And measured. But just going for it.

And then Francie went forward to the part where Chet's mom poked her head into his room and watched as he kept playing. And trying things. Because he didn't notice her. And his mom was so beautiful. With warm happy eyes. And a gentle smile. And long flowing blond hair. Like a goddess. And then Chet noticed his mom. And she smiled so lovingly at him and told him she was going out. And he said, "Okay." And Francie could tell Chet's mom loved him so much. And he loved his mom. And when she left, Chet turned to the camera and said, "Mum," with a cheeky smile, and Francie could tell there was no weirdness. And Chet kept playing the song for the camera. And Francie stopped the video.

They were so normal and happy and solid. And his mom was so loving. And Francie just wanted to crawl up into it. And be a part of their world.

Not hers. Here in the locker room. Wanting to escape.

She turned her phone to video and stared at her own face. She hated it. She stuck out her tongue. She hated that too. Even though it was kind of funny. And weird.

She hit play. She had nothing to lose. And had to do something. So she didn't disappear into the abyss of misery.

"Hi. Hi, Chet," she croaked. "I'm sitting in the locker room at the tennis club." She panned the room. "Coming to see you. Super angry. Like...I can't stand it. Because of my dad. But I'm trying to be positive so I'm making this stupid video." She turned the camera back on herself and made a funny face. "And I'm not embarrassing or pathetic at all. *Not.* But I am coming to see you and forgetting about him being a jerk. And confusing. And making me feel so crazy. And that's all I'm going to say because it's so boring, and I just needed to get that out. So I won't have to think about it when I'm there. Because I'm gonna see you soon. And you're going to be amazing!" And she smiled and shrugged and hit stop.

Oh my god. That felt so good. And maybe even a little normal. For a second. And she attached the video to a text and wrote: *A little misery and love. See you soon. FM*

And she felt SO. MUCH. BETTER.

She began putting her stuff in her bag and imagined Chet liking the video. And liking her. And hugging her when he saw her at The West. And introducing her to all his friends like she was super cool and he adored her and was proud to have her there. In spite of her family. Because he didn't care about them. He cared about her.

A text arrived: *Hey FM...on the radio dial! So sorry about Hank. You're amazing! Be my muse. See you soon. CJ*

11

Francie walked up the sidewalk to Stella's house. As soon as she'd gotten out of her car, she felt free again. Like in Austin. Like anything was possible. And everything was new. An adventure about to happen. Exciting.

She could literally feel herself walking taller.

Even the houses there seemed hopeful. Like they were nicer than where she lived, in her tract home. Fancier. And right on the lake. She wondered if they all had boats. And if Stella's parents did. Probably. She could just see Stella racing around the lake, being chased by lake patrol and out-speeding them. Yeah, Stella probably knew how to drive a boat even though she probably thought it was uncool.

Francie started up Stella's driveway. The house looked friendly with white paint and sage trim. A periwinkle door and English garden. Window boxes with flowers. And then she noticed the sheer black curtains blowing in a second-story window. Definitely Stella. And definitely not fitting in with the whole lakeside, country club thing.

She also noticed Stella's giant wooden set pieces and furniture on the porch. Black, silver, steampunkish, amazing. The ones from the *Game of Thrones*-Tim Burton sketch that Stella said she wanted to drop at RatBat's on the way to The West. That made Francie nervous. What if it slowed them down? What if Stella decided to stay in Agoura with RatBat? Instead of going to the show? And Francie was stuck, with no ride?

What if she just took her parents car?

No, that wasn't an option. It made her too scared. Like really alone-scared.

Like what if she were by herself in the car on the freeway and got in an accident and died. Scared. Because it was just her. With no one to save her.

No! That wasn't going to happen.

Because this was going to work. Stella would come through.

Because she was free. Finally.

And Stella was going to save her. From going alone.

She took a deep breath and stepped up to the door. Loud music blasted from somewhere in the house. Jane's Addiction or something. Definitely more rock than metal or punk. She tried to peek in the front window. Nothing but blinds.

She hesitated then knocked loudly. Nothing. Then rang the doorbell a few times. Finally, someone yelled back, "Hang on!" The music stopped.

Oh god, was it Eddie?

She heard running and yelling, "Coming!" Then the footsteps stopped and something banged into the door; it flung open, and there was Eddie, standing on the tile in his white socks and out of breath. He smiled ear to ear when he saw her, "Hi."

"Hi," Francie forced a smile.

"Hi," he said again with his stupid grin.

"Is Stella here?"

"*That* would be a big fat negative."

What?! "Really?" The nerves instantly clutched her stomach.

"But she will be. Soon. Like in twenty seconds. Come in." He held the door for her and bowed as if he were a butler or something.

Breathe.

He grinned. "Besides, I'm here."

What was his problem? She stepped inside. And really hoped he was right about Stella.

Temporary. It's temporary.

The place was very nice. And neat. Mostly. With cream-colored carpet and furniture, but a lot of stuff too. Tons of paintings and photos and odds and ends of furniture. And a piano and harp. And big cozy cushions everywhere. And a giant TV. And wooden elephants and masks and shrine-like things that were definitely from other countries. And tons of books and stacks of papers. And piles of newspapers. And jackets. And golf clubs and a can of tennis balls.

And sure enough, they were on the lake. With boats cruising around.

"I guess it's kind of a mess," he said.

To her it looked great. Totally relaxed and comfortable. She wished her house was like this. "It's fine."

"Yeah, I go for the je-ne-sais-quoi look too. But our parents get all the credit, except for the attractive rollerblades over there." He grinned. "They're lawyers. Never here and can't sit still for two seconds. I guess the apples don't fall far from the tree, right?"

He was insane. "Cool," she said and nodded. And why was he all hyper all of a sudden? Usually he seemed so chill.

"Okay, then. Nevermind," Eddie said, clapping his hands together. "You want something to drink? Water, coke, juice, beer, a peanut butter and banana smoothie?"

"I'm okay for now, thanks," Francie said, noticing a photo of Stella and Eddie as kids at a river. Eddie was carefully showing Stella how to hold a fly fishing rod. It was sweet.

"Well, I'm gonna go back in and work," he said, gesturing to the other room. "But you can come watch if you want."

"Watch?"

"I'm putting together my movie. It's kind of a documentary. Of our family. But mostly it's Stella being annoying. So more of a mockumentary."

"Oh."

"And then I add in other random stuff, like Stonehenge. I can show you if you want."

"No thanks, I'll just wait here." It sounded funny but she was getting more and more nervous about Stella so it was probably better to wait out there. As if that would make a difference.

Suddenly, he lit up, "Hang on!" and ran into the other room and returned with a camera, sliding across the tile in the socks and landing in front of her. "See!" He pointed it at her and started filming, "And here we have Stella's new friend, Francie Mills, tennis player extraordinaire, with a decent taste in music. Much better than Stella, I might add."

Oh my god.

"Would you care to say anything to our audience today, Miss Mills?"

"No, thank you."

"Nothing at all?"

"No."

"Would you care to elaborate on the suggestion by Mr. Plumb that you are quite excellent at running stairs?"

"No, but I would like you to turn off the camera."

"How about telling us what you think of how Mr. Plumb ran the stairs?"

"He did great. Now can you turn this thing off?!"

"Oh, c'mon, just give us a few words about fitness and footwork for tennis."

Was he serious? She looked straight into the lens, "Running stairs helps your footwork in tennis," then covered the lens with her hand. "Okay?"

"That's it?"

"Yes!"

"But you're so entertaining when you're mad."

She turned and headed into the living room, "I'm just going to wait in here."

He followed, still filming, "Does Francie hate the camera as much as Stella?"

"Yes," she said and covered her face with a pillow as she sat on the couch.

"It's just a home movie. No one's gonna see."

"I don't care! Go away!" she yelled from behind the pillow.

"Then will you help me with sound effects?"

"*Sound* effects?"

"A scream and a door slam. I need a girl to do a scream for Stella."

"I don't think so."

"Just come see then. It's cool. And you can help me edit. I mean, once I'm a famous movie director, I'm gonna need a great editor."

"I'm not interested!"

"In the editing or the scream?"

"Neither!" She flopped the pillow down and saw him grinning from ear to ear, clearly enjoying pushing all her buttons. And why would he think she could be an *editor*?!

"Okay!" he said, taking the camera down, continuing to tease. "Boy are you a killjoy."

"Excuse me?"

"Someone who kills the joy."

"I know what a killjoy is."

"Would you care to elaborate, Miss Mills?" he asked lifting the camera again.

"I never said I'd do it in the first place. It's like you're saying *anyone* who doesn't help you is a killjoy."

"Well, let's see." He grabbed a giant book from a pile, "Ok, killjoy...," flipping pages. "Here we go: spoil sport, party pooper, prophet of doom." He slammed the book shut with a grin.

"Why are you doing this?"

"Because you have such great stage presence, Miss Prophetess of Doom. And you could be seen as feisty."

"I don't want to be in your movie!"

"Okay," he said and brought down the camera. "Then I guess I'm just gonna have to do it myself. Let me know if you need anything." He turned and walked into the next room.

Oh my god.

She heard him turn on his music again and looked at the time: 5:20 p.m. Stella was twenty minutes late, which made Francie super anxious. But the show wasn't till 8:00 p.m. And they had time to stop in Agoura even if they left at 6:00 p.m.

She had to stop worrying.

And flopped back on the couch. It was totally comfy in this room. She looked at all the stuff and wondered if their family all sat around and watched TV together or read the paper or had an actual board game night or, better yet, sat around and talked. It sounded like fun. That never happened in her family. She could see Stella and Eddie hanging out in there together. Even though they were probably at each other's throats a lot. They probably had fun, too. Like in that photo with the fishing rod.

She wished she had a brother or sister. Then she wouldn't have to deal with her parents by herself. And would have someone on her side. To talk to about them. And do fun stuff with.

Ah!!! She had to get out of her head.

She stood back up. And looked around. She could hear Eddie slamming a door in the next room. Over and over. As if they didn't all sound the same.

He was so weird!

She went over and peeked in. It was a study with built-in, floor-to-ceiling bookshelves and a big mahogany desk covered in Eddie's equipment. He was slamming the closet door and then adjusting something on a screen.

She wondered if she should just help him. With the scream. For something to do. She didn't want to encourage him but it did sound kind of funny. Especially since Stella was so dramatic. And maybe it'd be fun to be in an indie-movie-slash-mockumentary. And have something to tell Chet!

She imagined the whole thing. The movie doing really well. And getting into Sundance. And her going, without her parents this time. And Chet going too and them snowboarding and going to the screening and hearing Francie's scream. And him kissing her. Because he loved it. And loved her. Because finally she was cool. And had something going on.

Yeah, she needed to do this. And stop being such a stick in the mud.

"Hey," she said.

"Hey! Prophetess of Doom!" His smile was goofy and happy.

Oh, god. "I was just thinking I could help you with your scream," she said, trying to sound cheerful.

"Perfect!" he said. "Come in!"

She stepped in and looked around as he did something on his laptop. There were photos everywhere. From all over the world. Photos of their family at the Eiffel Tower and in a jungle and even one of Eddie and his dad on camels by a pyramid. At least it seemed like his dad with that same curly brown hair.

"So what changed your mind?" Eddie asked.

She shrugged, "Better than just sitting out there?"

"That it is." He smiled and brought a chair for her. "Just one sec and we'll be ready."

She watched him adjust the mic and laptop attached to a huge monitor. It all looked complicated but he definitely knew what he was doing. Then she noticed four photo booth shots taped to the monitor of Eddie with a really cute girl playfully kissing him on the cheek while he smirked and looked off to the side.

Eddie saw her noticing and grabbed the photos and threw them in a drawer.

Okay. Was that his girlfriend? Francie suddenly felt dumb. She'd actually believed Stella that Eddie might have a crush on her. Totally embarrassing. *And* a relief. But what if it was his girlfriend *and* he was flirting? *Ew.*

"So you like the camel?" he asked and gestured to the photo of him and his dad. "He was a mean camel. Big spitter. And smelly. But a *dream* ride. Only a few blisters."

"Where was that?"

"Egypt. Gramps was stationed there for a while. Foreign service."

"Cool."

"Yeah, it was okay, except we hardly got to see them. But now they're in Carpinteria, so not too far. Okay, we're just about ready," he said, tapping on the mic. "You ready?"

She nodded.

"Okay, so it's gotta be loud and blood curdling and sound like Stella. Okay?"

She laughed and nodded, and her adrenaline started racing. This was exciting.

"And we gotta hurry, before she gets back." He tested the mic levels. "Testing, testing. One, two. Okay, now you."

She leaned forward, "Testing. Testing, one, two?"

"Perfect. Let's do it." He flipped a switch and pointed at her. "Aaaand, go."

She froze. Panic. *Don't know what to do.* And why was this mic so big? She could practically hear her future scream booming into the room. The blood rushed to her cheeks.

"You okay?"

"Yeah, yeah, fine." She took a breath to calm herself. But was still too nervous.

He told her to stand up, which she did, and she shook out her arms and jogged in place. That helped in tennis but wasn't helping now. Then he suggested doing the door slams first and told her to slam it like she was hitting a big forehand.

"I know how to slam a door!" She grabbed the door and slammed it shut, like a super topspin-y crosscourt.

"Excellent!"

Wow. That felt great.

"Now, again," he said.

She slammed the door again. Harder this time.

"Perfect, now, how about a few back to back?" He switched something on, and she slammed the door repeatedly, feeling stronger and stronger with each slam.

"That's it. Now, three more times then come to the mic and belt it out."

"Right." She slammed the door with all her might. *One. Two. Three.* Then went over and let out a long, loud scream.

"Perfect!"

She could feel the blood rushing down her arms. It felt amazing to scream.

He played the scream back for her. "Pretty scary if you ask me," he teased. "And now we can cut it in."

"That's it?"

"Yup. You nailed it."

She stood behind him as he showed her the scene, which was a shot of Stella coming home, going into the living room and seeing something totally annoying. Which turned out to be Eddie dancing. It was hilarious. And Francie laughed. And Eddie was so happy about that. And proud of the whole stupid thing.

"So the scream goes when she sees me. Watch." He added the scream and replayed it. Then stopped. The timing was off. "Shoot."

"It goes when she sees you turn, right?" Francie said, oddly knowing exactly what to do.

"Ahhhh!" he said, eyes brightening. "She knows of what she speaks." And he changed it. And it worked! "Schoonmaker!" He said and high-fived her.

She high-fived back, laughing, "What's that?"

"Martin Scorsese's editor," he said, "Whose style you could potentially model yourself after." And he grabbed his camera all excited again and pointed it at her.

"Oh my god! Stop."

"And here we have a *happy* Francie. With the gnarly scream. And boy can she let it rip."

Francie covered the lens. "Stop."

"Miss Mills, just a bit about your experience on set with director Plumb?"

"I don't want to do this."

"Then how about telling us what it feels like to be the new, upcoming scream starlet?"

"I don't want to be in the film!"

"Not even a little cameo?"

"No. I'm going outside to wait for Stella," she said and started to go.

"Wait!" he said.

She stopped.

"Thank you," he said and did a little bow.

Never in the history of the world was there someone this annoying. And polite.

She started to leave again.

"I'm sure Stella'll be back soon!" he yelled after her. "And then, we can all go see Loverboy."

She stopped again. "We?"

"Yeah," he shrugged, "That okay with you?" He smiled and suddenly looked all sweet and normal. Like a sweet big brother. And person, in general.

So weird.

And a relief. That he was going. Instantly.

But she acted as if it were no big deal. "Sure, why not?" she said and walked out, past the messy but calm living room and out the front door onto the porch.

Reliable.

Eddie was annoying but reliable.

And safe.

And if Stella got there soon, this would happen.

She checked her phone. No messages, 5:50 p.m.

Her heart started to race.

12

Francie sat on the porch on Stella's steampunk RatBat set chair. Waiting. Panicking. Wondering why Stella made a steampunk set for a metal band. Wasting her clearly amazing talent on their lameness with their stupid, big, rat-nest hair. And wondering how Stella could be so good and late at the same time.

Were creativity and tardiness mutually exclusive?

How about creativity and trustfulness?

No, they didn't have to be.

She looked at Chet's text. *Be my muse.* And all the posts and photos everyone was putting up about the show.

This had to happen.

6:02 p.m.

Should she drive? Alone?

No!

Then Stella pulled up in a Jeep. And Francie exhaled again.

There was a weird punked-out guy driving that had to be Scott. He was skinny with red-dyed hair that was curly and a mess and definitely brown underneath. And pale. Or was that makeup? Yeah, foundation and eyeliner. Weird. At least he wasn't wearing the cape.

"Hey! Sorry we're late," Stella yelled. "We stopped to get snacks and pizza, and it took forever." Stella jumped out. "Didn't Eddie let you in?"

"Yeah, but I just decided to wait out here."

"God, I hope he wasn't too annoying," Stella said, heading to the back of the Jeep.

"Not too bad," she replied.

"Well good." Stella grabbed two grocery bags and handed one to Francie. "Working at the club definitely has its perks."

Inside the bag was tons of candy bars and chips and red licorice and sweet tarts and hot tamale chewy things and ice-cream sandwiches. All items they sold at the club snack shop. Did Stella steal them?

"I'm Scott, by the way," said Scott, grabbing the pizza.

"Francie."

Scott winked and tossed the pizza box in the air, spinning it as if it were the actual pizza dough, while attempting to pirouette. Too slow. He fumbled it, and the box crashed to the ground.

"Man, they just don't make these boxes like they used to." He laughed and picked it up.

"You guys coming?" Stella yelled as she headed to the front door.

"Sure," Francie said and followed. She could tell they'd been smoking; their clothes and hair reeked.

Just as they got there, the door flew open. And there was Eddie with the camera, "Smile."

Stella smacked it out of her face and walked past, "You just have to ignore him!"

"So, tell me, lovely Stella," Eddie said, following her. "What're your plans this evening sans Mom and Dad? Free reign, free anything and with house guests no less."

Stella looked into the camera, "Don't expect me to incriminate myself," then continued into the kitchen.

Eddie turned the camera on Francie, "And how's our scream starlet doing?"

"Leave her alone. She's a guest," Stella said and put her bag on the table. "He does this all the time and he can't help it. It's like a disease."

Eddie turned the camera back on Stella. She flipped him off. "C'mon, let's have some snacks before we go," she said to Scott and Francie.

The kitchen was painted sherbet orange and filled with flowers and all kinds of knick-knacks with French and British sayings on them, like "C'est la fin des haricots" and "Keep Calm and Carry On." The walls were also covered in paper silhouette art. Little silhouettes of people cut out in black paper and pasted on a white or lightly colored backgrounds.

"Mom, collects those," said Stella, putting a few things in the fridge then grabbing a bag of M&Ms and shaking them for the camera.

"Where'd you get the stash?" Eddie asked.

Stella ignored him. "Grab anything you want," she said to Francie and Scott. "There's all kinds of junk in there and beer in that one. Although that should go in the fridge first."

She grabbed a few bottles of beer and put them in the fridge.

"That's not too incriminating," Eddie said, filming her with the beer. "Straight from the snack shop at the club no doubt."

Stella flipped him off again, "I'm scared," and handed a beer to Scott. Then changed her mind, "No, not till we're back," and handed him a soda instead.

Scott grabbed a magazine off the magazine rack and sat down at the round wooden kitchen table.

"Alright, this is boring. What's for dinner?" Eddie said and finally turned off the camera.

"Thank god," said Stella.

"Oh, c'mon, it's not that bad," Eddie replied, going to the sink and washing his hands.

Stella grabbed the camera and pointed it at Eddie. "Eddie thinks he's an *auteur*."

Eddie hammed it up for the camera then finished drying his hands. Clearly, none of this fazed him, and he took deep pleasure in driving his sister and everyone else nuts. "How about we barbecue?"

"We got pizza. And they have food there," Stella said.

"Fine," said Eddie, opening the pizza box.

"Hope that's okay for you guys," Stella said to Francie and Scott.

"Mmmm," said Scott, taking a slice.

"Great," said Francie, trying hard to smile and really hoping this didn't take too long. She glanced at her phone,

6:08 p.m. Eight minutes past the time they had to leave to get there on time.

Stella grabbed the M&M'S again and sat next to Scott. "So you guys've never met?"

"I don't know," Scott said. "Maybe I've seen you in Keller's class?"

Breathe.

"I don't think so," Francie replied, trying to deflect the whole school thing.

"No, she goes to that all girls' school in T.O., La Reina," Stella said.

Francie instantly felt the blood rush to her cheeks, so much for that.

"Oh, yeah. You told me. Lesbo city, right?" Scott teased.

Oh, god, here we go.

"You know, just because *you're* gay doesn't mean everyone else is," Stella said.

"What do you mean *gay*?" Scott replied, making a stupid face.

Stella rolled her eyes. Scott laughed.

Gay? Wow. Was he? Francie had no idea. And felt totally stupid. Like she had no clue. And hoped it didn't show. And that they weren't secretly making fun of her.

"Who's gay now?" Eddie said, chiming back in, teasing Scott.

"I was kidding," said Scott.

"Well, Francie's definitely not gay," said Stella, smiling at Francie.

"I didn't say Francie was gay!" Scott said, laughing.

"Because she *definitely* has the hots for Chet," Stella said and winked at Francie.

"We're just *friends*," Francie said, sounding way too defensive.

"Well, at least that's what Eddie said," Stella continued.

"He's in a band!" Eddie defended. "Girls always fall for stupid guys in stupid bands. That's why stupid guys join stupid bands in the first place. And smart guys hang around stupid bands."

Francie wanted to melt into the floor, "Whatever."

"I thought you liked the stupid band," Stella said to Eddie.

"They're okay, with their *one* song, but I don't want to date any of 'em."

"That's just stupid," Stella said.

"What're you talking about?" Eddie said, then turned to Francie and Scott. "She's in love with a guy in a punk band who wears dresses. And his thighs are thinner than hers. Not to mention she's about to go all groupie on this poor 'Billy' in your band."

"*Our* band?" laughed Francie.

"They're kilts," said Stella. "He wears kilts."

"Could've fooled me," Eddie said to Stella.

"Whatever." Stella turned back to Scott. "As I was saying, you probably saw Francie at the club."

Wow. Level ten to zero in seconds. How did Stella and Eddie do that, without actually hating each other?

"Maybe," Scott said, trying to place Francie.

"All you need to know is that she's super good and would kick our butts," Stella continued, giving Eddie the evil eye.

"She wouldn't kick *my* butt," said Eddie as he grabbed a soda from the fridge.

"Oh, please," said Stella.

"Twenty bucks says I whoop Francie's butt," Eddie said, then winked at Francie.

Oh my god. Francie just shook her head.

"What? You don't think I can beat you at tennis?"

"Maybe," Francie replied, knowing full well she could but not caring to prolong this.

"You're just pissed about your musician loverboy guy," said Eddie.

Francie groaned.

"*You're* just jealous," Stella said to Eddie.

"True."

"There's nothing to be jealous of!" Francie defended.

"See, *that's* what I'm talking about," Eddie said to Francie.

"And what about *your* girlfriend?!" Francie said.

"What girlfriend?"

"The one in the photo on the desk in there. In the photo booth."

"Emmy? Yeah, she would've gone for your musician too," Eddie said, taking a huge bite of pizza and not sounding so chill anymore.

"God, please, not Emmy again," groaned Stella. "I'm taking Francie upstairs to show her my stuff and get ready. And then we gotta go."

Yes, thought Francie, finally, and glanced at her phone, 6:11 p.m.

"Yes, ma'am," said Eddie to Stella and saluted with his pizza then took another bite.

Stella looked annoyed but didn't get into it. "Ready?" she asked Francie.

"Sure," Francie said and followed Stella out.

Breathe.

"We'll be back in a sec, Scott," Stella said, then whispered to Francie. "Emmy's a total sore subject. Really, I wish he'd just take that damn picture down already."

"He did. He threw it in the drawer when he saw me look at it."

"Well, that's progress," Stella said as they headed upstairs. "He was totally in love with her. So it's extremely good if he's jealous of Chet. I mean, not good for you, necessarily, but he needs to get over Emmy already. And you do kind of remind me of her. But really, you just have to ignore him."

"Right," Francie said and followed Stella to her room.

"It just takes practice. And then you turn into a bitch like me." Stella grinned and opened the door for Francie. They stepped in.

The room was black and covered with stuff. Everywhere. Posters and magazine cutouts of every indie, punk, and metal band ever, with pop, rock, rap and reggae stars scattered around. Fishnet tights in every possible color littered the floor, together with t-shirts and black shoes. Stuffed animals, some in spike collars. A Kindle covered in silver stickers. A gazillion CDs. And vinyl. A sewing machine. Lots of cloth, mostly black. Sequins. Scissors.

Ribbons. Metallic bobbles. Cans of paint. Cardboard. And tons of sketches. Basically, it was total chaos, but in a way that made sense. Like Stella probably knew where everything was, down to the last thread. And Francie loved it.

"There's a good chance he has a thing for you," Stella said, turning on music.

"Who?"

"Eddie!" Stella flipped on the speakers. It blasted. She turned it down, "Sorry."

"So, why is he so weird to me?"

"Because he's trying to impress you," Stella said, going over to the sewing machine.

"Really?"

"If you were into him, you'd think it was cute. That's what makes the world go round."

Francie got what Stella was saying but couldn't imagine ever finding Eddie cute.

"And some girl will think he's cute," Stella continued. "Even Emmy thought he was cute for a while." She searched through papers and found some sketches, "Ta da! The new batch. And here's the samples." She cleared stuff off the bed revealing four black outfits. That looked *awful.*

Cheesy goth, just like everything Stella showed Francie before. All black with tons of metallic stuff and plaid belts and silver things on tips of collars that made them look country western. And a green-and-black plaid kilt with an oversized safety pin.

"Oh, and check it out! Dog collars!" Stella said, showing Francie four black collars.

"Total geeks," exclaimed Scott as he came in. "I wasn't spying, I swear. I just came to get the charger." He rifled through some stuff, grabbed the charger and left again.

Francie looked at the collars. Totally unoriginal. Black with spikes.

"So, what do you think?" Stella asked. "About the costumes?"

Francie looked at them again and just wished she had something good to say. "They're great," she lied. "I mean, wow, the plaid really stands out."

"You don't like them. I can tell."

"No! No, I do. I just think I have to see them on."

"Crap," Stella said and sat down.

"Seriously, they're perfect. It's just not my thing. But they totally fit RatBat and then you added these really cool touches." Francie looked at the sketches trying to find something good. "And I really like the set out front. It's amazing."

"The set?"

"Yeah, and once they get on that stage, they'll totally blend in."

"They're not supposed to blend in. They're supposed to stand out."

What could she say? The truth? "They're not gonna stand out. They'll totally be overtaken by all the cool stuff on the set."

Stella stared at the costumes and dropped her head in her hands. "You're right."

Francie checked her phone, 6:23 p.m.

And the panic returned.

"But tomorrow *is* another day," Stella said and sat up. "*And* we can revise!" She grabbed a cigarette off her desk, suddenly all energized again. "Like, maybe the set should stay. And I can blend the costumes with that. Like different colors so they pop, but borderline steampunk." She offered the yellow cigarette pack to Francie.

Francie looked at the Native American on the label and felt the nerves growing in her stomach, "No, thanks."

"American Spirit. They're all natural." Stella said and tossed Francie the pack anyway. "No salt peter." She climbed up onto the desk by the open window to smoke. "They don't have the crap in 'em that's really bad for you that makes 'em burn fast so they can sell more."

Francie could feel her heart starting to race. Who cared about healthy cigarettes? Why didn't Stella just get ready? They had to go!

"Hey, would you mind shutting the door and stuffing that towel underneath?"

Francie shoved the black towel along the bottom of the door and the nerves gripped her stomach.

"Thanks," Stella said and lit up. "Have a seat." She gestured to the messy bed.

Francie looked at the costumes on the bed. And the nervousness surged. And her heart pounded. And she couldn't breathe. And the panic grew.

If she sat on the bed, this could take forever.

And it was too much.

Too much pressure.

Too much to process.

Too much stress. And panic. All the time. All day.

And being afraid they wouldn't go.

And she wouldn't see Chet.

And she didn't know what to do. What to be. How to act. How to seem cool. And patient. Like nothing mattered. Not pushing. Not caring. To get Stella to hurry up.

"You okay?" Stella asked.

Francie looked at her phone, 6:29 p.m.

And her breath caught. And she blurted out: "Maybe I can just take my car."

"What?" Stella said.

And Francie felt faint. And her mind went blank. And she just stared at Stella. And felt hot tears welling.

"Oh my god," Stella said and jumped up and grabbed Francie's shoulders like she was about to shake her. Or hold her up. And hopefully not choke her with her cigarette smoke wafting everywhere. "What's going on?"

Concern. Kind eyes. Genuine concern.

"I, I just, I just really want to get there on time," Francie stammered. "And it's been a really weird day. And my car's here. My dad's car. And I could drive. Because I really don't want to bother you. With Agoura. And your stuff. That's amazing. And a stupid waste for that stupid band."

And the nerves in her stomach went nuts.

And she wished she hadn't called RatBat stupid. But she couldn't help it. Because she felt crazy.

And Stella laughed. Warm. Happy.

And Francie looked up at Stella.

Who was right there with her cigarette breath in Francie's face.

"We could probably skip that *stupid* band," said Stella, amused. "With their *stupid* costumes that I need to fix anyway. Right? Who needs to go to *stupid* Agoura? When we're going to The West!"

Francie laughed. Nervously. Like she exhaled with a stupid laughing avalanche of relief. Like she hoped she didn't spit on Stella.

And Stella smiled. Like she understood. Somehow. Like a mind reader. Heart reader. Friend. "I totally want to go, you know," Stella said. "So don't think you can get rid of me that easily," she teased and stubbed out her cigarette. "We'll just have to hurry."

Stella quickly changed her black t-shirt into another black t-shirt but with silver skulls. And touched up her silver lips. And put in a *nose ring*! And grabbed a black sweater. "Let's go." And walked out the door.

Creative and reliable. Not mutually exclusive.

Impulsive and a friend. Also not.

13

Francie stared at the lens of the camera pointed at her from the front seat.

"Hang on," Stella said and unbuckled her seatbelt to reposition herself on her knees facing backward, lens pointing at Francie. "Alright, Miss Francie, tell us what's going on with you."

Francie groaned.

"C'mon, that's an easy one," Eddie said from behind the wheel. Francie was relieved Eddie was driving. He seemed way more trustworthy than Scott. But this whole camera/filming thing was driving her nuts.

"Okay, what's going on with me is I'm on my way to a Blues Harp Jones show at The West, otherwise known as Lyric Poet West," Francie said and fake-smiled for the camera.

"That's it?" Eddie said.

"Okay, your turn," Stella said and handed Francie the camera. "So you can get back at Mr. Kubrick here."

"Oh-ho, now there's a compliment," said Eddie.

Francie knew all about Stanley Kubrick because her dad was a movie encyclopedia. Clearly, Eddie was too. "Apparently, he shot a lot of film," Francie said and reluctantly turned on the camera.

"She gets the reference! Finally someone!" Eddie screamed. "Film nerd in da house." He did a weird arm dance and made loud noises for the camera.

Super annoying. Francie brought the camera down.

"You don't like my moves?"

"Just pretend you're making a documentary of us," Stella said, trying to encourage Francie.

Francie lifted the camera again, "Okay and here we are on a gorgeous summer night, heading into L.A. to the famous Lyric Poet West on..."

"Santa Monica Boulevard," yelled Eddie and Stella.

"In West Hollywood," Francie continued, "to see our beloved Blues Harp Jones. We have the lovely Stella Plumb sitting shotgun."

Stella did a peace-sign-eyes sexy dance.

"And her mad filmmaking brother behind the wheel."

Eddie danced in his seat again, waving one arm around.

"And next to me is Scott, pizza-spinner extraordinaire."

Scott flipped off the camera. *What a pain.*

"Woohoo!" Eddie hammed it up, blasting the music. Stella did some punk head-shaking.

"Okay, we get the idea and we want to actually make it there alive," said Francie.

Eddie turned down the music, "Okay, what should we do?"

"Tell us what you're looking forward to most about tonight, Mr. Kubrick."

"No brainer. Francie getting thrown around in the mosh pit and Stella drooling on Billy."

"And you, Miss Mata Hari?" Francie asked Stella.

"Mata Hari," said Stella and lit up yet another cigarette and rolled down the window. "Femme fatale who's up to no good." She blew the smoke at the camera and smiled all sexy. "The only no-good I'm up to is thinking evil thoughts about Eddie for driving so slow, and the only thing to look forward to is this," and she blasted "Louisa, Hey," and Eddie started bouncing off the seat.

Francie turned to film Scott. He flipped her off again and said, "Excellent music, Dude."

"And there we have it," Francie said, flopping back. They were all lame.

"Not bad, Dude," Eddie said to Francie in the rearview mirror. "You got mad skills."

Francie looked out at the Getty Center up on the hill. Another twenty minutes. She lifted the camera again and filmed the passing cars. "Another busy night on the 405. But none of them are as lucky as us. Because we're going to the rock-star-famous Lyric Poet West."

She put the camera back down and spaced out, thinking about how she was about to see Chet play at the rock-star-famous Lyric Poet West, which made him kind of like a rock star. At least for tonight. Or someday in the future. Actually, she knew he would be famous someday. He was too good and cared too much not to. Which meant she'd actually made out with a rock star. And was someone he might love. In some future reality. And it felt good.

Like she was special. And mattered.

Francie watched the doorman snap a white band on her wrist. "Thank you."

"No problem, little missy, you have yourself a good time," he said.

She walked into the club and felt tingly all over. Funky DJ music blared from the back, and it was so cool just to be in this place. Like she was part of something bigger. And important, just by being there. And knowing someone playing there. Even if they were no big deal. *Yet.*

"C'mon, let's check it out," Stella said, and they followed her back to the stage area.

It definitely wasn't crowded. Like about five people. But they were early, 7:45 p.m. Apparently, the band wasn't even going on till 9:00 p.m. So all that worrying for nothing. Again.

Two girls pogo'd around to the DJ music, and three people sat on the stadium-like bleachers in the back.

"And here we have people dancing to the pre-band DJ," said Eddie, filming from under his jacket, "A little bit punk-y and a little bit rock 'n roll and nothing even close to Blues Harp Jones's more ska-punk pop rock."

"What are you doing?" Stella asked.

He covered the camera, "It's called not getting my camera confiscated for the night."

"You know, you could just use your phone so you don't get kicked out."

"It's a matter of quality-over-confiscation risk."

Stella rolled her eyes and turned to Francie, "How about we get confiscated backstage to meet the band?"

"Sure."

"Okay, c'mon." Stella led Francie across the dance floor, past the stage to the guard at the backstage door. "Hi," Stella said with a super sweet smile. "How are you tonight?"

"I'm doing just fine, young lady," said the giant bouncer.

"We are too, except we're a little late. We're supposed to meet Chet here fifteen minutes ago."

"Chet?"

"Yeah, he's in Blues Harp Jones. And Billy. Billy Jones."

"Well, they're not here right now, Honey, sorry to disappoint you."

Stella shot Francie a "say something" look.

"It's okay, I'm a friend of Chet's. From Texas," Francie said.

The doorman chuckled, "I don't doubt you, Honey, but I can't let anyone back there, and they're really not here."

"Thank you," Francie said, turning red and starting away.

Stella forced a smile, "Thanks anyway," and took Francie's arm and led her to Eddie.

"Sorry," Francie said. "I didn't know what else to say."

"It's okay. You're definitely a newb, but we're gonna break you in. And the first trick is to pretend you're *supposed* to be backstage, *right now*, and *of course*, you know Chet, and *of course*, he's waiting for you, and *of course*, the bouncer's gonna let you in. You have to be confident. That's the key. And then you can go anywhere."

"He's not even here."

"You have to make the guy think he's here. Even if he's not."

"Right," Francie said. *Oh my god.*

Stella beamed. Clearly, she knew her stuff, but it seemed insane and Francie knew she'd never do it anyway.

"Hey, so why don't we just call him? Or text?" Stella said.

"Oh, right," Francie said. Of course. That was the logical thing to do. But when she grabbed her phone, she started to feel super nervous. She'd already sent that video. And he'd sent that sweet text. And this was just too much. Like she was bugging him. And not her style. But Stella was watching. And *he texted you to be his muse!*

So she called. And it went straight to voicemail. And she hung up. Without leaving a message. And the nerves went crazy in her stomach. And she didn't text either.

And she felt like an idiot. Because she knew Stella was annoyed.

And Francie's hands were shaking. Like she was scared. *Why is this happening?*

But Stella smiled knowingly. "Okay, so you really like him," she teased. "And I'm obviously the only one who doesn't love this DJ so I'm going out for a smoke. And to try to message Billy." She pulled out her phone.

"Out?" Francie said.

"Yeah."

"They won't let you back in. If you're under twenty-one. The guy said they don't even let you out, even if you're on the list."

"Yeah, well, watch this."

Francie watched Stella go up to the front doorman, with Scott at her heels, explain something to him and then go out, waving back with a grin on her face then disappearing.

Oh my god.

Francie looked at Eddie.

"Don't look at me," he said. "I don't know anything about being a groupie."

Kill me now.

"And I guarantee by the end of the night, Stella will be backstage and running the show."

"I'm gonna go get something to drink," Francie said and left Eddie and his laissez faire uber-positive annoying smile in the middle of the empty dance floor. When she came back, with a really expensive bottle of water, he was chatting with some girl on the bleacher seats that he introduced as Anna.

Even more annoying. But Francie lurked. Because it was better than feeling stupid just standing there on the dance floor with those girls making total asshats of themselves.

It turned out Anna and her friends were there to see one of the other bands. They lived in Santa Barbara, and clearly, one of them had a huge crush on one of the band members because she wouldn't stop talking about him. Anna said they met the Blues Harp Jones guys in the parking lot earlier and that they had gone out to eat.

"Oh my god, how did we miss them?!" Francie said to Eddie.

He shrugged. "Because we didn't have a plan?"

Francie groaned, audibly.

"Let's see what Stella's up to then," he said and led her to the front door to look outside.

"Not with that, Sweetie, sorry," the doorman said to Francie about her wristband.

"Hey, you let my sister out and she's, what, sixteen? Maybe?" said Eddie.

The doorman stared at Eddie and raised an eyebrow.

"The mouthy goth chick and her sidekick?" Eddie continued.

The doorman just stared.

"Alright, maybe a threat isn't my best angle, but I'd really like to see what my sister is up to. You know. My neck is on the line here if anything happens to her."

Francie chimed in, trying to be as confident as Stella, "Look, I'm a friend of Chet's, in the band, and we're supposed to meet him backstage."

"Yeah, your little goth friend is a friend of your friend Chet too. And she went with the manager to go pick them up at the restaurant."

"Yeah, that Chet's pretty popular with the ladies," Eddie said, and the guard actually laughed, which annoyed Francie, and Eddie pulled her away.

Then he checked his phone. "Three messages. From Stella."

Oh my god, how did he not notice?!

Eddie listened and fed her little bits: "Tried to get backstage. Met some kid named Hugh. Hit it off. Invited to Swingers. And that's it."

"Swingers?!" Francie said, incredulous.

"Like I said, Stella'll be running the show by the end of the night."

"What about us?"

"Chopped liver," he said and dialed Stella and put her on speaker. "Hey, it's us."

Stella's voice blared, "We're at Swingers! And leaving soon, so we'll see you there."

"We?" Francie said.

"Blues Harp Jones," Stella yelled. "Chet's a hottie, and the road-manager-slash-junior-manager is even hotter."

Eddie laughed as if this were the stupidest thing ever.

"You're *with* them?!" Francie said. She couldn't believe it.

"Yeah, he said he's happy you're here!" Stella yelled. "Oop, gotta go. See ya in a few."

"Chet? Chet said that?!" But Stella hung up.

Eddie laughed and put his phone away. "C'mon, let's get food. Who needs them anyway?"

I do, Francie thought and followed him to the diner.

Francie stared at The West snack menu, holding it up to block Eddie's face. She really was not in the mood for this.

"Well, I know what I'm getting," he said, putting his menu down.

She could feel him waiting for her to ask.

"Hello?" He knocked on her menu and peered over. "See anything interesting?"

"Not exactly." She pulled it up higher.

"Well, if you're having trouble finding something, I'd highly recommend the exquisite fries. With a tasty side of mayo or delicious ranch dressing. The onion rings could also be good but a no-no if you see Loverboy later. Excuse me, *when* you see Loverboy later. Because Stella will surely have us backstage."

"Which we could also potentially miss," she replied.

"Not now that I have my phone, right here, by my ear," he said, trying to make her laugh. "We could also share fries. Which would be great since I only have enough money for one thing. And we could bond." He pulled down her menu to see her reaction.

"No, thank you," she said and jerked the menu up.

"You know if this is about Loverboy, I totally get it. It's tough being in love with someone unavailable. But eventually, you realize there are other fish in the sea." He pulled her menu down again and grinned, as if he were one of those fish.

She stared.

"What?" he asked.

I have zero interest in you!

"You're totally judging someone you don't know."

"Who's in a band and has tons of girls in love with him and lives all the way in The Valley so it's kind of difficult to be friends. Like, real friends. Which you keep alluding to."

"All because he's in a band?!"

The waitress walked up, "Ready?"

"An order of fries please, with mayo and ranch on the side. Anything else?" he asked Francie.

Francie fumed.

"Nope, that's it then, one order, thank you." Eddie handed the waitress his menu.

The waitress tried to take Francie's menu but she didn't let go. "I'm gonna hang onto to this. Thanks." She couldn't bear giving it up. She needed a shield between her and Eddie.

"Look, why don't we just start over?" said Eddie. "Put the past under the rug to haunt us later. And go forward, hanging out like normal people. And only fight during the full moon."

"That's exactly why this isn't going to work."

"There aren't enough full moons?"

"We cannot be friends!"

"How about civil?"

She hid behind the menu again until the waitress brought the fries. He dipped a couple in the mayonnaise.

"That looks disgusting," she said.

"It's how the Belgians do it."

"The Belgians?"

"Try."

She dipped a fry in the mayo. Surprisingly, it was pretty good.

"Here. Have some more."

She did, which made him really happy, and he started talking about music, and she zoned out and fantasized about Chet as he rambled on.

14

Francie stood next to Stella on the dance floor. There were definitely more people now, like fifteen. She recognized a few from online, like YoYoMatilda! With her spikey green and purple hair! She was talking to two guys with Mohawks.

Stella kept looking over at this totally nerdy guy with horn-rimmed glasses named Hugh, who was supposedly Billy's best friend and managed the band. Francie didn't recognize him. Maybe he had a fake name online.

Hugh looked over and Stella waved, "Cute huh? And so friggin' smart. He's totally gonna make these guys happen."

What the hell?

Francie couldn't believe all this happened while she was eating fries with Eddie.

And then she noticed Chet's mom walk in. She was with an older guy in jeans. Was it Chet's dad? Even though he said they were split? Like, maybe they were friendly for their kids. Or maybe they were back together! The guy definitely seemed close to Chet's mom though because he put his hand on her back when they went to sit on the bleachers. She seemed slightly agitated but smiled warmly at him as she sat down. She took a deep breath and looked around. She seemed proud. And a little excited. And was even more beautiful in person than in the video.

Why is she so beautiful to me?

Because she seemed so real? And present? And agitated, but proud? And excited? Not trying to pretend she wasn't feeling anything?! Like Francie's mom did.

Still, there was a bit of sadness in Chet's mom's eyes and that *was* just like her mom.

Suddenly, the lights and music went down and the lights above the stage came on. And everyone cheered. And Chet's mom vanished in Francie's mind, because right in front of her, the band was walking out the side door, past the bouncer and up onto the stage.

And there he was. Guitar round his neck. So cute! And smiling. And wearing the blue plaid jacket! Right at the front of the stage. Where he could see her. Did he see her? Francie got goosebumps all over.

Stu sat at the drums and Billy was on one side with his guitar. And there was the new guy on bass, Memphis. Super tall and lanky with short brown hair and nerdy glasses.

"Good evening, L.A.!" Chet boomed in the mic to all fifteen people, as if it was a stadium.

And Francie got chills. And the two girls screamed. And Chet smiled and looked back at the guys and counted and then started playing.

The two girls immediately started dancing. And everyone else just stood there listening and watching the band.

Francie moved to the back to get a better view. She glanced at Chet's mom who was practically glowing with joy. Which made Francie so happy.

Safe. Her love feels safe.

And then Francie looked back at Chet. And was instantly drawn in, mesmerized and in disbelief that she was actually there. But she was. Because Chet was right in front of her. So close. So happy. Playing. Doing his thing. And sounding amazing. The whole band was amazing. But Chet was really, really good. His guitar. His voice. It had so much power. And she could feel the energy of the sound inside her. Rising up from her stomach into her heart and throat.

Is that what it was? Was it the sound and the song and the voice? Or was it him? And that thing? That inexplicable thing!

But she didn't care. Not now. She just wanted to be there. In the moment. Listening to the song. Feeling the song. Feeling him. And his music. The new song. One of the new songs. One of the ones she helped him with. And it was really good! And the parts he was worried about were really good. And Billy was good. All of them were.

And then it happened. Chet looked right at her. And she waved. And he smiled. And instantly, her heart melted and she felt so happy and beautiful and smart and creative and cool and none of it mattered—missing Swingers or the fight with her dad or her family being so awful or Stella meeting a guy in two seconds. She was in a magic bubble of happiness. And everything in the world felt like it made sense and had purpose.

She stayed in her bubble until the next song, which was "Louisa, Hey," and everyone cheered and came out to dance. Scott was even into it and Stella too, dancing all ska-like and looking hilarious because it really wasn't her style and looking at Hugh every two seconds. And Eddie looked hilarious too with his outward-pointing duck feet moving.

Francie caught Eddie's eye and laughed, and he laughed too, at himself, and that's when she saw the green light of his camera under his jacket. *What the heck?* He was going to get caught!

"Hey, Francie! C'mon!" Eddie yelled.

"No! I don't dance! And turn that thing off!"

"Sure you do," he said and pulled her out.

And there she was. On the dance floor. Frozen. Lame. Eddie grinning and dancing around her like a total moron. He was so weird. And goofy. And she just wanted to run. Because she felt so awkward. Because people would see her if she danced.

And Chet might see her. And her heart. On display. And how much she loved this song. And felt it inside her.

Her soul would be naked.

But if she ran off, that'd be weird too. If Chet saw.

So, she started to move. A little. Slowly. Measured. Awkward. Keeping the rhythm inside her as still as possible. Not letting it go. Not letting it just be.

And she felt completely ridiculous. But apparently, that was okay.

Because Stella bellowed at her, "Woohoo."

And Eddie started filming her, "See!"

And she just kept moving and started to feel a little okay. And glanced up at Chet. And he looked right at her again. And smiled. And her heart leapt out of its measured cage, and she started to move more. Let more of the rhythm seep into her arms and legs and shoulders.

Dancing. She was dancing to his song.

Which is when Eddie handed her the camera. "Go for it!"

Oh my god. "What are you doing?!" She caught the camera as it started to fall and quickly hid it under her blouse.

"You're a natural. Just hold it up."

"No! I don't want to get caught!"

"No one's gonna see!" And he started bouncing around through the people.

Oh my god! She tried turning off the camera. Impossible! So she kept it hidden under her blouse, dancing, trying to blend in, so no one would notice. But YoYoMatilda did and bent down and sang right into the lens, close up, then spun all around—the colors of her hair passing with the beat, purple, green, purple, green—before she jerked back, pogo-spinning into the other bodies.

Oh my god. If Matilda noticed the camera, so would someone else! Francie tried to get Eddie's attention, through flailing arms. But all she saw was the doorman, looking right at her.

Shoot!

She tried to get off the dance floor, slamming into someone, getting pushed back, then tripping and almost falling flat on her face. Luckily, she was gripping the camera tightly. But then a strong hand clutched her arm. It was the doorman from the front.

"You're gonna have to come with me, Miss. There ain't no cameras in here. No how."

"But..."

"It's policy and policy says you're goin' out that door. No matter how polite you are or how you had no idea."

15

Francie clutched her double mocha tightly, spreading her fingers, trying to get as much of her hands on the cup as possible. It was friggin' freezing in there.

"This is amazing!" Eddie yelled from across the table. "Look! She's singing into the camera!" He tried to show her the footage of YoYoMatilda.

Francie was too mad at him and just shook her head "no."

"Oh c'mon! It's not that big a deal. And you're in good company. I heard John Lennon got kicked out of there."

"Right."

"Yeah, you and a Beatle. And you've got it on here forever."

Francie wanted to take his camera and just smash it down. "I don't believe it," she said and looked at the time.

"Stella's gonna text. Chill."

She couldn't chill. She wanted so badly to be at The West.

"Oh, and look at the pan to Chet! Maybe getting thrown out was worth it."

"You mean the 'omigod-the-bouncer's-coming' pan to Chet?" Yeah, she hated him right now.

"And we can cut it together. And get interviews after the show."

"Why are you doing this? You don't even like them."

He shrugged. "It's fun?"

Francie screamed inside her head and pretended to look at her phone until finally Stella texted that they were done.

She and Eddie hurried the few blocks back to The West, where a bunch of people were standing outside and Eddie started filming and asking them how they liked the show.

Francie immediately started to feel super nervous. Worried that Eddie was annoying people. And wondering where Chet was. And his mom. And when and how she would see him. And what if she didn't see him? And what if she did and had to tell him she missed most of the show? And what if it was awkward? Or he was with other people? And didn't try to talk to her? Her heart started pounding. She was insane.

"Hey, I'm going round back," said Eddie. "C'mon."

Francie followed and immediately spotted Billy and Stu smoking. Her heart pounded faster.

"Hey, let's interview them," Eddie said. "You know them right?"

She was frozen. What if they didn't want to? What if they thought Eddie was weird? What if Billy didn't know who she was? Because they'd never actually met.

"Hello? Earth to Francie."

"Fine, yes, I don't know."

My heart is going to explode. Where's Stella?

"I'll see if they're into it," Eddie said and went over. "Hey, you guys up for an interview? The show was great. I'll throw it up on your page."

That didn't sound so bad.

"Yeah, sure," said Billy.

Relief.

"Hey! Cool!" said Stu, and he gave Billy a fake hit in the stomach, and they started to fake wrestle, as if that looked cool, and then stopped abruptly and grinned into the camera.

"Hi, we're Blues Harp Jones," said Billy. "Minus Chet."

"Who's inside, chattin' away, I'm sure," said Stu. "Chatty, chatty."

Oh my god, this was terrible.

"And we love L.A.," said Billy. "And our new bassist. Memphis!"

Memphis looked over from a group of people.

"Dude, introduce yourself," Billy yelled. "He's from Memphis."

Really terrible.

The lanky bass player came over and waved shyly into the camera. "Hi, I'm Memphis." Then he turned to Stu for help but Stu just cracked up like there was an inside joke.

"I love you, Mate," Billy said and grabbed Memphis, and *they* started wrestling.

Super-duper lame. Francie felt embarrassed for *them* now. She whispered to Eddie, "Ask them about the club."

"Huh?"

Francie leaned into the mic, "What do you think about the club and tonight?"

Billy stopped. "The club? Terrific. I mean, it's an unbelievable venue. It's The West, for chrissakes. Legendary. A total honor. And it felt great and the new songs felt great. And our L.A. fans came out and were really supportive. It was perfect."

L.A. fans? Francie chuckled knowing Chet's take on that. *All ten fans!*

"Hey, and here's our fourth mate. Chet!" yelled Stu.

Francie turned and everything went into slow motion as Chet walked out after Stella and Hugh. Looking so, so cute she almost couldn't stand it.

Hugh yelled, "Let's go! Uncle Pete's out of here!"

And Chet waved to Hugh with a cigarette, "Just one!"

"Fine, but hurry it up," Hugh said then turned to Stella with a big love smile.

"Hey, Chet, over here. This guy's interviewing us," Stu yelled to Chet.

"Right on," Chet said to Eddie. And then Francie saw Chet's gorgeous green eyes move from Eddie to her.

She felt the blood slowly filling her cheeks.

"FM on the radio dial!" he said with the biggest smile ever.

And it was totally genuine.

And her heart raced. And she couldn't speak. And luckily, he just gave her a big hug. "I was worried I wasn't gonna get to see you," he said.

Smiling, happy eyes looking into hers.

"Yeah, I, uh, was too," she said, awkward and hoping he wouldn't notice her voice shaking.

"Yeah, I'm sorry. I'm slacking on my FM stalker moves. Are you okay? I left my phone in the van again," he said and checked out her hair.

Again paralyzed. And happy. Feeling special. And seen.

"All right, all right, let's get a move on troops," boomed a voice, and this super tall, long-haired, older guy came barreling outside clapping. "You need your beauty rest. Let's go!"

Stu mouthed to the camera: "Uncle Pete."

Uncle Pete looked straight into the camera and stared it down. Then went back to clapping and yelling, "Let's go! In the famvan! Say goodbye to Miss Lily, boys!"

Which is when Chet's mom walked out with the jeans guy.

And Chet said, "Shoot," and quickly hid his cigarettes in his jacket pocket.

And Billy went over and gave their mom a kiss, "Mom!" And talked to her for a moment before pointing to Chet, and Chet's mom beamed at Chet and walked over, and Billy shot Chet a "C'mon-Bro,-say-hi-to-Mom-already" look behind her back.

And Chet ignored Billy and said, "Hi, Mom," and kissed her cheek gently.

"You did it," she said to him with her kind, tender voice. And Francie could see she totally adored him. And Chet adored her. And Francie almost couldn't stand it. And felt embarrassed for being so drawn to them. For no good reason other than they looked so happy. And supportive. And normal.

Then Chet introduced her, "Mom, this is Francie. We met her in Austin. Francie, this is my mom, Lily."

Francie blushed as Lily took her hand and gave her the kindest, happiest, most loving smile ever. "Nice to meet you, Francie." Her hand felt warm, and Francie wished she'd never let go.

But she did. "We'll see you at home, Honey," she said to Chet and glided away over to the guy in jeans, who waved at Chet. And Chet waved back.

"Is that your dad?" Francie asked.

"Nope. That's Steve, her boyfriend." Not sounding at all thrilled.

"And your dad?"

"I'm pretty sure Billy told him not to come. So it wouldn't upset her. More than usual. Which, of course, it wouldn't, so he may as well be here." And then he turned to Francie, playfully, "So do *you* have a boyfriend?" And he looked like he hoped she didn't.

Her cheeks immediately got hot. "Uh, no?" she laughed nervously. "Do you? Have a girlfriend?"

He shook his head no. "I seem to attract the fiercely independent type. That always leaves me in the dust," he joked. And sang, "Violet hair, like she's going somewhere."

"Louisa?"

"Actually, her name's Violet," he said and looked down, like he suddenly was embarrassed. "So be kind to me, Francine," he sang. And smiled. And was blushing.

It was so charming. And disarming. And she just loved him more. Because he was so honest. And funny and sweet about it.

Then Uncle Pete came barreling through again, "Let's go," and grabbed Chet's shoulders and redirected him toward the van, pushing him along, giving Francie a smile and yelling to Stu, Billy and Memphis, "Five minutes is now going on forty here."

Chet yelled back to Francie, "Write me, FM! Sorry we don't have more time!"

And they all piled into the minivan "famvan."

And then that was it. And Francie felt excited and totally empty at the same time, standing there with Eddie, who was looking at his footage, next to Stella and Hugh, who were making out, next to Scott, who was leaning on the wall chain smoking and talking to some random people.

"Hughbie!" bellowed Uncle Pete, and Hugh pulled himself away from Stella and joined the rest of them in the van. Through the tinted window, Francie could see the outline of Chet's head looking at his phone. Like one of those paper silhouettes from Stella's kitchen.

Francie wished she could run over and talk to him. He was so close.

But also a million miles away. Again. Already.

How could it be? All that planning and hoping and emailing and talking and getting away from her parents. And all she wanted to do was to be with Chet.

Suddenly, she felt so far away. From everything. Starman looking down from space.

Stu rolled down the window and yelled, "Get your butts up to Santa Barbara!" And Chet yelled, "Bring the limp!"

And Francie's heart leapt back to earth, and Stella smiled, warm and bright-eyed and hugged Francie tight, which was totally weird, and Francie felt like maybe there was hope.

For a second.

Until they drove off. And she was just standing there. And Eddie ran off to pee. And Stella started texting. And Scott was texting and laughing with his new friends.

And she felt stupid.

And small.

Like she cared too much.

And alone.

Wanting more.

Wanting to be part of something.

Wanting to belong to something important.

And relevant.

To her.

16

Francie sat on the cream-colored couch listening to Eddie stopping and starting "Louisa, Hey" over and over in the study while she stared at the blank email, trying to decide if she should write to Chet now or go to sleep.

Eddie was cutting together The West video, which he'd asked her to help with but she'd said no and he seemed pissed.

Which was totally annoying because *she* was the one who deserved to be pissed. *He* gave the camera *to her*! And if that hadn't happened, she would've been there the whole time and heard all the songs and been a part of it. And it would've been magical and amazing like it was supposed to be, like in Austin, sharing a magical experience.

But no, she'd taken the stupid camera. And she hated herself right now.

She tried to focus on Chet and how happy he'd been to see her after the show, even if it was just a few minutes.

And how cute he was. He was *so cute!* And he looked at her hair in that way. And made her feel special. And introduced her to his mom. And told her about his ex, Violet. Which weirdly made her feel closer to him. Like he trusted her enough to tell her. And wanted her to know him better.

And he wanted to see her in Santa Barbara. And then, maybe, they could be together. And she could be a part of his life.

Not hers. Here. All depressing. And alone. Even if Stella and Scott and Eddie were in the next room, which made her feel more alone. Why was that?

She hated to feel alone.

She was always alone.

Even when she played tennis. Singles.

But *that* was okay. Like it was a good alone. In-control alone. And she was good at it. And tomorrow, she'd be hitting. *Backhands. A lot of them.* She loved backhands. She could control them. With topspin. And her left hand. And that'd help her win in Ventura. And get ranked. Nationally.

Hitting up, left hand. Making the ball go anywhere. Control.

She could feel it. As if she were there. On the court.

Relief.

She heard Eddie start to drum and sing off-key. And Stella and Scott giggling in the kitchen. They were probably still stoned or drunk or whatever and reenacting scenes from *Star Wars*. Which, actually, was pretty funny.

They had all drank beer. The beer Stella "borrowed" from the snack shop at the club. Francie had just taken a tiny sip so as not to look weird. Somehow she couldn't do it. Instead, she watched Stella and Eddie and Scott like she was in a fishbowl looking out. Part of her envied them. They could just be. In the now. And do whatever. And be risky.

Like she'd been in Austin. Maybe she could only do that with Chet. Why was that? Why did sipping beer with Chet make her feel calm and this didn't?

And why did she feel so empty right now? And separate?

She thought about how Stella and Hugh had met so easily and how it was like they were already together. Probably because Stella was so confident and positive and thought everything was going to work out no matter what. Like with her costumes. And how she said it didn't matter that Francie got kicked out because they were definitely going to Santa Barbara in two weeks. And how she'd spent the entire ride home talking about Hugh and how great he was and how he was helping with the band and how they couldn't do it without him and how he had all these great ideas to promote them, even though he was only seventeen, and how Uncle Pete had agreed to mentor him and let him be an intern all summer, and how she was going to help and was so glad they'd gone to The West because otherwise she might never have met Hugh, even though it was total destiny...

Was Chet total destiny?

...And how they had to come up with a plan for Santa Barbara, to get their parents to let them go and how

Francie had to get into it so it would happen for her with Chet and how Eddie should too so he could see that girl from Santa Barbara, who obviously liked him.

Francie groaned. It was too much.

She looked at the blank email, which was *her* reality. Not Stella's. Chet and her under the bridge. Shy. Self-doubt. But seen. And accepted. And okay. More than okay. Connected. Somehow. Like they understood each other in so many ways. Maybe destiny. And love? What was she supposed to do with this feeling?

Stop!

She started the email.

Subject: Your awesome show
Dear Chet,

You guys were so great tonight and I'm really sorry I didn't get to see the whole show or talk to you more. I got thrown out because I had Eddie's camera on the dance floor. But he seems to think something good will come of it and is making a video with what we filmed. Hopefully he'll send it to you for your website or something.

I'm so glad I got to meet your mom. She seems very special. And I'm sorry that your dad wasn't there because I can tell you wanted him there even if it would make everyone sad, but not more than usual. I'm sorry. And that you didn't seem too keen on the boyfriend.

She stopped. Way too much. And started the last paragraph over.

I'm so glad I got to meet your mom. She seems very special. It's really cool that she came to see your show! I can tell she loves you so much and is happy and proud too.

Sorry if that's weird. Pls tell me if I ever say too much.

Anyway, just wanted to say that you were really awesome. All of you and the first two songs that I did see. Thanks!

FM on the radio dial

Francie hit send. And stared at the screen. And immediately felt empty again.

She clicked over to the band's Facebook page. A bunch of people were asking about the show. And the band and YoYoMatilda were commenting and posting photos.

Like normal people.

With friends.

While she was sitting alone with her friends in the next room. Emailing a guy. Hoping he would love her.

Alone.

Loser.

She left the page and googled Chet's mom, Lily Jones. She had a Facebook page. Private. And all Francie could see was two photos of her in the desert with a camera. Her long blond hair blowing in the wind. She looked so free. And brave. And strong. Beautiful but full of experience. Beautiful still. In spite of it.

She was a photojournalist. Or had been. And maybe a peace activist. "Defender of social justice," it said.

And the dad too. Will Jones. Documentarian.

Normal. They were normal. And successful at life. Saving the world. And Chet was too.

Still a loser.

She laid down and pulled the throw blanket over her head and pulled her knees in tight.

Left hand pulling up. Hard. Pulling up on the ball. Spinning it up and over cross court. It bounces in and blasts up.

Francie awoke to Stella whispering in the middle of the night. Francie was on one couch and Eddie on the other and Stella was trying to wake him up. "What?!" he grumbled.

"Why the heck are you sleeping down here?" Stella asked. "Scott was supposed to sleep here."

Scott was sitting on the arm of the couch checking his phone.

Oh my god, they were all insane.

"He can take my bed!" Eddie said. "Push whatever's on it off." And he turned away.

"Did you finish the video?" Stella asked, poking him.

"We'll look at it in the morning!" Eddie pulled the blanket over his head.

"C'mon. I want to see it, so we can send it to them," Stella yanked the blanket off him.

"Hey!" Eddie yelled, and she ran, and he chased her down and swiped it back.

She beamed, "Now, can we see it?" Cleary, this was exactly what she wanted.

"Oh my god, you are such a pain in the ass," Eddie said and went and got his laptop.

Stella clapped like a little kid. "Francie, wake up! Eddie's showing us the video!"

Francie got up and wrapped the blanket around herself, and they all gathered around Eddie as he played the video—the car ride, songs, audience, dancing, interviews, everything.

And it was awesome. And hilarious. Especially when Francie got caught by the guard and when they were driving to the show. Eddie even added one of Francie's screams. Which made Francie laugh, which made Eddie very happy.

They watched the video a few times, and Stella got all excited and told Eddie to send it to the band. "They could put it on their website! It's totally professional."

"Oh, so now she appreciates the master at work," Eddie said and told her he had to at least finish it first.

"It's done. Stick a fork in it already," Stella said, as if she knew what she was talking about.

"Your Highness," Eddie said, bowing.

"Hey, and we can make another video at the show in Santa Barbara!" she said. "But bigger and more like a documentary, with more interviews and stuff!"

"Who's we?" Eddie asked.

"You," Stella replied. "It's the perfect excuse to go up there. I mean, what parents wouldn't let us go if we're making a documentary?"

Eddie grumbled.

"C'mon! We can stay at granny and gramps' and just go to Santa Barbara for the show. *Or* have the car 'break down' *in* Santa Barbara and spend the night. It's brilliant!"

Eddie pretended to drop off to sleep, snoring.

"What do you think?" Stella asked Francie. "Our grandparents live in Carpinteria."

"I think it's extremely odd that suddenly you're interested in my filmmaking skills," Eddie interrupted, "when just ten hours ago you wouldn't give my camera the light of day."

"That's because this has purpose," said Stella.

Purpose.

"I think documenting you and your escapades has purpose," Eddie grinned.

"Well, I think you're weird," said Stella.

"Well, I think I'm going to bed," Eddie said, standing with his blanket. "The couch is yours, *Skywalker*." He nodded to Scott and headed upstairs.

"Thanks," Scott said and flopped down.

"Whatever!" Stella yelled to Eddie and turned to Francie. "He'll be onboard. He lives for this. So what about you? It's perfect, right? Filming art in Santa Barbara. Your dad'll love it."

He'll think it's amateurish. "Maybe," Francie lied.

"Oh, c'mon, we'll invite you to our 'family getaway,' and it'll be super fun. We'll come up with a plan. I gotta tell Hugh," she said and disappeared upstairs.

Clearly, it didn't matter what Francie thought. Stella was on a roll and was way more focused than Francie thought.

Francie wondered why Stella wanted *her* to go to Santa Barbara. Or why she liked *her*. Or cared. Maybe it didn't matter why.

Francie also wondered if she could trust Stella. And if she really was a part of this.

She pulled the blanket over her head.

Right hand down. Forehand. Hitting up around the right side of the ball. Spinning it up. Blasting up. Ball curving up crosscourt, arcing down just inside the line. Then springing up and off to the side.

She was going to win next week. All of her matches. She had to.

17

Francie stared at herself in the mirror. She was wearing her lucky tennis skirt and told herself the luck was real if she believed it. But she was too nervous for it to make a difference. She'd be on the court in almost three hours.

Left hand down. Brushing up and over. Hard. Ball spinning, curving, crosscourt, down inside the line. Perfect.

She went back to her laptop and Eddie's Lyric Poet West video. She'd watched it a gazillion times and reread the emails with Chet and still wasn't bored of any of it. The video was hilarious. It was the best thing she'd ever been a part of. And everyone else loved it too. Gazillions of likes!

She clicked over to Chet's reply to her after the show.

Subject: Your awesome show
FM!

Thanks so much for coming to the show! Not so many fans (yet) but everyone's happy. And the video is great. So maybe getting thrown out had a perk??? Tho would've rather had you and the limp there for the whole thing. But seriously really, really, really dig the video! Hugh's gonna get it on the website tonight and wants to do another in SB so now you definitely have to come. No excuses. Nice work Eddie! We want more.

And hey, thanks for the thing about my mom. You hardly say too much and you're always kind. Now hopefully I haven't said too much!

Onward FM!

CJ

And then there was her reply.

CJ,

You never say too much. In fact, I appreciate you so much. That you listen and that I can be honest with you and tell you stuff I never tell anyone.

Francie's heart started pounding.

Especially about my family.

She took a deep breath.

They're totally different from yours. Yours seems amazing. But I can somehow relate. And you understanding me makes me feel so much better.

She exhaled.

And yeah, I thought so too. About Eddie. He's totally talented. He gave me his old camera to practice with cuz he wants me to help him but I dunno.

And Stella's got a plan for Santa Barbara that involves convincing my parents to let me go. Starting with Stella and Eddie driving me to this tennis tournament in Ventura so my parents see they're responsible. Haha! Actually, Eddie drives real slow. So I guess he is. And Stella is apparently a planner. (And enforcer! ☺) Weirdly. I'm so nervous. Not about them but the match. Just, I really hope I win. And it's not even my knee because I can push through it. It's just that sometimes I get so nervous that I freeze and panic and start pushing the ball and lobbing and can't go for it. That probably sounds like gibberish but maybe you get the idea ☺
FM

And then she read his reply, the one that made her feel even happier.

Dearest FM on the radio dial,
Stop pushing the ball already and go for it! Kidding. You are so amazing now go be amazing in Ventura. Let me know when you win. And have fun. Make sure the limp has fun too. Take a photo.
I love that you love my family. And understand.
CJ

Francie wished she could stay in this email bubble forever. But Stella and Eddie would be there soon. And she'd be playing soon. And now she wanted to win even more so she could tell Chet. And be amazing. Like him. And his family.

The nerves came back immediately.

What if she didn't win? What if she got distracted by Stella and Eddie? She hated when people watched her at tournaments. What if it messed her up? Why did she agree to this?

Shit!

And they were about to show up on her doorstep. And they were going to meet her dad. And then she'd have to worry about that too! Because it was all getting so weird with him. Like yesterday, drunk at 3:00 p.m. Again! And what about Saturday? When they had those people over for dinner and he just got up and fell asleep on the couch, snoring with his fly half open? He didn't even get up to say good-bye! And her mom lied and said he'd been working way too much and was under the weather. How was this possible? Who even *were* her parents anymore?!

Francie hated them both in that moment.

The doorbell rang.

Oh god!

She grabbed her shoes and rackets and ran downstairs hoping her dad wouldn't talk too much. Or be obnoxious. Or brag. Or anything!

"I've got it!" Francie yelled, barreling towards the front door. Too late. Her dad had the door open. And Stella and Eddie were there.

"Mr. Mills?" Stella said.

"Yes?" he replied.

"Stella, Stella Plumb, and this is my brother, Eddie." Stella shook his hand with her friendliest smile. "We're Francie's friends."

"From the club," Francie added, stepping up next to her dad and smiling at him as if this were normal. "Sorry, I forgot to tell you. They're taking me to the tournament." She noticed his hand shaking as he held the door open and the smell of stale beer.

Francie turned back to Stella and Eddie, smile plastered on her face. They were totally dressing the part, Stella in her mom's tennis skirt and top that were way too big, spiky hair covered with a scarf and nose ring *gone* and Eddie fully decked out in Adidas.

"Well, c'mon inside," Francie's dad said, turning up the charm. "We've got pancakes. Always good before a match."

"We gotta go, Dad, I just gotta put my shoes on," Francie said.

Stella and Eddie stepped inside anyway and were luckily on their best behavior, which was surprisingly really good and really stuffy. And Stella looked eager to check it out.

"I thought you were going with Ricky," Francie's mom said from the kitchen.

"He looked at the time wrong," Francie lied. "He's playing later. But this is Stella and Eddie Plumb, and they're happy to give me a ride."

"You should've told me you needed a ride," her dad said, "I would've cancelled my tee time," then hammed it up for Stella and Eddie. "Golf. Who can resist?"

Oh my god, this was going great!

"We're both really big fans of your movies, Mr. Mills," Stella said. "Especially Eddie. He's really into those cool cars."

"That Edsel you got for that Mac Mitchum film last year was just great," Eddie said.

Sweet.

"Well, you let me know, and I'll get you out there some time," Francie's dad said.

"That'd be great," said Eddie, totally working it.

"Yeah, Francie came out with me to Austin a few weeks ago, and we even had her practicing her driving in the '64 Mustang. She did pretty well considering it was stick."

Francie felt her cheeks turn red. The story wasn't even true. She'd sat in the Mustang and revved the engine and that was it. But her dad loved to exaggerate.

"Oh, cool," said Eddie.

"Yeah, and then she got in our rental car and backed into a pole," he said, teasing.

"Dad, they don't want to hear this!" Francie said.

"Oh, no, we'd love to hear this," Eddie grinned.

"*And* we have to get going," Francie said, glaring for Eddie to stop. He laughed.

"Actually, we're not in such a rush anymore," Stella said to Francie's dad.

What?!

"Abigail Mitchum was coming with us," Stella lied, "but then she decided to drive herself because she has to be back early. But I think she's coming with us tomorrow."

"I thought she wasn't playing anymore," Francie's dad said to Francie.

"She's just gonna watch," Stella said, totally winging it.

"Well, I think it's an excellent idea to drive together like that," Francie's dad said, buying it all. "Eliza, come say hi to the Plumb kids."

Francie's mom came out of the kitchen.

"Hi Mrs. Mills," said Stella, jutting out her hand to shake. "I think we met at the club, and you know my mom from doubles maybe."

"Oh, yes, yes," Francie's mom said, clearly not remembering at all.

Because they were probably all lies, too!

"I'm just gonna get my water and then we can go," Francie said. She ran to fill her water jug and wondered if they should stop by the club so she could warm up. She never went to a tournament without warming up. But it was the first round and a summer tournament and no one good would be there. They'd all be at nationals, like Mallory, so she'd have an easy draw, at least for a couple rounds. She could relax. Go with the flow of it. Like now. This was totally working and amazing. Especially how they mentioned Abigail. Her dad was eating it up! Maybe it'd be okay to have Stella and Eddie with her in Ventura after all. Maybe it'd be lucky.

"Okay, I'm ready," Francie said and came out of the kitchen smiling.

"Alright, good luck, Kiddo," her dad said and gave her a warm hug with his shaky arms.

Eddie shook his hand and no one did anything weird, and then they left.

They did it! And piled in Eddie's car and waved good-bye to Francie's parents, just like a postcard, and as soon as they turned the corner, they all cheered and high-fived.

"That was great!" Francie yelled. "Especially the thing about Abigail!"

"Yeah, I think we're off to a good start," said Stella, pulling off her scarf and checking her pink spikes in the visor mirror, then flipping up the mirror. "Okay, so, bookstore?"

"You got it," said Eddie.

"Wait, what?" asked Francie.

"I gotta work and I wanna get this book about music management for Hugh," Stella said, dialing on her phone. "I could order it but it's gonna be a great excuse to see him before S.B."

"Right, like you can't just mail it," said Eddie.

"No, because we're gonna read it *together*," said Stella, grinning as Facetime rang.

"So you're not going with us?" Francie said.

"You guys'll be fine," Stella winked at Francie as Hugh answered. "Hughbie!"

Crap! This meant she had to ride all the way to Ventura with just Eddie.

"Check it out, we're all country club for Francie." Stella held up the phone so Hugh could see. Francie waved. Hugh made a peace sign with a nerdy straight face under his glasses.

Stella turned the phone back on herself, "Hey, wasn't the Country Club a venue in The Valley? My mom saw Oingo Boingo there! That was a rhetorical question."

Hugh laughed, and Stella rambled on, totally in love and not even letting Hugh speak. How was this happening? They were totally into each other!

And she was going to have to be alone with Eddie.

Shortly before The Oaks Mall, Eddie pulled into a strip mall. And Stella hopped out, yelling, "kaaay," as she ran into a pub.

What the...? "Wait, what about the bookstore?" Francie asked.

"She's dropping a key," Eddie said. Then Francie saw his hands squeeze the steering wheel and his knuckles get all white, and his voice did a weird thing and his energy got all dark, like there was a shadow wrapping around him, as he added, "for our mom."

Wait, what?

Then Stella ran back out and hopped in all happy and normal. Until she saw Eddie. And Francie. And must've realized she had to explain because Eddie didn't. "That was our mom. Our other mom is actually our step mom. This one is somewhat of a free spirit. Hippy. Right, Jerkie?"

Eddie couldn't even look at her and just shook his head as he drove off. This was heavy. Francie could feel the anger coming off his back. Even Stella got weird and cloudy.

Was this why all the photos of them as kids just had their dad in them?

Wow. Totally unexpected. They seemed so normal.

Francie wondered what the deal was. But she knew she'd never ask. Not in a million years. Just like she hoped they'd never ask about her dad. But she knew it was something similar.

And she understood. Like Chet understood her. That Eddie was embarrassed. Angry. Furious. Full of rage. At his mom. And hurt. She could feel it. In herself. The hurt growing. *No!* Anger rising. As if coming out to meet his.

Stop! You can't do this. You have to play!

"Wooooo!" Stella yelled all of a sudden and blasted the music, waving her arms and singing along. She must've known. Known what to do for Eddie.

That's what brothers and sisters do.

Eddie cracked his neck with an eff-you crack and took a deep breath.

And they were back to normal. And by the time they pulled up to The Oaks Mall, everything seemed light again, thank god.

Stella got out and looked into the back seat at Francie. "You coming up here or you want him to chauffeur you?"

Francie reluctantly got in the front seat.

"Good thing," said Eddie. "Or I'd be expecting a rather large tip."

"Well, break a leg," Stella said, slamming the door.

"Thanks," Francie managed through the open window.

"I don't think they say that in tennis," said Eddie.

"Well, then, good luck," Stella said.

Francie nodded.

"Oh, c'mon, Mills, smile! You're gonna kick some ass!" Stella said.

Francie forced a smile and wished it was that easy.

Eddie pulled away and Francie stared out the window, hoping he'd let her be.

"How about we listen to something good?" he said and blasted some hip hop thing, singing along. Then turned it down when she didn't join in. "Whad up, Mills?"

He didn't let it be.

"I don't feel like talking. Okay?" she said.

"You're still mad about The West."

"I'm not mad!"

"Okay. You're not mad." He turned up the music, sang along for a sec then turned it down. "Did you try the camera?"

"A little," she lied.

"And?"

"It's great," she lied again.

"See, that wasn't so bad."

"What?"

"Us having a conversation. You and me talking." He grinned as they came to a red light.

Francie groaned.

"I do love pushing your buttons," he said. "And that everyone loved the footage you shot."

That's when she made the mistake of looking him in the eye. His smile was honest and kind. And their eyes connected. Like really connected. Like he could see right into her. Like, *ah, naked!* Way too much to stand. And it scared her.

"Yeah," she said. And looked away. Super quickly. Heart racing.

"You know what I like about you? You wear your heart on your sleeve and you think no one notices. And I get to take pot-shots at it." The light turned green and he drove on.

What did that even mean?!

"Actually, I have no idea what you're thinking. Except that you want me to stop talking now. So I will." And he turned up the music and pulled onto the 101 Freeway.

Francie watched the hills passing and thought about Chet. And that first moment he looked at her. And how different it was from what she was feeling right then about Eddie and that intense, awkward, eye-meeting, see-right-through-her connection. Chet made her feel better. And Eddie made her feel super weird.

Hitting up and around the right. Hard. Brushing up. Forehand. Ball spinning up and down crosscourt. Inside the line and blasting up and out.

Relief.

18

Francie was feeling super positive as they pulled into the parking lot of the Racquet Club of Ventura. She just kept imagining emailing Chet when she got back and telling him how she won and how relieved she was that her knee was okay. She could practically feel the win.

But then she saw two girls walking in with rackets and water jugs. She'd beaten one of them before and the other she'd never played but knew she was good and would probably be in the top sixteen that year. Apparently, she'd beaten someone good at sectionals then lost in the round of sixteen. Francie probably wouldn't play her today, but still. The thought of playing at all and the pressure suddenly took over.

"Here we are," said Eddie as he pulled into a spot.

"Perfect." Adrenaline coursed through Francie's veins. She grabbed her rackets and water jug. "Just don't go anywhere until I'm sure I'm playing here," she said and got out.

"I'm not gonna leave you here! I'm coming in."

Oh god. This was exactly what she didn't want. But he looked so eager. Whatever. She'd just ignore it. She slammed the door shut and went in and straight for the draw.

Eddie followed. "Hey, look, you're seeded five!"

Sure enough, her name was in the fifth spot. Her stomach suddenly jumped and felt excited. In a good way. This was great! It meant she'd at least get to the quarters. And then she'd have to play Tara McDonald, who was seeded fourth.

But that was okay because she'd beaten Tara before. Twice. Oh my god. And then she'd be in the semis and play Leah Schwartz. She could probably beat her but she'd have to play great. Alright, first things first. Today, she was playing Emily Brenner. Emily…Emily…that sounded familiar. Maybe she'd just see her name before. Whatever, she couldn't be that good.

But then Francie went to sign in and saw Emily. "Oh my god," Francie said out loud.

"What?" asked Eddie.

"That's totally not fair!"

"What?!"

Francie felt panic coming on. "She's playing up. The girl I'm playing is playing up from the 14s, and she's totally good. Mallory used to play her all the time."

"Mallory's just a kid. You can beat her."

"Yeah, and she's gonna be top four in the country. And they didn't seed this girl. And I think she's even beaten Mallory once. She should be at nationals. Why is she here? It's totally not fair. Why do I have to play her in the first round?"

Eddie shrugged and made a "yikes" face, clearly wanting to help but making it worse.

Francie felt desperate. And rattled. By Emily. By him. She just wanted him to leave. But was too chicken to tell him. She didn't want to hurt his feelings. She felt her armor go up, like it did when she was with her mom.

And she turned away, trying to calm down. But then, everything got worse. Because there, standing with Emily, was Hawk. Her coach.

No!

She quickly turned her back. He'd freak if he saw she was playing on her knee. And why was he there? With *Emily*?! He only came for the really, really good people.

"Hey, there's Hawk," Eddie said and yelled, "Hawk!"

"No!" she whispered and turned further to hide as Eddie waved. She peeked back at Hawk. Still talking to Emily. And a woman who was probably Emily's mom.

Francie felt sick. Was he there to watch Emily? But Emily lived in The Valley! Then again, other people came from The Valley for lessons. He was an amazing coach, with tons of ranked juniors. But he coached Mallory, too. That'd be weird, since Mallory and Emily were rivals.

"Okay, do you want to check in?" Eddie asked.

Francie took a deep breath and gave her name to the lady at the desk.

"You're going to be right here on the second court," the lady said. "Emily Brenner?"

Emily came bounding over with a big sickening smile, "Hi."

"Hi," Francie replied, forcing a smile back. "We're on the second court."

Eddie gave her a "go get 'em" fist bump and Francie started to the court, praying Emily wouldn't want to chat. She had to stay focused. She could beat her. She knew she could. Even though Mallory was ranked super high, she was only twelve, and Francie could beat her sometimes, because she was stronger, and Mallory had beaten this girl a few times. So she definitely had a good shot. But she was so nervous, she really thought she might be sick.

Francie stood at the baseline.

"Thirty love," said Emily and fired off another serve down the center.

Francie pulled her racket back late and went for it anyway, hitting the ball as hard as she could towards Emily's forehand. It flew out wide.

"Topspin!" Francie yelled at herself. "Can't you even hit up on it?!" Francie was so angry she smashed her racket into her ankle.

Ow. She cringed in pain. *Dammit!* How could this be happening? She had to win this point. There was no way she was going to be down 0–2. She had to win at least one game. This was totally embarrassing and impossible! How the heck did she even lose the first set 6–0?!

"Forty love," said Emily, bouncing, ready to go.

Francie paced at the baseline making Emily wait. She had to calm down and pump herself up. Her heart was racing. She straightened her strings and tried to psych herself up, but she was too nervous and her hands were shaking and she couldn't stall forever. She took a deep breath and got into position.

"Hit up, hit up, hit up," she said to herself as Emily served to her forehand. Francie pulled her racket back low, ready to hit up for topspin, but suddenly, she lost all courage and strength in her arm and choked, pushing the ball towards Emily's backhand, totally afraid to hit out on it. It didn't even make it near the top of the net and fell back on her side.

"What the hell are you doing?!" Francie screamed at herself. "Godammit!" She chucked her racket at the pole in the back fence. Bang, it hit dead on. Good shot, she thought and wanted to cry.

Suddenly, the door to the court flew open, and Hawk stepped in. What was he doing? He looked furious. And he was. He walked straight over to her. "One more word out of you and I'm pulling you off this court," he said, his voice unusually tense. "You shouldn't even be out here on that knee and your behavior is unacceptable."

She nodded, and he turned and walked off the court, slamming the door behind him.

Francie felt the tears welling up. She picked up her racket, grabbed her towel and tried to hide her eyes as she walked to the other side. She didn't even stop at the bench for water so Emily wouldn't notice. Who cared if she had water? She just wanted to die. She deserved it. What was the point of anything? She didn't care. She stood in the back and cried. "C'mon, you have to at least finish this," she told herself.

Francie picked up the balls and went to serve. She was so upset that her arms were like mush, totally relaxed, and bizarrely, without even trying, she served an ace. And then another. And then she proceeded to win the next six games straight. It was a miracle. Somehow, as soon as she stopped caring and trying and pressuring herself, she played amazingly. She hit out on the ball, moved it around, kept it deep, mixed it up and just hit winner after winner.

She grabbed the balls and walked off the court without even a glance at Emily. It didn't feel great not to be friendly or not to say anything but she didn't care. She had to stay focused.

She went straight to the desk to get new balls. "Hi, we split," she said, handing the woman the old balls and waiting for the new can they gave you when you split sets.

"Hey," said Eddie, nonchalantly putting his hand on her shoulder. "Good job."

"Thanks," Francie said to the lady, taking the new balls, then looking at Eddie. His eyes were kind, and she knew he wasn't judging her. He cared and wanted the best for her. "Thanks," she said and walked back to the court putting an imaginary bubble around herself so she didn't feel like she had to look at or talk to anyone. She just had to win this thing and not think about anything else.

Francie's heart was pounding. She could hear it. Literally. Shaking her chest like it would explode out. Match point. She had to win this point. Just one more point and this would be over and she could go home. She bounced the ball at the baseline, ready to serve.

Halfway into the third set, the nerves had started to come back, and it got really bad as soon as they'd started the tiebreaker. Her hands were shaking. She stopped bouncing and stood up and wiped her racket with her shirt and took a deep breath.

She got back in position to serve, bouncing the ball then looking at her target. She tossed it up. Too low. Her hand shaking too much. Her stomach in a knot, and Emily over there looking totally sure of herself and annoying, bouncing around on the baseline waiting for her serve.

Francie started again. She bounced the ball and eyed her target, crosscourt wide in the corner, and imagined how it would feel: *Tossing, reaching, slamming up and over, ball spinning, dropping in, popping up and out to the side. Perfect.* She tossed the ball up. *Too low, too low, too low.* But her shaking arm went for it, pushing the serve over. *Why?!* It arced high over the net, bounced in and up and just sat there, and Emily stepped in and ripped it crosscourt for a winner.

Shit!

Francie toweled off and tried to relax. *C'mon!* Then got back in position to serve again. "Seven all," she said and pushed the serve over. Emily stepped in and ripped it down the line.

"Oh my god, what am I doing?!" she yelled in her head. She took a deep breath and wiped her hands. Emily hurried to serve, "Eight, seven."

Emily tossed the ball up and served it down the middle. Francie pulled her racket back and hit up on it as hard as she could to get spin. Emily stepped in and hit it back down the middle. Francie nervously pushed it back, and Emily stepped in and hit the winner and continued running up to the net to shake hands.

Francie felt the tears immediately. She shook Emily's hand without looking at her, grabbed her stuff quickly and left the court. Normally, they would walk off together and chit-chat but that was not happening this time.

Francie focused her eyes on the sidewalk, kept her chin down and walked right past Hawk and then past Emily's mom and past Eddie and just kept going. She didn't know where to but she couldn't bear facing any of them. She immediately started to cry. And heard, "Francie!" And saw Eddie following her. What a nightmare.

She went to the car and realized she couldn't get in, so she dumped her rackets and water and just kept walking. Maybe she'd get lucky and someone would steal them.

She continued down the driveway of the club and onto the street heading towards the ocean. She walked through the freeway underpass and ended up on the beach and just kept going down to the water.

It was a gorgeous day. But she didn't care. She lay down in the sand and curled up in a ball and just cried until she couldn't anymore and closed her eyes. Finally, totally relaxed.

Eddie woke her up, double-fisted with ice cream cones that were so melted he was licking both. *Gross.* She took one anyway. The ice-cream place should've bought those drip catchers from those inventor kids on *Shark Tank*.

Eddie sat down next to her and didn't say anything, and they just ate their ice cream.

Then he started talking about movies and Martin Scorsese and *The Last Waltz*, which was a movie Scorsese made of The Band, which was a band called The Band, and all these other great musicians, on Thanksgiving. A really long time ago. And he told her how it was one of the first really cool music films, a cross between a film and a documentary and a music video. Really long for a music video, but before its time, so that was okay. Francie knew some of this from her dad but had never seen it.

"You should," he said, eyes lighting up. "They have all this concert footage and these kind of random interviews with the band, literally The Band, but no structure and just the perfect amount. I think we could do that too. In Santa Barbara."

Francie knew that'd never happen. But she didn't say it. She didn't even want to go to Santa Barbara anymore. *Not as a loser*. She just wanted to curl back up into a ball and never feel anything ever again.

"They can talk about whatever," Eddie continued. "And then we cut it in. And more with audience and fans. I think that's the good stuff. You definitely should watch it."

His eyes were friendly, as if trying to gauge where she was at and if this was helping.

Did he have to be so nice?

"My dad might have it," she managed in hopes that he'd stop talking or go away.

"Or you can borrow mine."

She nodded, and they both turned back to watching the boogie boarders in the water. She thought about the tennis match and how angry she was at herself. He must've known.

"How you doin'?" he asked.

She shook her head and the tears came again, "I don't want to do this anymore."

"What?"

"Tennis. Why do I even try?"

"Because you're really good."

"No, look at me. I practice so hard and I lose to a thirteen year old!"

"Barely. And you have the knee thing."

"But I practice ten million times harder than Mallory and I'll never be as good as her."

"Not many people will be."

"Thanks."

"Not many people will ever be as good as you either. Or as totally obnoxious and rude on the court."

She felt her cheeks turn red.

"Kind of like our doubles match. So you're a little crazy and totally emotional and angry. I still like you." He smiled. And then gave her his ice-cream napkin that was totally covered in mint chip, for her face, that was totally covered in snot. "Oh, hey look at that guy," he said.

There was a boogie boarder doing fancy spins on a wave.

"Let's see if he'll let us interview him!" Eddie jumped up. "And some of those other lazy dudes hangin' out." He put his hand out to help her up.

She didn't want to and said, "You go."

And he said, "Okay," and went.

And she watched him and felt totally numb but was grateful that she could just sit there and be.

And feel safe. Because of Eddie.

And not really admit that to anyone.

Even herself.

19

Francie and Eddie pulled up to Francie's house. The lights were on, and she really didn't want to go in. "Your parents await," Eddie said, honking the horn long and loud.

"Oh my god! What're you doing?"

"We want them to see me dropping you off safe and sound," he said, amused.

She groaned and got out. Her mom waved from the front window.

"See," he said.

Francie slammed the door shut. Eddie looked out the open car window. "Be sure to practice with the camera. We've got ten days to Santa Barbara."

She *so* wanted to latch on to his optimism. And how he and Stella were doing all this for her. Lord knows why. But all she could think about was how much she didn't want to go in her house and how she knew that once she did, everything would get even more miserable.

"Alright thanks," she said and headed to the door. Her mom was waiting and waved to Eddie.

"He seems like a nice guy," her mom said.

"Yeah, he is."

"Oh, honey, I'm sorry about the match."

"It's okay; I'm fine," Francie lied and went in. She was so relieved she'd texted them ahead of time. So she didn't have to say it out loud, that she'd lost.

"I made fried chicken," her mom continued. "Your favorite."

"I'm not really hungry. We had some food at Stella and Eddie's," she lied again.

Her mom tried to hide her disappointment, "Wonderful," and went into the kitchen.

Her dad stood at the counter taking a bite out of a piece of chicken. He looked up and waved with a goofy smile and full mouth. "Hey there!" He covered his half-full mouth with a napkin. She could see his hand shaking. "Your mom made some excellent fried chicken. I couldn't wait."

He laughed at himself and his eyes sparkled as he walked over and give her a hug. Francie instantly started to cry. This was the dad she loved, and she knew he was there to make her feel better.

"Are you hungry?" he asked.

"No thanks. I just ate."

His hands were shaking so bad he had to let go of her. She could tell he was embarrassed, but for a change, he stayed focused on her and cheering her up. "Well, put your rackets away and let's watch a movie. It's my last night here and I want to spend it with my girls. And as for that match today, forget it. They shouldn't let anyone play up."

Again, he smiled warmly. And relief washed over her. He totally got it.

"What should we watch?" he asked.

"*The Last Waltz?* You have it, right?"

"Of course, I do. Now we're talkin'. Right, El?" He looked at her mom, his eyes full of charm. Her mom seemed to blush. *Weird.* He got up to put his plate in the sink and even gave her a kiss. A rare moment. Her mom seemed embarrassed in front of Francie and turned away.

"How did your friends do today?" her mom asked. "They both seemed nice."

Francie thought about lying, but at this point, she didn't care. She didn't care about anything let alone what her mom thought. "Actually, they didn't play. They just watched."

"Really?" her mom said, surprised.

"Why not?" her dad defended. "Francine has wonderful friends."

"Oh, of course," her mom said. "So, do they play at all?"

"Stella works at the snack shop and designs clothes and Eddie played at Westlake and makes documentaries."

"That's interesting," her mom said.

"It is!" her dad added.

That made her feel good. Like he was paying attention. And actually understood what mattered to her. And what she needed. How was it possible? He could make her feel so okay when he wanted and listened and when he wasn't being all obsessed with himself.

And he got her. Way more than most people. Way more than her mom. In fact, it wasn't even close. Because Francie and her dad were alike somehow.

Was that bad? Or good?

"You could always invite him for dinner so we can get to know him," her mom said.

"No, it's fine," Francie said. "We're just friends. And Stella, too."

"You can still invite him over," her mom said. "It might be nice for you to have someone."

Like I'm not okay if I don't?! That's how it felt. Like she was a loser for not having someone.

"My darling Francine will always have someone," her dad said, again saving the day. "Starting with me." He looked at her with that sweet and goofy smile and she just melted.

Francie watched her dad try to open a video file. His hands shook on the mouse as he attempted to hover the arrow in the right spot. It was painful to watch, but he got it.

"There we go," he said. "This is the one Rolf and I shot at Lollapalooza. It's no *Last Waltz* so you tell me when you've had enough. Or if you don't want to see it at all."

"No, I want to see it. All of it!"

He made a "yikes" face for effect and hit play. It was so weird to see him so humble.

Together they watched the video. Mostly concert footage and him and his buddy Rolf and her Uncle Mike being totally stupid. Her dad was the sanest one and narrated with history about the festival and each band. He was like a walking music professor. So crazy-smart and funny.

And he was totally enjoying it, laughing, remembering being at the festival and making the video. And for a moment, one split second, Francie saw *him*. The real Hank. Full of joy.

"That was really good," Francie said when it finished.

"Naw, it was just fun. We were just goofin' around." He closed out the video, and Francie watched the joy drain from his face.

"Can we watch another one?" Francie asked. There were tons in the "Concerts" folder. "Oooh, and what's that?" she asked about a folder called "All-Star Francie."

A smile came across his face. "Let's see," he said knowingly.

It was all videos of her. He opened one called "Jane Says Francie's an All-Star." And there she was, probably five years old, dancing with her dad to "Jane Says" and laughing.

Someone else was filming, probably her mom, and Francie and her dad were completely and utterly happy: He picked five-year-old Francie up and threw her in the air; they did an Eskimo kiss, and then he just looked at her and totally adored her and she knew it and hugged his neck.

Then the video ended, and Francie and her dad were both silent. It was awkward and almost worse to have seen it because they had been so happy.

Her dad quickly changed the mood, "Whelp, alright, Kiddo," and closed out the folder. "Your old man needs to relax before his big trip tomorrow." He popped *The Last Waltz* out. "But thanks for watching this with me."

Her heart sank. She could feel this heaviness return as he put the disc back in the sleeve. "And feel free to goof around with Premiere all you want. And if you have any questions, ask Uncle Mike. Er, me!" He laughed, a forced laugh, and in that instant, she knew he was going to go downstairs and have a beer.

He put the disc back on the shelf. "And check out whatever you want here, *Some Kind of Monster*, *Don't Look Back*. That's another classic."

"Yeah, great, thank you," she said, watching him meticulously straighten out his DVD collection. He was so ordered and had everything labeled, all professional. Why was he not making more videos? And doing what he loved? It had importance to him.

He stood up. "I'd better go eat some more fried chicken so I stay on your mother's good side." He put his hand on top of her head and squeezed it playfully then headed downstairs.

She stood at the door and watched him disappear.

Francie sat down and turned on her laptop. She went to her favorites and clicked on Chet's site. "Louisa, Hey" started. She turned it off. She really didn't feel like hearing anything.

She went to the band's Facebook page and looked through a couple posts but couldn't concentrate either. She just kept thinking about her dad and how sad he felt and that just made her feel totally empty and alone. And there was nothing she could do to help him. Nothing.

Then her stupid tennis match came flooding into her mind and she hated herself for it. And made a fist and slammed it down onto her thigh. And did it again. And again. Harder and harder until it really hurt. Maybe it would bruise and she could remember how much she hated herself.

She took a deep breath. Then clicked on the video from The West and watched it with the sound off. Everyone was so happy, and she watched herself dancing.

Then she opened a new email for Chet. But couldn't focus. She hated herself. And how stupid she was about him. Just waiting to write to him and for him to write back or Facetime and to see him. *Loser. Worthless.* She grabbed the camera sitting on the edge of the desk and turned it on herself.

"Hello, this is me. The girl who totally freaked out on the court today. Who lost to the stupid thirteen year old that I know I could beat after having two match points. That's me. I work really hard but then I still suck. It doesn't matter how hard I try. I'm lame and useless."

She stopped the camera. The tears welling. "And here is my room. Bed, poster, collages, laptop," still talking as if to some camera audience, crying, "and there's the Blues Harp Jones site," gesturing to the screen like Vanna White, "because really I'm a fan. And I really love Chet. And his family. Even though I really don't know what that means. Or why he would ever love me back."

She sat down and just cried until she couldn't anymore. Then deleted the video.

She looked at Chet's smile on the website and opened his last email. The one where he was so excited for her about her match and thought she would win for sure. He was so encouraging and cute, and now, she was just a disappointment.

She hit reply and just started to write whatever. Without thinking. Because she didn't know how to be anyway. And her inner editor sucked.

Dear Chet—

Today was awful. And I'm not even sure why I'm writing except that you wanted to know how I did. And I feel really weird and am not sure what to do. Well, I lost to a 13 year old I could've beat. Because I was too scared. I got really mad at myself too and threw my racket and my coach came on the court and yelled at me and said if I made one more peep he'd pull me off. The whole thing was totally humiliating and I just hate myself. I hate that I get so mad and that I can't control it and that I can't make myself win. And I feel totally worthless. I usually can pick myself up. But right now that feels impossible. Like I'm such a loser that nothing will ever help. Or be okay.

And I feel sad. And sad too about my dad. He is so miserable and there's nothing I can do. And it makes my heart hurt to think about it.

We watched The Last Waltz together, which was amazing and he was so happy about it. And he showed me some Lollapalooza video he made and told me how he has Don't Look Back and Some Kind of Monster. And he was so proud and then he just got really depressed. He's going to

Vancouver tomorrow for work for three months. I know he doesn't want to go. He only likes his job because it makes a lot of money. And I think seeing his amazing video made it worse. I've never seen him this sad.

I don't know why I'm telling you all this. Maybe because you know my dad. Sort of. And I don't really talk about him to anyone. I'm sorry I'm so messed up and that this is such a downer.

Tomorrow I'll ask my mom if I can go to SB with Stella and Eddie. If she says no at this point, I don't even care. It can't get any worse, so whatever. And maybe it's totally unrealistic to think I can actually go to shows and see you and support the band, which is the point, right? Maybe the stars aren't aligning for that. Like they did when I met you.

Thanks for listening.
Francie

She hit send and closed her laptop and curled up in a ball on her bed, squeezing her eyes shut and doing her best to keep her mind blank, hoping she'd just fall asleep soon.

She did. And then her phone rang. The Facetime ring. It was him. She pulled the phone under the covers with her, watched it ring a few more times and answered.

Chet's face filled the screen. With glasses she hadn't seen before, black nerdy ones like Hugh or that Elvis Costello guy her mom liked. Actually she liked Elvis Costello too, and Chet looked great in the glasses. Especially because she could still see his gorgeous green eyes. Intense

and looking right at her. Drilling into her like he was serious but smiling too. Which instantly made her happy.

Like magic. *How? How does he do this to me?*

Her heart pounded.

"Hi," Chet said, turning up the adorable Aussie accent.
"What the hell are you doing?"

Her stomach leapt into her throat and her cheeks got
really hot and she couldn't speak.

"I can't even see you, you know," he said.

"It's so late," was all she could think of to say.

"Hugh and Stella are still up and talking," he said, as
if that made a difference, and panned into the room that
clearly was the carport and over to Hugh Facetiming with
Stella, then back to himself. His eyes sparkled, "But
they're kind of over-the-top gross, wouldn't you say?" and
he cracked up.

Which made her laugh too, and she pulled her head
out of the covers.

"Oh, so much better," he said.

She laughed again.

"And a laugh. Mate! I was worried. What is up, gorgeous FM on the radio dial?"

She had no idea what to say and felt embarrassed, and
it was all too much, and suddenly, she felt the tears coming. "I don't know." She hid the phone and cried.

"FM?! Look at you. You're gonna be okay!"

"No, I'm not."

"Yes, you are! Now please let me see your face!"

She lifted the phone again and forced a smile.

"Ah, so much better. Tears and all! The only thing
missing from the screen is your limp."

This made her laugh again. And then she snorted.
Oh my god.

"Oh, finally, I get my old FM back!"

She blushed. Even though her heart was swelling with joy. He cared! But why? And then she just said it out loud. *Oh god.* "Why do you even care?"

"Because I like you?" he said.

Really?

"And I want you to be happy? For no reason? Do I have to have a reason? I mean, other than how amazing you are. Kind and observant and a hesitant dancer and renegade videographer who gets thrown out of important L.A. clubs and a gorgeous demure girl with a limp that liked me and trusted me enough to go see bats?"

And she burst into tears again because she believed him.

"No, no, no, I'm sorry. FM, look at me."

And she did and forced a smile through the tears because he really did make her feel better. "Thank you," she said.

"I mean, you're putting a lot of pressure on me here, FM," he joked. "And the tennis. I mean, maybe Limpy needs a break."

And she knew he understood. Again.

"I mean, I get it. Like how I think music is going to fix things. And pretend it's all Billy. And blame him. But really, it's me too. Music is going to fix my family. You know?"

He really understood.

"Even if it doesn't. But you also get an A-plus for determination, FM."

And she couldn't help but smile and laugh, not knowing why. Maybe because it was true. And embarrassing. But she felt relieved.

"I mean, you know even if you never win the U.S. Open, I think you're amazing. And please come up to Santa Barbara. So it's not just a whatever. And we can actually spend some time together this time. Okay?"

And once again, her heart swelled, and then she heard yelling from somewhere in his house.

"FM?"

She nodded.

"Be good to FM. Chill on the tennis. Just let it flow." And there was more yelling, and he waved, "bye," and hung up.

Did that really happen? Yes, it did. He called her. Not for the songs. But for her. Because he cared. For no good reason. And maybe because he understood her.

And she had to get to Santa Barbara. No matter what. It was the only thing that mattered. Chet was the only thing that mattered. And she had to see him.

She had to make this real.

20

Nothing could have prepared Francie for what happened the next day and the days that followed. All of it, from her dad saying good-bye the morning he left to him not calling for a few days to finding out he never went to Vancouver for the TV show and totally bailed on the job and was just somehow gone and in Reno and spending all their money. And even worse was that her mom wasn't telling her anything at all and she had to sleuth around to figure it out.

It made it impossible to think about anything or even care about Chet. Even though she kept making herself disappear into her head and imagine being with him. That escape worked when she got there but she had to get there first. And it wasn't easy.

She also got out of her house as much as possible. Which helped, too. First, she asked Stella if she could come over, and then Stella kept inviting her over and never asked what was wrong. She just let Francie hang while she was doing whatever, which was mostly drawing and talking to Hugh or about Hugh and watching movies. Probably Stella knew it was better to just not talk about stuff sometimes. Or maybe it was easier. Even if it was just sitting out there, like Stella's mom. And maybe Stella knew it was just too painful and you would shatter into a million pieces if you uttered it from your mouth. And that it was your job to hold it all together.

Which is what Francie was doing, sitting there on the piano bench at Abigail Mitchum's house watching Eddie interview Abigail's friends with his camera. It was part of Stella's grand scheme to get Francie to Santa Barbara. Stella figured that if Eddie chauffeured her and her mom to the party as kind of a pseudo-date-slash-chaperone, it would ingratiate Eddie to Francie's mom and dad forever since they loved Abigail's parents, director Mac and Libby, so much.

The whole Eddie thing was working but Francie was having a hard time just being there. She hated it, in fact, but was going along because she was out of hope and ideas and had been following Stella around like a robot, or puppy, all week. And now, she was supposed to be helping with the interviews but couldn't even get herself to go over there.

She was in her own nightmare, and being at Abigail's sweet-sixteen party was just another nail in the coffin. She always felt totally lame and depressing next to Abigail and her friends, even though Abigail was really nice. They were all perfect and had perfect lives and she knew she was just invited because her dad worked with Abigail's dad and they were friends.

There were some tennis people too from when Abigail played but that made it worse. It made Francie feel stupid for caring so much about tennis and for being jealous. Abigail was a natural, and if Abigail cared half as much as Francie did about tennis, she'd be amazing. Like she made the team at Westlake freshman year without practicing ever and played number one and beat people at other schools who played all the time and were serious.

And now, Abigail never played at all. Ever since they moved from Westlake to Malibu and their super amazing house that felt more like a ranch than a house. And she started at her cool "progressive" school. Francie wished all the people at the party were from Abigail's school so she didn't have to see the tennis people and be reminded about her own reality.

Whatever. It was stupid, like Chet said, and she was just going to stop caring so much about tennis anyway. And she probably only had to be there at the party for a couple more hours.

She looked at Eddie again. Her mom really liked him so he was definitely scoring for Stella's Santa Barbara scheme. And he'd totally saved Francie's butt from the collage vase she'd made Abigail. Which was totally lame. The invitation had said to bring a homemade gift or a donation to charity, but Francie was the only one who did. Everyone else brought cool presents, like clothes and music and stuff. Abigail acted like she liked Francie's homemade vase but was probably faking, and everyone else just stared at it like a dirty diaper.

Luckily, Eddie whipped out a copy of the Lyric Poet West video and said, "Here's the other part to Francie's homemade gift, *and* we're making a party video starring all of you!"

Francie was worried her mom would see her in The West video, but her mom wasn't watching. Instead, her mom was in the next room talking to Libby, and Libby was consoling her.

Seeing her mom made Francie sick, and she wanted to bolt. It was the same feeling she got when her dad drank and embarrassed her. But worse because she was scared and knew that running wouldn't help because she couldn't escape the black vortex.

Francie felt dizzy and got up and went into the bathroom and locked the door. She leaned back on the floral wallpaper and put her palms flat against it to make sure she was there and it was real. It felt cool. And she started to feel better. She took a deep breath and played out the events of the previous week in her head for the millionth time, starting with her dad coming into her room the morning he left.

It was probably like 5:00 a.m. He had a really early flight to Vancouver and sat on her bed and woke her up and gave her the tightest hug ever and told her he loved her and looked at her for a really long time. Then he got tears in his eyes and hugged her again really tight and left. Kind of like when he woke her up to talk about the job but a gazillion times more intense.

It was so weird and scared her because her dad looked so frightened and vulnerable, and she didn't understand it.

So, she'd just focused on Chet. She was so grateful. And lucky. And it felt like her destiny. She even eased up on tennis. Maybe Chet was right. And maybe if she didn't push so hard, she'd actually do better. Maybe there was destiny and flow to tennis, like he had with music. He stayed relaxed and good things came in. She had to believe it could be true for her too. Because they were so connected.

That worked for a few days until she found out something was up with her dad. Then she panicked about easing up on tennis. What if it kept her from getting ranked? Going to nationals? She had to go to nationals. Nationals would make it all okay. Make her dad's mess okay.

She had to play. And she knew Chet would understand.

That's what she was thinking right then in the bathroom when she decided she'd go to the club and hit on the ball machine after the party. Her heart started to race. She could do that.

But then the anxiety in her stomach screamed and she told herself to think about Chet.

Elvis Costello glasses. Green eyes. Laughing.

Nothing was working!

Stop!

She was going to get to see Chet in a week. He would make it okay.

She thought about when she'd told her mom about Carpinteria and Santa Barbara. It was the day after her dad left. Her mom was so happy for her and said yes. Francie was worried her dad wouldn't agree but her mom said she'd wait until Francie was in Santa Barbara to tell him and only if it came up on their daily Skype.

Her mom thought her dad would probably be okay with the grandparent visit near Santa Barbara. He liked both Eddie and Stella and would love that the grandpa was in the Foreign Service because it was so adventurous and important.

Francie slid her hand along the cool wallpaper in the bathroom and thought about how she'd emailed Chet that she was going for sure and how he'd been so happy. And had called her about another new song. And again, he was so kind and caring and made sure she was okay, and she thought she was.

And she spent days at Stella and Eddie's, and Eddie kept trying to get her to practice with the camera. She went along with it even though she couldn't get into it. And Stella was practically married to Hugh. He visited her, and they all Skyped when Francie was there, and she saw Chet in the background, and they waved.

And Francie wished Chet could visit her too. But she knew he was too busy with his music. And that they'd all be together in a week, making a video in Santa Barbara. And that was amazing.

Francie could hear them singing happy birthday to Abigail in the dining room, and her stomach started to hurt with anxiety, and she felt like she was going to cry. She was so happy about her new friends and Chet and was so excited about seeing him, but she couldn't block her parents out of her thoughts, no matter how hard she tried.

She thought about how her mom had started to look worried two days after her dad left. And how weird it was that they hadn't talked to him. And how she'd heard that terrible phone conversation of her mom's, where she said,

"No, I don't know where he is. He never showed up? I don't understand. No, I'm sorry. I know it's a huge show and a lot of money. Of course, I'll tell him." And then, her mom had cried and texted.

And for days nothing was said and Francie didn't ask. No one ever asked anything in her family about what was really going on. It was like if she asked, it'd make it worse for her mom. She had to go along with pretending everything was okay so maybe it would be. And maybe that would help her mom.

But she was terrified. Had something bad happened to her dad? Why was no one doing anything? But if something bad had happened, they'd have to tell her! *Right?*

And then she'd snuck a peak at her mom's texts, and there were a bunch to her dad's phone with no reply: *Where the hell are you? They want to know where you are! What is going on?!! I can't take this anymore! The Hyatt in Reno?!!! $500 a night?!!! The credit card called to see if it was stolen!! How are we going to pay for this?!!! Please stop! You have a family!*

A knock on the bathroom door.

"Francie?" said Abigail from the other side. "Are you okay? Please come out."

"Okay, just a minute," Francie quickly washed her face, fixed her hair and went out.

"Hey," said Abigail, standing there with a piece of cake. "You missed the candles." She smiled genuinely, clearly feeling sorry for Francie and knowing something was up. Abigail suggested they sit on the sofa.

They did, and Francie couldn't help notice how absolutely perfect Abigail looked even though Francie felt like shit and Abigail was just wearing jeans and a vintage t-shirt and tennis shoes. Somehow everything looked great on her. Maybe it was her long goddess-like straight brown hair. Or the fact that she was nice and funny and smart and had the coolest parents around and got to go to a normal school and got a new, adorable red VW for her birthday. Not to mention she had a gazillion guys in love with her. And a super nice boyfriend for over a year.

I am such a loser.

"What's going on?" Abigail asked, concerned. "Your mom looks kind of sad."

"Yeah, no, she's fine, I mean, she and my dad had a fight or something." Francie smiled, hoping that'd be enough. But she could see Abigail needed more and added, "Honestly, she never tells me anything really."

"Yeah, I get that. My parents are the same." Abigail smiled warmly, and they laughed as if their parents were the same. Francie didn't believe it for a second. Abigail's parents probably talked about everything honestly and listened and her dad probably was supportive all the time and happy. She knew Mac loved his job as a director and her mom loved being a writer. Even the dog, two cats, bunny and egg-laying chickens were happy. She just hoped Libby wouldn't tell Abigail about what was really going on with her dad.

"Well, your parents definitely know how to throw a great party," Francie said, trying to shift the conversation. "At least you can give them that."

Abigail laughed. "Yeah, it's pretty cool." She waved at her friend Lisa. "And great present."

Oh my god, so not true.

"I'm serious," Abigail said. "You're the only one that made something! And how fun is this video?" She looked at Eddie interviewing someone. "It's *so* cool!"

"Thanks."

"And Eddie seems really cool. You never told me about him."

Francie just nodded. She didn't feel like getting into the fact that Eddie wasn't her boyfriend. Not with Abigail. Let her think she had a boyfriend for a change.

"And The West video! I love those Jones guys. So cool. My dad had them over before the shoot, and they were really funny."

Francie was instantly jealous.

"Yeah, I wanted to go to that show but I had a paper. But Lisa, from school, her right there, we're thinking about going to another one. I guess they're playing in Santa Barbara."

Panic. "You're going to that?"

"Maybe. I think it would be a blast. And that Chet is really cute."

Francie caught her breath. "What about Josh?"

Abigail grimaced. "We broke up." She honestly looked sad.

"Oh, no. Yeah, I noticed he's not here."

"Yeah, I don't know. I kind of hope we get back together, but for now, I have to look at the bright side. Like cute guys in bands."

Francie's heart started pounding. What if Abigail went? What if Chet thought she was cute? Why wouldn't he? She was perfect. Francie smiled, doing her best to hide it.

Eddie came over filming. "And here we have another gorgeous guest." He smiled at Francie.

She turned red and just shook her head.

Eddie laughed, "And the lovely Abigail."

Abigail beamed.

"Hey, I have an idea!" said Eddie. "Let's Facetime the band and have them sing happy birthday. For the video."

It was a great idea and Francie hated it. But she couldn't let anyone know how insecure she was about Abigail. How like in two seconds Abigail thinking Chet was cute made all hope about Chet vanish. Francie knew he'd love Abigail. No doubt. But she grabbed her phone anyway and Facetimed him.

"FM on the radio dial!" Chet's face filled the screen, honestly happy to see her.

Eddie butted in, "Hey, Dude, we have the lovely Abigail Mitchum here, and it's her sweet sixteen. Any chance you guys would give her a song?"

And Chet yelled for Billy and Stu, and suddenly, they were all on the tiny screen singing happy birthday. And Abigail beamed, and her friends came round, and Eddie filmed, and Francie wanted to disappear as she held the phone out, feeling sadder and sadder by the minute. Finally, she handed the phone off to whoever was next to her and went into the kitchen trying not to cry.

A few minutes later, Eddie came in with her phone. "Hey!" He stopped when he saw her face. "Yeah, um, Loverboy said to say bye and he's looking forward to seeing you next week. And talking to you before. Whatever that means."

Francie took the phone, still emotional. Was Eddie telling the truth? Or just trying to make her feel better? Both were oddly comforting in that moment. Even if Eddie was annoying as hell. And Francie latched onto that hard. And was going to stay right in the middle of it.

She was going to go hit on the ball machine as soon as they left. And block out everything about her family forever and just tunnel-vision on Santa Barbara. When she would be free. With her friends. And Chet. And her own life. *Safe.*

21

Francie's tunnel-vision to Santa Barbara lasted almost a week, until her dad came home.

Francie had been hitting on the ball machine for about an hour after camp. And it was amazing. She kept thinking about the new tournament next month and how she was going to win and make up for what happened in Ventura.

And it totally helped get her out of her head. Standing there focusing on the ball and nothing else. Hitting with perfect form and feeling the satisfaction with each hit as it spun up and curved back down to land deep and just inside the baseline. It felt like little bursts of positive energy and relief. Over and over. It was about balance, and this was balancing out, even wiping out all the fear about her dad.

That's when she got the text from her mom that her dad was back. And that she should come home in time for dinner. Her first reaction was relief. He was alive and there, but then her heart started racing with fear. Fear about what it would be like when she got home.

So, she just kept hitting on the ball machine, hoping it would go away. And it did every time she hit the ball perfectly on her racket and the ball went in. But then the fear came crashing back and she'd hit the next ball. She kept going for probably an hour until finally someone else had the court and she had no choice but to leave.

Francie stood in front of her house. She was so afraid of what her dad would be like and was pretty sure it'd be more of that sad man. And now, he'd also probably feel bad about what happened and hate himself more. And hate whatever he did. She felt it for him without even seeing him

And she knew her mom would be weird and it would be overwhelming and embarrassing for her dad and all of them and super hard to even look at them. But there was nothing she could do. She had to handle it.

Finally, she just donned an imaginary suit of armor. And went in.

Her mom was cooking and checking her laptop at the kitchen island like nothing had happened, and her dad was standing in front of the sliding glass door, staring out at the perfectly manicured garden, his back to her, hands in his trouser pockets.

"Francie!" her mom exclaimed, overly cheerful and with a giant, be it real, smile.

Her dad turned to her. He looked smaller than usual, which was totally weird. And frail, as if his strength had been sucked out of him. And there was that pain and sadness and fear and feeling bad in his eyes.

But he smiled anyway, and that part, that smile, seemed real. Like he was relieved to see her and loved her. But like it was almost too much for him. Like his love for her hurt and was wrapped in some kind of sadness that she could never understand.

He came over and hugged her. He was shaking and kissed her cheek and whispered, "I'm sorry, honey." And when he smiled, she could tell he felt even more sad than she could imagine. "I've been on a little adventure," he said, oddly, with a weird forced grin.

He glanced at her mom for support, but she didn't look up at all. Francie knew her mom was beyond pissed and punishing him for what he'd put her through.

"And, I am an alcoholic," he said to Francie.

Francie caught her breath. It was like a punch. That word. *Alcoholic.*

"Luckily, I've hooked up with some mighty fine people in a very successful group," he said, again glancing nervously at her mom, "where everyone is exceptionally professional."

Francie just stared, trying to understand. What group? What was he talking about?

"And, I got quite lucky in Reno."

Her mom shook her head at this part, visibly furious.

"And I made a plan." And his eyes flashed at Francie with that mischievous grin he got when he was about to tell her a fantastical story. An exciting, unbelievable adventure. Like he always did. "Because you see, there was a train that came through every day. Every day at the same time. Like clockwork. And I decided that was to be my grand finale. I could go out there on the tracks in the dark. They'd have no time to stop if they saw me. And boom. Done."

Francie gasped under her breath, and her mom got up and checked the dinner on the stove as if nothing earth-shakingly terrible had just been uttered from the lips of the man she loved.

"But, the day before I had this planned, someone else had the same idea. And beat me to it," he mused for effect. "You see, some people are just quicker to the draw I guess. Read it in the local morning paper: Man Dies on Train Tracks. I mean, that's luck if I ever saw it."

And he laughed as if this were the best news ever.

And Francie felt a weird tightness in her throat that got hot and turned into tears rising. She tried to force them back but they escaped, filling her eyes as she looked at her dad's forced amusement, his brow furrowing beneath it as he saw her eyes brimming.

She quickly wiped her tears. Her mom was now back to her laptop scanning Facebook, seeming determined to not react. Was she not hearing this? Why wasn't she stopping him?

"So," he said, with renewed zeal, "I called up a friend of Mac's, Jack Reynolds, an amazing circuit speaker in AA, that little group I was telling you about, and he's taken me under his wing. Given me the indubitably crucial job of being in charge of literature at one of the biggest weekly gatherings." Again, he looked at Francie's mom, "Right, El?" and Francie realized he was trying to get her approval.

Francie's mom turned and smiled, "You're definitely on the right track."

Relief filled his eyes. "So, there you have it. I'm going to help Jack with his speaking engagements and make sure everyone is in possession of the A.A. books needed for success, and in a few weeks, I'll jump back into working on a show."

Francie had no idea what to say to any of this. "Cool," she croaked and eked out half a smile. Once again, he'd twisted everything around to be about how wonderful he was, even though it was the worst thing she'd ever heard. And she had to get out of there. Or maybe she needed to stay. She didn't even know.

She turned to her mom for help, but her mom just smiled as if this was all a good thing. "Dinner will be ready in about half an hour," her mom said. "And you can take it up to your room if you want. Daddy is probably heading over to meet with these new friends."

"Or I might just stay here tonight," he said. "And head over in the morning."

Francie saw her mom's lips tighten as she turned back to the screen. Francie just forced a smile and a really fake nervous laugh at her dad and turned and walked up to her room without saying a thing. She was sure she made him feel more awkward and worse by leaving like that. But she had no choice. She couldn't help him. At all.

She closed the door behind her and leaned against it. For the first time in her entire life, she felt absolutely nothing. Not sad. Not relief. Nothing. And her mind was blank. It was the weirdest sensation ever. She thought about her dad. No tears. It was as if suddenly a switch went off inside her and he was someone she didn't know. As if *she'd* just read an article about this man and his family and she could understand it was miserable and tragic but had no feelings. And he'd just said he'd wanted to kill himself, right? It was so twisted.

She wondered if feeling nothing was bad. Did she suddenly not care about him anymore?

She sat down and googled "alcoholic" and "alcoholism" and "AA" because she had to know what this was and knew her parents would never tell her.

She read how AA was Alcoholics Anonymous and how alcoholism was a disease of the body, mind and spirit, which she didn't get at all.

She read the list of things that were signs that someone was an alcoholic, like how they drank every night or more than a few times a week or drank at home alone or didn't think it was a problem but it was to everyone else around them or how they "blacked out," which she realized was when her dad didn't remember things that happened or that he said, or how they "passed out," which was like when her dad fell asleep early and was really hard to wake up, or how they drove drunk, which was when her dad tried to make her laugh by swerving all around the road on purpose, which never made sense because otherwise he was the best driver.

She read about how it was really helpful for alcoholics to go to meetings, which were probably those gatherings her dad was talking about, and they needed a sponsor, who was like a friend and mentor. She figured Mac's friend, that guy Jack Reynolds, must be her dad's sponsor. The one that he said was a good speaker.

And then she read about how there was a program for families of alcoholics to help them deal with it and get support. And they even had a version for teens called Alateen!

Alateen. Oh my god. Thank god.

Relief came over her. Like there was some hope. But then she went downstairs to mention Alateen to her parents and they panicked and told her it wasn't for her.

"Oh no, no need to bother with that," her dad said. "You don't need that."

"No, you're fine," her mom added, looking away as she said it.

"But they have a whole thing for families, just like what dad is doing, but for us," Francie said to her mom.

"But we're not alcoholics," her mom said, finally looking at her, fear, sadness, pain, all in her eyes. All at once. "We don't need anyone to think that."

Fear. Gripping stomach.

"No, it's for families of alcoholics," Francie said, immediately feeling embarrassed and ashamed saying the word alcoholic, as if she was making the whole thing worse.

And her dad laughed as if she had it all wrong. "We're fine. I'm fine. I'm just helping Jack with his speaking career a little and these other people that are really in trouble."

Francie knew that instant that he was an alcoholic. It was just like what she read. He was saying it wasn't him but he just bailed on his job and them and drank every night and passed out and blacked out all the time.

And she knew her parents weren't going to get that. And that she'd have to deal with this on her own. And that they were wrong about this teen thing. That it would be good for her. Because there'd be other kids like her.

Eff them!

But she knew she'd never go. Because it was too embarrassing for them. And that made her so unbelievably angry. And totally afraid. And alone.

Francie smiled and nodded at her parents as if she agreed and went back upstairs with her dinner. And in that moment, she told herself she didn't need them. Or anyone. Ever.

And that she would never be like them. She'd never ever drink alcohol at home because that would make her an alcoholic. And when she did drink, it'd only be with friends. Like when she had that sip of beer with Chet under the bridge. She remembered how good it felt. And how fun it was. And that was okay. Because it was really Chet that made her feel okay.

And she would never ever have a boyfriend or marry anyone who was an alcoholic. Because it was just totally unbearable. And then she started to cry and cried for a long time until her whole body felt like it had no more strength and she had nothing more to lose.

She looked at her laptop and opened it. She hadn't written to Chet all week but now she was going to. She didn't even know why.

Subject: Sorry I haven't written
Hey Chet,

Sorry I haven't written since we Facetimed. Thanks for checking on me. I like the new song. I also have to confess I broke down and played tennis. Even though I said I was going to ease up like you suggested. I hit on the ball machine. I just had to. My life got worse, if you can believe that, and it's the only thing that helps.

The thing that happened is that my dad disappeared for a few days. He was supposed to go to Vancouver for work but instead he went to Reno and stayed in a really expensive hotel. And just bailed on the job. And didn't tell my mom what he was doing. And my mom didn't tell me what was happening so I was super scared that he was hurt and would never come home. But then he did. And said he's an alcoholic. Which is so strange and scary that I don't even know what to do.

She thought about telling him about the train suicide thing but that was just too much. She couldn't bear the thought of writing it down where it could exist forever.

And that's all. Sorry this is all so down. Bye for now. FM

She hit send and curled into a ball on the bed.

After a few minutes, Facetime rang. It was Chet.

She put the phone long-ways on the pillow so it was like Chet was lying next to her. His face filled the screen with the dark-rimmed glasses. This time she could care less about the glasses. Or how cute he was. Or how his eyes crinkled when he smiled. She felt nothing.

"Hi," he said.

"Hi."

"I'm sorry, FM on the radio dial."

"It's okay."

"No, I hate that you feel like this."

She shrugged, and the nothing she was feeling started balling up in her chest. And expanding. Outward. Like a ball of pain. Swelling. Up into her throat. She tried to stop it.

"I wish I could make it okay," he said.

But it forced its way up, flooding her eyes and brimming over into hot tears.

"Francine," he sang. "I understand."

And she shook her head, and the tears fell like angry daggers. Angry that she couldn't control them. Or this. Or anything. Or understand what was happening to her dad. And mom.

"I do," he said.

"It's impossible," she whispered.

"No, I understand," he whispered back. "Uncle Pete's an alcoholic. Sober. And my dad. My dad drinks too much too."

And she looked up at him through her hot tears and saw it was true. And the ball of pain grew bigger, hot, searing, like it was reaching out to his pain. *No! Stop! Please, stop!* Clouding her senses, building in her chest again, flowing down her arms, weak, fingers tingling.

"And my mom hates him for it," Chet said. "She hates him for everything. Booze. Work. Drugs. Food. Success. More success than her. Saving people. Never stopping. Good. Bad. Everything. It's all too much. He even loves *her* too much. He's too much."

And their eyes met. And a ribbon of pain shot out from her heart to his and connected them. *Help.*

"Francine," he sang again. "You're going to be okay."

"I'm sorry," she said. "I'm sorry about your family."

And he smiled. And his voice got all choked up. "My mom couldn't handle it. So he left. And met someone else. Who loves him the way he is. And he's happy. Without us." And his eyes got all watery, and then, he laughed, trying to keep it light, but not quite managing: "And I blame her. For pushing him away."

And he made a weird choking sound and had to put the phone down.

And she felt terrible. And wanted to tell him it was okay. That he was going to be okay. And it was okay to hate his mom for pushing his dad away. Because Chet loved her too. And his mom was strong. And normal. And she could make it okay for all of them.

And give him strength.

But Francie was paralyzed. And he came back, sniffly but smiling. "Okay, totally embarrassing, but I got something that is going to fix everything." And he produced his guitar. "Voila! Fraaancine," he sang and strummed. "A song for youuuu."

And he propped up his phone and started to play "Wonderwall." And sang the original lyrics. Kind of over-the-top serious and cheeky. And then he started to make up his own lyrics about her for the chorus: "Aaand Fran-cie...she's limpin' away so I can't see...Her freedom now, Is all that I want for me; Aaand Fran-cie, Sweet green shoots of a Maple tree, Fighting through the Storm; For the love she wants to be. And Quicksand, her Chucks flit to my Wonderland..." And then he cracked up.

And so did she. And he was so happy about that. Like he was relieved he could make her laugh.

"How about this?" he said and grabbed the harmonica and made up a hip-hop rap about Santa Barbara. "And you and me. This Sa-tur-day. And the limp. And be-ing free. From in-san-ity. In-ten-sity. Just the limp. And mu-sic. And you and me." And then he made boom-chucka sounds and did a little dance.

And it was so silly. And funny. And in that moment, she was so happy he was there. And could make her feel better. And she felt love.

His dad is an alcoholic. Or something like it.

And her skin tingled. In a weird way. Like electricity. And magic. Like it was important. And after they hung up, she wrapped herself up in it like a blanket and closed her eyes.

He understands. Saturday Santa Barbara. Forehand hitting up hard. Spin. Up and over. Spinning fast. Down inside the line. Blasting up.

Relief.

Chet. Saturday. Escape. From here. Safe.

22

Living in a Chet fantasy and knowing she was going to be safe in Santa Barbara with him worked for some days. She texted him and thanked him for being honest about his dad and said she couldn't wait for Saturday to spend time with him. She didn't say more about his dad though. Maybe they'd talk about it in Santa Barbara. Or not. It didn't matter. What mattered was forgetting. And being together.

And then Friday afternoon came. The day before Saturday, when they were going to Santa Barbara. And Francie came home from the club. And her dad was there. And his fear took over. And he became that crazy man. That made no sense. And had crazy paranoid, worried thoughts. And made crazy plans. And tried to control her. And her mom. And everything. And became that person she hated because he had the power to control her. And he did.

"I hate you!" Francie sobbed at her dad through the bathroom door. She was crying so hard she could hardly breathe, the anger clouding her head. She punched herself in the thigh because she had to punch something because she wanted to punch him because she hated him so much and was so angry and didn't know how else to get it out. And she screamed deep inside her throat like a roar, trying to keep it in but then not caring and letting it echo through the bathroom.

"Please come out," her dad begged, as he tried the door knob for the thousandth time. "Please come out so I know you're okay. Please. I need to know you're okay."

Francie roared another scream. "Go away!" She slid down the wall to the floor, pulling her knees to her chest, squeezing them, scratching them, gouging skin, sobbing, not even knowing if her dad was still outside the door or not.

She got flashes of what just happened. Bits from all over because she couldn't think clearly, chronologically. Her memory was like a collage of anger. She heard his voice, "No, I'm sorry, I can't let you go. We don't know those kids. It's not safe for you to go to Santa Barbara."

Not safe? You're not safe!!!!!!!!!!!!!!!!!!!!!!!!!

And then she remembered what came before that, coming home from tennis, after teaching, coming in the door, her dad on the sofa staring at the TV, looking bored out of his mind, agitated.

Then, the flash of anger that rose in her as she realized her mom had told her dad about Stella and Eddie taking her to Carpinteria and Santa Barbara.

Then, she remembered how nice he was at first. Asking about tennis, like that listening and caring guy, saying, "Forget about Mallory and Abigail. I'm so proud of you."

And she believed him. Oh, why did she believe him? Why did she let him lure her in? Why? Why?! She knew better! But she did it because she wanted to. She wanted him to care.

Please see me.

And she let her shield down. And let her heart be vulnerable. And then, he turned on her. Because it was a ploy. To control her. And get her to like him. And approve of him. No matter what crazy decision he made.

And she heard it again, him saying, "I'm sorry, I can't let you go to Santa Barbara."

She tried to breathe in. Calm down. But the anger rose like fire. Higher. And higher. Sucking all the air. *Can't breathe. Can't breathe!* And then it hit a critical mass and turned.

And suddenly, it flattened into a hard stone slab of calm. And there were no more tears. And she felt her own strength build, from deep inside. Like a warrior. Peaceful strength bracing her heart. She would fight for herself. She was strong. And she was going to be okay. She was going to separate herself from her parents in her mind. And go to the show with Stella and Eddie. And protect herself because her parents didn't know how. But she did. Her connection to Chet made her safe.

She felt invincible.

She lifted her head and listened. Nothing, except the muffled sound of the news on the TV. She wondered how long she'd been sitting there. She had no idea. She got up and washed off her face, stood tall and opened the door.

Her dad was sitting on the armrest of the big reclining chair, hunched over, staring at the ground. Vulnerable. Small.

He came over and hugged her. "I'm sorry." He looked like a little boy.

She just stood there, still, not reacting. And he cried into her shoulder.

"And your mother," he sobbed, shaking. "I love your mother so much, and I didn't want this to happen. I told her it wouldn't be the same. As her father. I was protecting her. And now, I don't know how she'll ever forgive me." She saw the desperation in his eyes.

"Please, let her forgive me," he said as if Francie had the power to make it so.

Francie had no idea what to do so she just imagined her armor coming from her heart and shielding her whole body from his pain.

And then he forced a smile. "It's okay. We're going to be okay. I hope you understand about the concert. You'll have another chance to make a movie with your friends. I just wouldn't be able to face your mother if I allowed it and something happened to you."

Francie nodded, poker faced, "I'm gonna go up to my room now." And she walked past him and upstairs to her room.

She grabbed her backpack and carefully packed her pajamas and toothbrush and mascara and the outfit she'd been planning and trying on all week—her jeans and a kind of dressy, black, beaded halter top. She'd wear her other favorite jeans and a t-shirt and Chucks in the morning and then change before the show.

She shoved the backpack under her bed for now, grabbed her rackets and headed out. She'd practice on the ball machine for as long as they'd let her. She didn't care if it hurt her knee. She had to do something that felt okay. Stella would be off work by now so she wouldn't have to talk to anyone. She'd text Stella later and tell her they'd have to meet at the club in the morning instead of them picking her up at home.

Francie's dad was gone when she got back from the club but her mom was there in the kitchen looking at her laptop.

"Hey," her mom said, cheerfully. "Looks like you're back to hitting again."

Francie stayed poker faced and just went straight up to her room. She felt strangely powerful when she didn't talk to her mom. It felt safe.

She took a shower and got online. There was a lot of excitement about the show the next day. There was also a group text with Stella and Eddie, excited about going. She texted back to say she'd have to meet at the club in the morning. She'd just get up at 6:00 a.m. and ride over.

She'd leave a note for her parents about an early practice game. She honestly didn't care what they thought at this point. They were crazy, and if she didn't communicate clearly or truthfully, they'd just have to deal with it. It's not like they communicated clearly. Or truthfully!

There was a knock on her door and her mom peeked in with a guilty smile. "Your dad went to a meeting. Won't you come down for dinner?"

Francie shook her head, keeping her eyes on the screen. She could sense her mom looking at it and closed her laptop. She didn't want her mom to see the band's page. She didn't want her mom to have any connection to them at all.

"I'm sorry, honey," her mom said.

Francie ignored her. But her mom just stood there. Finally, she couldn't stand it. "I thought you weren't going to tell him till I left."

Her mom instantly looked apologetic. "He wanted to go to Palm Springs. For the weekend. Like we used to. So I had to tell him. I wanted to be honest." Like there was nothing she could do to help her daughter?!

Francie felt tears of rage inside. She used all her strength to keep them down, bracing her heart. She felt betrayed and she knew her mom would never help.

But then her mom said, "I think you should go anyway."

"What?"

"It's the right thing. I know your friends are nice and you really want to do this film thing."

Francie just stared.

"Just go, and I'll tell him I said it was okay and that it's not fair that we keep changing our minds. I'll wait to tell him until you're there and make it seem like you just went to the grandma's house or with Abigail or something."

"What if he gets angry?"

"Let him. I've got it under control."

Francie knew her mom had nothing under control but in that moment, she didn't care. Maybe for a change her mom would stand up to her dad. She would be so much better off without him. Maybe one day she'd leave him, even for a little bit. Like how Chet's mom looked out for herself and everyone when his dad drank. Or maybe her dad would stop drinking forever like she'd read about online or Uncle Pete, "sober." Maybe someone would help him, like Mac's friend Jack.

"But you'd better hurry and pack now before he comes home. And go to bed early and get out of here early so it doesn't come up."

Francie nodded at her mom, "Thank you."

And her mom hugged her and said, "I love you, Francine Mills. You are going to do what I couldn't do. Because you are so smart. And strong." She pulled back and smiled. "Because you can do anything you set your mind to. I know that about you."

And Francie felt the weight of the world on her shoulders all at once. She was her mom's everything, the one that was going to make this family okay, that was strong enough to deal with her dad, and that was completely overwhelming.

She had to escape.

23

Francie had been sitting on the front steps of the club since about 6:30 a.m. People kept walking by, and she'd say hi, like a greeter.

She tried to sneak out of her house without anyone noticing at 6:00 a.m., but her dad was up, staring at the TV like a zombie, still in his clothes from the night before. For a second, she felt his misery but then just told him she was going to the club, without trying to explain why she was in jeans, and just hurried out. It was like being Stella, getting in backstage, doing exactly what she was meant to do, with confidence.

And surprisingly, or not, it worked. Probably because he was in his own miserable world.

At 9:00 a.m. sharp, Eddie and Stella pulled up and she got in. She put her phone on airplane mode and shoved it to the bottom of her backpack. If her parents tried to reach her, she'd never know. Which was exactly what she wanted.

Some old-school song was blasting. Like, really old. Like Frank Sinatra old. And Eddie high-fived her, "Da scream queen is in da house!" *So weird.*

And the color of her world changed from black to white. And she relaxed a little.

Stella's phone rang. "It's Hughbie!" She answered Facetime and sang, "Hellooo..."

"As if it would be anyone else," Eddie teased.

"How's my girl?" Hugh said.

"Look who's here!" Stella held up the phone so Hugh could see Francie.

"Francie!" Hugh shouted, then yelled back into the motel room, "Hey, Jones Two, interview crew is onboard." He panned over to Chet, still in bed, but reading.

"FM!" Chet yelled with a big smile, "You made it!"

Her heart leapt. The blood rushed to her cheeks. She waved, and her world changed from white to neon. She stopped bracing her heart. And everything else fell away like it didn't exist. Her family vanished. Her tennis ranking disappeared. Everything that scared her. Everything that bored her and that she hated about herself. Gone. She was just right there, in that very moment. And it was going to last all day. Maybe even forever. And she was going to have fun. And be a part of something she cared about. And there was hope. And she knew she did the right thing by defying her dad. He had to be wrong because nothing that brought so much joy could be the problem. And her armor fell away.

Hugh panned back to himself. "I'm gonna text the address. Just park anywhere and come in back. We're gonna set up in a bit and do soundcheck at noon."

"Nice," said Stella.

"And!" Billy exclaimed, popping onscreen out of no-where, "KJET is cool if you film."

"Awesome," said Eddie.

"Yeah, Uncle Pete's radio interview magic," said Billy, voice super deep for effect.

"Nepotism," yelled Chet from the background.

"I say, Uncle Pete pullin' strings for Blues Harp Jones. Because he *loves* the music and we effin' rock," Billy corrected.

"Nepotism," repeated Chet.

They all laughed.

"That's at two," said Billy. "And then we can film around S.B. Cool?"

"Word," said Eddie.

"Word," replied Billy and did some gangsta hand sign and then was off again.

"And don't forget the YouTube thing!" Stella said, as Hugh's face filled the screen again.

"Podcasting music-festival YouTubers who book gigs. I'm workin' on it," said Hugh.

And Stella started air kissing at Hugh, which turned into tongue air kissing. *Gross!* Which turned into Stella's tongue actually licking the screen. Lipstick everywhere.

"Oh, c'mon, disgusting!" said Eddie.

Stella laughed and ended the call, "Ciao, Bello," and flopped back in her seat, smiling and drifting into her thoughts with that mischievous smile, clearly thinking about Hugh.

Eddie and Francie laughed, and then Eddie blasted Frank and they headed onto the 101, in the slow lane, going sixty miles per hour.

Francie grabbed Eddie's camera off the seat and zoomed in on the speedometer. "And here we are with Eddie Plumb *speeding* up the 101 at almost sixty miles per hour, a full *five* miles per hour under the speed limit, for the Blues Harp Jones show at Elliston's on State Street in Santa Barbara tonight." Francie turned the camera on Eddie. "Here he is."

Eddie grinned for the camera, "You know it, Scream Queen."

Francie's heart started to race as they pulled into the parking lot for Elliston's and got out. She could hear Stu on drums and Memphis on bass and wondered if Chet and Billy were there too. Which made her more nervous. Stella disappeared as soon as they parked and was probably making out with Hugh somewhere by the time they reached the door.

Eddie filmed as they entered, "Yo, Blues Harp Jones is in da house for soundcheck!"

Francie's fingertips went numb. Like, in a good way. Because of Chet. Like she felt so nervous and shaky. Adrenaline shaky.

She looked around the restaurant. Brick walls. Stage in back. Small tables. Still closed. And dark.

And then, she saw Chet. In the weird plaid jacket and an "American Dad" t-shirt and checked Vans this time. Smiling. At her.

And every nerve ending in her body tingled.

And he came over. And hugged her. Tight. And she broke down and sobbed without knowing why. And he hugged her tighter, and she buried her face in his chest, and he smoothed her hair. His arms felt so strong, and he told her it was going to be okay.

She heard Billy yell, "Dude! You're here." And she felt embarrassed and wiped her tears and lifted her head, just as Billy gave Eddie and the camera a bro hug. Jostling them around. And Eddie laughed, "What a reception."

And then Eddie looked over. At her and Chet. And she saw disappointment in his face.

"And here's Francine," Chet sang, "on the radio dial."

And Eddie hid the disappointment. And lifted the camera to film.

"Hey, and we're gonna be on the KJET FM radio to-day!" Chet continued and pulled Francie in cheek-to-cheek for the camera, "And here's our girl with the ador-able limp, in Santa Barbara with her biggest fan...me!"

And Eddie disappeared from Francie's mind.

Because she was so happy.

And Chet was saving her.

And making her whole.

"That's right," Chet continued. "I am her number-one fan, and I want to see what she's up to. Future U.S. Open champ, future *collage* artist extraordinaire. Yeah."

And Francie's heart expanded as Chet turned and looked at her. So close. She could feel his breath. Smokey breath. And there was the light beam again. Like when they first met. Intense. Straight to her heart.

Love. Forever.

Then Billy yelled for Eddie to follow him with the camera and put his finger to his lips, "Shhh. We're goin' on a Petee hunt. If we're quiet, we'll catch him mid-crossword."

Eddie looked at Francie before he followed Billy, for a split second. And she saw him trying to connect with her. But then he let it go.

And they all followed Billy over to Uncle Pete, sitting at a small table, intently doing the crossword. He wore horn-rimmed glasses and a stylish hat pulled low and was drinking tea, which totally clashed with his old-school casual rocker look—straight shoulder-length hair, casual t-shirt, shorts and K-Swiss sneakers. He looked up over his glasses at them, amused.

"Uncle Pete," said Billy. "What's the word on the street?"

"Five letters," said Uncle Pete. "Waves of it fill your ear and go with the word 'check' to create a noun for the task you should be doing right now."

Billy put his face up to the camera lens, "Uncle Pete is all work and no play when it comes to *sound*check," then gestured for Eddie to follow him to the kitchen. "And this is where all the love happens, filling our bellies with warmth and joy. Hey, Jones Two, front and center."

And Chet went over and played a note on his harmonica. And he and Billy launched into a barbershop duet, about a girl called Lida Rose, from *The Music Man*! But they changed the words to be about the people working there at Elliston's. It was just like on the set in Austin with the craft service lady, and it was amazing and charmed the staff. And Uncle Pete looked proud. And

Chet kept looking over at her while he sang. And she felt like she was part of it. And in love.

Then everyone clapped, and Billy and Chet bowed, and Uncle Pete boomed playfully, "Soundcheck!"

They headed to the stage, and Chet winked at Francie.

And Eddie filmed the soundcheck. And Francie sat in a chair on the side and watched.

She felt alive. Present. And full of joy.

24

Stella and Hugh finally emerged right as the band was about to leave for the KJET radio interview. Francie and Eddie were standing by the "famvan" next to Uncle Pete waiting for everyone else. Eddie seemed back to normal and was asking Uncle Pete tons of questions.

When the guys finally came out of the restaurant, Billy had his arm draped over Chet's shoulders, and he, Stu and Memphis were singing the words "good enough" over and over to a familiar but ancient tune, like from the 1950s or something, teasing Chet: "Goo-oo-ood enough, good, good, goo-ood, when Chet sings his so-ong, all he needs is goo-oo-ood enough, good, good, goo-ood..."

Chet looked at Francie and was clearly embarrassed by this whole thing and laughing, too.

"It's a thing we do," Billy explained. "Right, Jones Two?"

Chet nodded, "Yep."

"Whenever someone's worried, we put it to the Everly Brothers' *Dream* song," Billy continued. "And Chet's a little nervous about this radio interview and playing his new song, and he's worried it's not good enough, so it's goo-oo-ood enough, good, good, goo-ood."

"It's not ready," Chet said to Billy.

"Aw, c'mon, it's great," Uncle Pete said, teasing Chet. "And I'd never put you up for something I didn't know you could handle." And he grabbed Chet and knuckle-rubbed his head. "Now, get in, all of you," Uncle Pete continued. "You, too, Hughbie. Stella, Francie, Eddie, we'll see you there. You got the address, right?"

Eddie nodded.

"Excellent. In case I lose you."

The guys laughed knowingly, and they all got in their vehicles.

"Apparently, Uncle Pete drives fast," Stella said. "So, try to keep up."

"Yessir," said Eddie as he followed Uncle Pete's minivan onto the street.

Five minutes in, Uncle Pete veered into a fast food drive-thru. Eddie had do a U-turn, and then, Uncle Pete abandoned them before they got their order. Stella Facetimed Hugh and called them "bastards," to which they all laughed. It was all so impulsive. But fun.

They found the station easily and were a little early. Apparently, Uncle Pete was incredibly punctual. Which was one reason, according to Stella, that he was so incredibly successful in music. Francie knew this, but Stella filled Eddie in about how Uncle Pete had been a super successful music agent since the '90s, with huge, huge bands. And now, he manned the ship from afar but was helping Billy and Chet himself.

"Because he totally believes in them," Stella said. "Hugh says he thinks they've got a lot of talent. And Hugh does too. Which is why Uncle Pete is going to mentor him."

"Aw, Hughbie is gonna be an agent-let," Eddie teased.

Stella punched him in the arm.

"Ow!"

Stella had definitely drank the Hughbie punch.

They found Uncle Pete and the guys inside the station, waiting for the interview, eating and talking about music. They joined them, and the conversation continued.

Chet was so intense and animated. Totally into it. And in his element. And excited. And Francie loved that about him. And getting to see him with other people.

Eddie jumped right in, too, and he and Chet both knew a ton about music and were both really into movies, too. And movie scores. Super nerds.

Francie just listened. Entertained. Lost in it.

Then the conversation segued into ideas and philosophy and art and creating stuff, and it felt so real. Like they were all stepping into something bigger than themselves but that they could make their own. And Francie felt excited because it was so different from what she was used to, which was either tennis talk or her dad telling her about cool stuff but talking *at* her and repeating so much that she just tuned it out. This was like a real conversation back and forth.

And it excited her. And she wanted to jump in. She hesitated at first. Worried they'd criticize. Or make her feel dumb. Like her dad did. But this was different. Because they asked her what she thought. Chet did. And everyone listened. And they discussed. And were inspired to new ideas. And even disagreed. And no one felt bad. They were all included. And respected.

And Francie talked. And laughed. And even toyed with Chet, suggesting Eddie turn the camera back on after the interview to catch the excitement. And *nerves*. Billy and Stu sang a round of the "good enough" song, and everyone, including Chet, laughed, and he gave Francie a super flirty smile. And she did it back!

Oh my god, I'm free!

The radio interview went great, and Eddie caught the band coming out of the studio, and Francie asked them how it went. And Billy and Stu sang, "Goo-oo-ood enough, good, good, goo-ood." And Chet laughed and couldn't stop talking about how honored he was to get to be on the show and how the DJ loved his song and how cool it was to guest DJ when the real DJ went to the "head" and he played his favorite Bowie tune.

Francie watched Chet feeling connected, and she connected back, somehow feeling his joy as if it was hers.

And her world expanded. And so did her heart.

Again.

25

The rest of the afternoon was probably the best time Francie ever had.

First, they piled back into the vehicles and headed down to State Street. This time, Stella and Hugh drove Eddie's car and everyone else went with Uncle Pete so Eddie could film the band driving. Billy thought it would show "forward motion!"

Chet sat next to Francie and kept flirting, and their legs touched, and her whole body buzzed with joy.

Meanwhile, Uncle Pete talked the whole time so it was less about forward motion and more like "The Uncle Pete Show." He just kept telling tour stories. He also talked about Stu and how he was the Jones's neighbor and got the band started when they were little, banging pots, waking up Uncle Pete, who was living on their couch, thanks to Chet and Billy's mom, who was a saint and allowed his snoring ass in the living room. He also talked about meeting Chet's parents, Lily and Will, at Northwestern and how they asked him to be Chet and Billy's godfather. And how that was the most important job of his life.

Billy and Chet teased Uncle Pete about "The Snore." And Uncle Pete roared, "Well lookout, because whoever's staying tonight is gonna hear The Snore."

"Even in the next room," Chet added, and everyone cracked up knowingly.

Next, they parked and walked down State Street towards Stearns Wharf and filmed everyone being silly. Eating ice cream. Singing. Dancing. Jumping on and off planters. Billy was definitely the ring leader and had a plan.

They stopped in a hat shop and went nuts trying everything on. Chet immediately found Francie a hat. It was camel-colored felt and funny-shaped, with a wide brim and a big tall, round middle part, like a strawberry. She looked in the mirror, and the hat was cute. And hilarious. And Eddie said it looked like the "Pharrell hat," and Uncle Pete said it was '80s punk Malcolm McLaren, and Stella said it was Vivienne Westwood. And Stu looked it up on his phone and said it *was* the Pharrell hat which *was* a Vivienne Westwood buffalo or mountain hat, clearly, a knock-off. *And* McLaren wore it in a Buffalo Girls video. So everyone was right.

Then, the hat shop guy corrected them all saying it was an antique Stetson.

Then, they tried on more hats, and Eddie filmed, and it was super fun. And Uncle Pete bought everyone Stetsons that looked totally old-time urban western, and they posed a bunch and wore their hats out of the store.

Then, they walked down to the harbor and ended up renting kayaks. It was Billy's idea, "for the video!" And a total blast. Chet and Memphis weren't thrilled, but Francie was totally in her element. And Chet teased her about it, which she loved.

Francie and Chet rode in one kayak and Billy and Stu in the other. And they got in a battle and all went in while Eddie filmed and everyone else sat on the wharf and watched. Chet hugged Francie, and they wrestled in the water. And she was beyond happy.

After kayaking, Hugh hurried everyone back to the van. The podcast interview was on and they had to go. "And then we'll see you all at Elliston's," Hugh said to Eddie and Francie and then turned to Stella and kissed her. A long, long kiss.

Francie caught Chet's eye and got super embarrassed because she could imagine *him* kissing *her*. And Chet smiled, and she *knew* he felt it too. And that it was going to happen.

Finally, Uncle Pete herded the guys into the "famvan" and waved to Stella, Eddie and Francie with his ever-amused smile, and they were off.

Francie felt so happy in that moment that she almost couldn't stand it. Like her heart would explode. So much good stuff was happening. A totally new sensation. All of them honestly happy to be with each other and about the show. And it seemed like it'd continue. And was real. And mattered. And she was a part of it.

"Alright," Stella said. "I have an idea about where we can get ready."

"Nana and Papa's," said Eddie.

"Too far," said Stella with a mischievous smirk. "Something better."

Eddie looked annoyed. And wasn't looking at Francie *at all.*

"What?!" said Stella, "I thought we weren't going there till after the show."

"Look, you may end up staying up all night with Hugh, but I'm sleeping there, and I don't want to just show up in the middle of the night. I want to go and be nice and get some Nana love and tell them we may or may not be back."

Stella grumbled, "Fine, you're right. I'm a jerk." She made a stupid frowny face.

Eddie exhaled slowly under his breath, trying to stay calm. "Fine. Go. Just text me where to get you."

Stella threw herself at him and hugged him and kissed him all over his face. "The spa! Pick us up at the spa!"

Eddie shook her off. "Just text me the address." And he walked away.

Stella smirked. "He loves me. He can't help it. He's way too nice."

Francie knew Stella loved Eddie, too. She couldn't help it.

And Francie couldn't help noticing that Eddie hadn't looked at her that whole time.

26

Francie looked at herself in the spa mirror. She loved the beaded halter and felt cute. She put on her Stetson and felt really cute. She was so happy she'd gotten to take a shower and wash off that gross kayaking water. And all thanks to Stella sneaking them into this resort pool area with her I'm-so-confident-I'm-just-gonna-walk-in-here-like-I-own-it thing.

Of course, it totally worked. They waved at the pool attendant and walked right into the spa and sat in the sauna and Jacuzzi and went swimming.

And weirdly, Francie felt like she belonged in this place. Like she was important and part of something important, even though the band wasn't staying there. But if they were, they would totally own it. Like they owned wherever they went and could do anything, no matter how stupid or silly. Because they stuck together and supported the weirdness, no matter how weird. And maybe now she was a part of that.

With Stella. Who was dressed and wearing her Stetson and furiously texting Hugh.

"Okay, I'm ready," Francie beamed.

"Nice! You look awesome," Stella said. And Francie felt awesome. And Stella seemed to mean it, and Francie blushed, which was weirdly okay, too.

Then, they walked to the lobby and sat on the sofas to wait for Eddie to pick them up.

Stella kept texting and giving Francie updates, like "Apparently, the podcast went well, and they're back at the motel getting ready" and "He says we should park there and walk down to the club since they're both on State Street, and he's gonna get there early so he'll meet us."

Francie kept nodding and people watching. The resort guests kept looking at them as if they were important and trying to figure out who they were. Was it the hats? Probably. Not to mention Stella was in goth garb, looking *extremely* cool with the Stetson on top.

"Did you see all the likes that video of you and Chet is getting?" asked Stella.

"What?"

"Yeah, and the photo of you guys with the hats."

Oh my god. Francie's heart started to race. That was so exciting. But her *phone*, she hadn't looked at it since that morning. And didn't want to. What if her dad had called? And what if he did something stupid?

Her heart raced faster as she fished her phone out from the bottom of her backpack.

She hesitated to take it off airplane mode. What if her dad was freaking out? What if he was pissed and tried to come up there and get her? Or what if he was mean to her mom for helping her?

Her palms and feet were sweating.

"Cool, huh?" said Stella.

"Uh, huh," Francie lied and her heart raced as she took her phone off airplane mode. Three texts. She ignored them and went to see the videos and photos.

The video was her and Chet battling Billy and Stu in the kayak. She was laughing and Eddie was narrating and she was totally included and looked great, and her heart swelled. And Chet even wrote "FM saves the day! Against the evil Bill and Stu's Wild Ride."

And then there was the photo of her and Chet with their new hats, and they looked super cute together! And a bunch more photos of the guys and Stella too and Eddie filming them and one of her and Uncle Pete! And a gazillion comments and likes from all the band's friends.

"See," said Stella.

Francie agreed. And liked everything.

And then she looked at the texts. All from her dad: *Please call me; We need more details of where you are;* and *Francie, please give us the number of the grandparents.*

Her heart sank. She couldn't get away. And what if he got the number and called and ruined everything? She had no idea how, but she knew he was capable of it.

"What's up?" Stella asked. "Something's up."

Francie knew she couldn't hide it and told Stella about her dad wanting Stella's grandparents' number. And how he'd said no to Santa Barbara. And how she came anyway, obviously.

Stella unbelievably thought it was hilarious and brave of Francie and told her to just give her dad the number. "It's no big deal."

"Unless he does something crazy."

"Like what?"

"I don't know, call them and ask for the address and come get me or, who knows, ask *them* to drive me home. Or come to Elliston's and make a scene. Or get paranoid and call the police to check on me."

Stella agreed that was crazy. And Francie wished she'd never looked at her phone. But then Stella rallied: "He has no right to ruin our show just because he's irrational!" Which Francie knew already, and they both laughed at the thought.

Then Stella started making up a song to Madonna's "Material World." "Li-ving in an ira-tion-al world. Our parents li-ving in an ir-rational world."

Francie joined in, and they sang and danced, like, literally stood up. And people looked at them, and it was hilarious. And Francie laughed so hard she cried. And felt so much better and not afraid of her dad, for at least three minutes.

Then Stella rallied again and told Francie exactly what to do. And Francie texted her dad verbatim: *Left phone in car all day. Everyone taking showers before dinner. Will get phone number and text it later. May take a while but all is great here.*

Short. Sweet. Genius. Francie was super grateful. And Stella must've sensed it because she gave Francie a hug, which was so un-Stella but felt right, especially when their hats bonked. They were like sisters, band sisters. And

Stella understood. And they didn't have to talk about it anymore.

Then Eddie pulled up in front of the resort and Francie felt elated. They were together. And were going to the show. It was perfect. Especially because Eddie wasn't ignoring her anymore. He even smiled at her, like he was back to his normal annoying-but-nice self.

27

Eddie didn't want to walk from the motel on upper State Street so they found street parking near Elliston's in a loading zone, which, apparently, according to Stella, you can use at night. Legally. Not a commonly known fact, unless you're Stella Plumb.

Uncle Pete and the guys were getting to Elliston's right before the show since there was no backstage. But they were meeting Hugh early to film the crowd and the band's entrance.

Francie and Stella peeked in. The place was not very full, maybe twenty people, mostly their age and some grownups. Francie saw Santa Barbara Anna from The West with a group of friends.

And there was YoYoMatilda! Only now her hair was pink and purple with a pink boa to match. She looked like an Easter egg. Her whole table stood out, all neo-hipster-slash-avant-guard-glam-rock. There were the two guys with Mohawks and a more toned-down but ultra-hip girl.

And when she turned, Francie saw it was Just Jez from the band's Facebook page. The one who was in Shout! Shout!

"Hey, I think it's that girl from Shout! Shout!" Francie whispered to Stella.

"Jezebel Crane? Cool," Stella shoved her face in the door. "Yup, that's her. They drove up from Burbank. You've gotta interview her. And I've gotta tell Hugh."

"Why? What's so big about her?"

"Nothing, but we're gonna make it big and get a buzz going." Stella squeezed past Francie through the door. *Whatever.*

Francie spotted Abigail and her friend Lisa and her parents, Mac and Libby. Francie's stomach tightened, but just for a second because somehow it didn't matter anymore that Abigail was super cute and nice and smart and had amazing parents. Because Abigail was out *there*, and Francie was with Stella and Eddie and Hugh and the band. She had a purpose and felt special.

"Alright, Scream Queen, you're on," Eddie said to Francie, butting in on her bliss and handing her a mic. "Let's do our thing."

She followed Eddie in as he filmed, and they interviewed people in the audience.

Abigail and Lisa jumped up and down like cheerleaders.

"And what about you, Mr. Mitchum?" Francie asked Abigail's dad. "I heard you have Blues Harp Jones in your latest movie."

"That's right," Mac said. "They came out to Austin and were a complete joy to work with. Billy and Chet, super talented. Nice guys. And Stu and Memphis. What can I say? Rhythm machine. I'm lookin' forward to seeing it all tonight."

"Thank you, Mac Mitchum," said Francie, feeling stupid for sounding like a TV news person. Whatever. She was going with it, and it was fun.

Next, she turned to Jezebel Crane's table. "And over here we have Jezebel Crane from Shout! Shout!" Francie led Eddie over to her table. "Hi!"

Everyone at the table screamed when they saw the camera. Total hams. "We love Blues Harp Jones!" yelled YoYoMatilda, and they all screamed again.

"So, where are you all from?" Francie asked.

"The Valley!" boomed the two Mohawk guys. "Huaaaa."

Francie wanted Jezebel to say something but was too chicken to ask. Luckily, Eddie did: "And how is the gorgeous Jezebel Crane tonight?"

Jezebel's face lit up. She truly was gorgeous. And when she looked at the camera, it was like electricity. Francie wondered if this was that star-quality thing her dad talked about and if one day Jezebel Crane would be famous. Francie's dad made it sound like almost no one actually had the star thing and anyone who thought they did was fooling themselves and a loser and wasting everyone's time. But Francie knew Jezebel did. And maybe Chet, too. Though she couldn't tell about Chet because she was biased.

"I'm doing fine," Jezebel said. "Looking forward to seeing the guys perform."

Even when she spoke, there was some kind of magical, magnetic thing. Like you just wanted to watch her and listen to her. Even though she didn't say much.

Francie wanted to ask Jezebel about her voice training and songwriting, which she'd seen somewhere online, but she chickened out again. "Thank you, Jezebel Crane, from Shout! Shout!" was all she managed. *Dork!* Francie smiled and felt the blood rush to her cheeks.

Jezebel returned the smile and again that crazy light and charisma shot out of her eyes and made Francie feel like she was totally special. *Bizarre.*

Francie and Eddie continued interviewing people until Hugh got on the stage and nervously announced that the show was about to start. The audience cheered, and Francie and Eddie hurried to the parking lot just as Uncle Pete's van pulled up and the guys piled out like they were debarking a plane, waving at the camera. Chet winked at Francie, and the whole thing was pretty campy.

Eddie panned round, following the guys inside, getting their POV as they went on the dark stage and the twenty-some audience members cheered. Francie and Uncle Pete moved in behind Eddie in the doorway as the band started and the lights went up and everyone cheered again.

They listened to the first song, and Eddie handed Francie his phone. "I'm going to the back for a wide shot. You take this and get them from the dance floor."

"Me?"

"Yeah, go dance, Scream Queen." He winked and moved into the audience.

But Francie was too self-conscious to move as "Louisa, Hey" began. YoYoMatilda screamed and started dancing. And so did two other girls, and Abigail and Lisa waved for Francie to join them. And Uncle Pete pushed her out.

And there she was. In the middle of the dance floor. Like a complete idiot. Again.

Abigail tried to include her in their little dance circle. And Matilda kept ramming into her with her pogo moves. And all she could think was: *Just kill me now.*

But then, she noticed Chet. Watching her. Amused by her awkwardness.

And he started singing to her, over the top, to get her to dance, making funny eyes to lure her in. Until he did. And she finally started to dance.

And he kept singing to her. And the room. And her.

And again, she let the music course into her. And just danced. And knew the music was for her. She was in her own world, with Chet, and it was perfect.

Until Eddie came out and reminded her she was supposed to be filming, which was fine too, somehow. And she held up the phone. And danced. And watched Chet.

He called Jezebel Crane up to sing with him, and their voices together were amazing. And Francie was so happy she was out there to get close-ups, even though she'd never admit that to Eddie and laughed to herself that he was right and just kept filming.

They played new songs and covers, and Chet seemed super comfortable onstage, like he fed off the band and the crowd, even though he was so shy in person.

Then, the band left the stage, and the crowd cheered and stomped their heels on the ground, and the guys came back out and did another song. And Francie just stood on the side and watched, disappearing into her bubble of joy.

28

Francie walked alongside Stella as they all headed up State Street from Elliston's to iHop. Chet was in front of them talking to Trevor, who apparently did the band's sound board and was a family friend through Uncle Pete. He had a long, skinny beard that he braided, and he looked older, like twenty-three or something. He had a band too, in Phoenix, but was living in Ventura and thinking of moving to L.A. Chet seemed to think that was a great idea and that Trevor should come stay with them in Encino.

Behind Francie and Stella were Abigail, Lisa and Stu. Francie quickly glanced back and saw Abigail seriously flirting with Stu and vice-versa. Then, Stu hit the back brim of Francie's hat, teasing, "Hey, FM," which made her feel special, and they all laughed.

Then Stella spotted Hugh catching up to the group and stopped to wait for him, which is when Francie locked eyes with Mac, Abigail's dad. He had that look grownups get when they have something serious to say. Francie smiled and quickly turned back, hoping he'd go away.

He didn't. "Hey, how's it going, Francine?" said Mac, catching up to walk alongside her. "You look like you're having fun here."

"Yeah, totally," she said, seeing in his eyes that this was serious and had to be about her dad. Because what else serious would they have to talk about?!

"Good, good," he said. "And you know, I just wanted to say, I know your dad's been having a tough time of it, and I'm sorry if it's been difficult for you and your mom."

Oh, god.

"But I think he can do it. Jack Reynolds is a great guy so he's got a lot of support. I've got friends that've won that fight and came out all the better for it. Like Uncle Pete."

"Really?" she said, pretending she didn't already know about Uncle Pete.

He laughed, "Oh, yeah, back when we were starting out, he was a wild man. Totally fronted a punk band and had quite a drinking issue. In fact, it kind of put an end to the band."

"That's the band you were in?"

"Yup. And your old man was in the other amazing punk band in Reseda. Quite the front man, *he* was." Mac laughed. "Yeah, it took Uncle Pete a while to get it but he really needed to, fast. And he's had a lot of success since as an agent. Actually, he had a lot of success before, but honestly, I'd say if he didn't get sober, he might not've made it."

Francie's heart lurched into her throat. *Might not have made it?*

"But hey, your dad's gonna be okay. Everyone's different and has a different path."

Francie nodded and fake smiled but was terrified inside. Mac didn't live at their house and see her dad drunk every night. But he did seem to know she was worried.

"Francie?" Mac said. He was serious but his eyes were kind and so was his smile, and she knew he wasn't going to twist anything around or try to control her or tell her something crazy. And for a moment, she believed him and felt safe and like maybe it would be okay. "Okay. Thank you," she said.

He gave her a hug. "My pleasure. Now let's get dessert! Abigail? Lisa? Stu? Dessert?"

They cheered, and Mac put his arm around Abigail and kissed her head, and they all went into iHop.

Uncle Pete was already there with Eddie, and they had a huge table. Francie felt awkward. She really wanted to sit by Chet but was frozen and just standing near him. And Eddie was waving to her to come sit next to him, bizarrely. She pretended not to see.

Luckily, Chet noticed her. "FM!" he said. "Come sit with me and Trev. Trev, this is our fabulous future Wimbledon winner, Francie Mills. Francie, meet the uber-talented banjo player extraordinaire, Mr. Trevor Waits."

"Banjo?!" said Trevor.

"Excuse me, anything with strings." They cracked up, clearly an inside joke, then guy-wrestled and then Trev slid in the booth.

"After you," Chet gestured to Francie.

She scooted in, followed by Chet, and tried not to look at Eddie, hoping he'd stop staring and start talking to Santa Barbara Anna.

Chet and Trevor talked nonstop, and Francie was happy to just sit between them and listen, except when Trev snuck out a flask and poured something into his hot cocoa and asked her if she wanted some, "Jägermeister?" She said "no."

"Yeah, good call," said Chet. "That stuff is like cough medicine."

Francie got a chocolate shake, and Chet and Trevor got burgers and fries, and Chet kept asking for sips of her shake, which she loved. She ate some of his fries too, but her stomach was so nervous and way too excited to really eat.

Then Uncle Pete banged his spoon on his water glass. "Alright, I'd like to propose a toast. To Billy, Chet, Stu and Memphis for an awesome show."

Everyone cheered and toasted. And that's when Francie's phone vibrated in her bag and Chet noticed because he was right next to it and handed it to her: "Mom."

Francie's stomach tightened and her heart started racing. She didn't want to get it. But felt guilty not getting it. And Chet was watching. So she answered, "Hello?"

"Francie!" her mom said, her voice oddly cheerful.

"Mom? I can hardly hear you. We're in a restaurant."

Chet gestured for Francie to go outside. She mouthed "no," but he slid out for her anyway. "Hang on, Mom," Francie said, reluctantly. "I'm going outside so I can hear you."

"Okay, take your time," her mom said, still sounding all happy.

Chet held the door open as Francie went outside, forcing a smile as she passed. "Okay, I can hear you now," she said and waved to Chet, hoping he'd go in, but he just stood there.

"Oh, yes, much better," her mom said. "I have your dad here who wants to talk to you."

The panic set in immediately. "Okay." She turned so Chet couldn't see her face.

"He's changed his mind about you being there so everything is fine."

More panic.

"Francie?" her dad boomed. "I was wrong. And you and your mother were right." He was yelling, overly enthusiastic. And in that moment, she knew. He was drunk.

Her heart sank.

Pulling up round the right. Hard. Forehand. Spinning up. Round. Landing in. Blasting off.

"And I fully support you being at that concert," he went on, orating and slurring. "Those boys may not be The Beatles, but they can fully hold their own, and I fully endorse that and you being there. And I commend you for putting on your filmmaking cap. And I insist that you get a hotel and invite your friends and I will pay for it. And you take them out to dinner on me."

Francie couldn't move, paralyzed.

"Francie?" her mom said, taking back the phone.

"Enjoy the show!" her dad yelled from somewhere in the room.

"Honey?" her mom said.

Francie couldn't talk. Or breathe.

"Are you okay? It's good news, right?"

Francie stared at the sidewalk, trying to comprehend.

"Francie? Are you there?"

"Uh, I don't know," Francie managed. "I just, what happened? I thought he wasn't going to drink."

"No, it's fine. He just had a couple beers."

"But he's an alcoholic," Francie said, feeling a stab like a knife in her stomach as she said it. "He can't do that. I read it. It says it everywhere."

But she knew her mom would never listen. She never did. No one did. Even when Francie was right.

"He's not really an alcoholic," her mom said in a weird don't-worry voice, as if she totally believed it herself.

"Yes he is," Francie said, feeling the anger rising.

But she believes him. Always him. Never me.

"No, it's really okay," her mom continued. "He just was having a tough time, but he's going to pull it together and he's got a new show next week."

Francie held the phone away and stared at it as her mom continued. She was being pulled back into a void like a rabbit hole into a parallel universe, knowing there was nothing she could do. She couldn't fix it. Or change it. It just was.

"Now, just go have a fun time, and we'll see you tomorrow," her mom said, her voice sounding weird and distorted in Francie's mind. "Okay?"

Francie continued staring at the phone from her alternate reality.

"Are you having fun?" her mom asked.

"Yes," she said, and her voice reverberated in slow-motion sound waves into the phone.

"Okay," her mom said, and Francie heard that weird, desperate, longing pain in her mom's voice as she added, "Love you."

And Francie just hung up. And zapped back from the parallel universe. And stared at the ground, trying to process this. And then, slowly, the pain gripped her heart. And it just stayed there, seeping into her body. Paralyzing her. How was this possible?

She felt a hand on her shoulder. "You okay?" It was Chet.

"He drank again," she said and looked him straight in his gorgeous green eyes, feeling nothing. "My dad drank again."

"I'm sorry," Chet said and just wrapped his arms around her and held her so tight, and she just let him, melting into him. She wanted to cry but she couldn't, and he just let her be without saying anything. Just understanding.

And finally, she looked up. His eyes were concerned. But calm. And reassuring.

"You okay?" he asked.

"Confused."

He nodded, "Yup, that is what it is," and grimaced knowingly. "And now you get to forget about it. Because we're here and we're gonna have fun and go to the motel and play music. Francie Mills with the cute limp."

He smiled, kind of bittersweet. And she just really wanted to believe him.

"I know it may not be the sanest solution, but it sometimes works for me. To forget. Maybe it'll work for you, too."

She nodded. "Thanks."

"Anything for my FM on the radio dial."

His eyes. I can see through them to the parallel universe. The stars are there, twinkling.

Warm. Love. Wrapping around her. Arms tingling. Electrical. Joy. Safe.

He understands me.

"C'mon," he said and offered his arm and escorted her inside and back to the table. She felt her heart turning to magical goddess-warrior steel as they went.

Everybody smiled as if they couldn't tell something happened, but obviously, they could. She was so embarrassed but sucked it up, especially when Abigail rubbed her arm and gave her a sympathy look, "So sorry, I hope you're okay." Of course, Abigail was sincere, but still.

And then Stella looked at her and said nothing, which was perfect and comforting. Francie didn't look at Eddie. She couldn't, and she didn't know why. She knew he was over by Santa Barbara Anna at the next table, and she could sense that he was watching her again.

Instead, she scooted back in next to Trevor and told herself to just have fun and not think about anything else and not worry and just totally be herself. Because she could, because she was with people that totally cared about her and loved her and wanted her there just the way she was.

And she knew she had to be herself if she wanted a relationship with Chet. A real one. And she had to go for it. Whatever *it* was, and stop second-guessing herself and everyone else.

So when Trevor offered her the Jägermeister again, she said "yes."

"What?" Chet laughed. "Fine, I'll have some too." And he flagged down the waitress, and they all ordered hot chocolate and discretely poured in Jägermeister.

It tasted intense and like cough syrup, like Chet said, but was also sweet, and as it went down, it warmed Francie's throat, all the way to her stomach, then radiated through her chest and into the front of her shoulders and over her shoulders and down her arms at the same time as it went up into her head and down her back. Her entire being relaxed, and she felt giddy and free.

She drank more, and suddenly, she was funny and saying whatever without worrying, and everything was funny, especially out of Chet's super cute mouth. And her heart swelled. And whenever he made her laugh, she hugged him, and he laughed and gave her that flirty look, and it suddenly felt like they were together. And she was *really* free.

And Abigail winked knowingly and gestured with her eyes to Chet, happy for Francie, and it was like everything she ever wished for was coming together right then.

Uncle Pete and Mac had a friendly spat over who would pay the bill, and then they split it and everyone went out front and talked some more and said good-bye to the people who were leaving, like Abigail and her family, who were staying in a hotel in Montecito.

One of Santa Barbara Anna's friends snuck up and snagged Billy's hat right off his head, the one from Uncle Pete, and then skipped off.

Francie, feeling all warm and brave, took off after her, "Hey! That's his hat!"

The girl was embarrassed and returned the hat to Francie. But then Billy came over and gave the hat back to the girl, who ran off giggling with her friend.

Billy got tease-y with Francie and hit the brim of her hat. "I'll get another one, but thank you."

Francie was super embarrassed and sad that the hat didn't mean as much to Billy as it did to her, but then Billy dragged her back to the group and they walked up State Street to the band's motel and she quickly forgot it.

29

Uncle Pete had his own room and bellowed goodnight, "Be good and quiet, people; this old man needs his beauty sleep," then disappeared for the night.

Everyone else piled into Chet and Hugh's room then moved to the adjoining room where Billy, Stu and Memphis were sleeping to put space between them and Uncle Pete's room.

People were drinking beer and smoking on the balcony, and Trevor had more Jägermeister for Francie. She didn't hesitate. She was having too much fun and told herself not to worry. She'd never drink just a little and think it was nothing, like her dad. She was drinking to have fun tonight. With friends. And all inhibition left her.

Jezebel and Stu and Chet started singing and playing music and Matilda started dancing. Francie joined her and danced on one of the beds. Matilda got on the other. And they laughed and danced in sync until Francie fell off and hit her head really hard on the nightstand.

Chet ran over and looked to see if she was okay, and she felt all warm and flirty and smiled. "Well, I guess so," he said, and everyone laughed and went back to what they were doing.

And from that moment on, Chet kept smiling at her with this new intensity, flashing his gorgeous green eyes, and it made her stomach flip every time. And she knew he liked her. And she felt it too. And she felt brave. And relaxed. And didn't try to make it go away.

Hugh and Stella came over to Francie with a bowl of water and made her lie on the bed and let them drip water onto her forehead.

Weird!

"What are you doing?" Francie sat up.

They looked both serious and hilarious at the same time.

"We're giving you healing tonic," Stella said and pushed Francie back down and did a few more water drips. Then she and Hugh peered at Francie in sync and cracked up.

"You guys are meant to be," Francie said and sat back up. She couldn't lie there when this music was happening and Chet was there. She had too much energy.

"We love you," Stella yelled to Francie, and then she and Hugh started making out.

Francie got back on the bed and jumped and danced with Matilda, song after song. Jezebel and Chet sounded brilliant together. And Chet kept looking at Francie and singing to her, and there was all this electricity and tension.

She felt so happy.

Then Chet and Stu took a smoke break and Francie and Matilda drank water and did a Jägermeister shot.

Which was when Eddie came over, looking seriously annoyed. "Sorry to interrupt, dancing Scream Queen, but I think we gotta go."

"We can't go now," Francie said. "It's too fun."

"I don't want to get there too late."

"Oh, c'mon, don't be a party pooper," Francie laughed.

He didn't think it was funny.

"Let's just stay a little longer. It's so fun."

He shook his head.

"Don't be sad," she said and hugged him.

He shrugged her off. "I don't know what you're talking about, and you're drunk."

"I'm sorry," she said, looking at his furrowed brow—cloudy again, like outside that pub when they stopped for his real mom.

"Francie!" Stella yelled. "Just let the sourpuss be. C'mon."

But Francie felt sorry for Eddie. "C'mon," she said, trying to take his arm, "on the balcony, we can talk."

"Nevermind," Eddie said, angry and disappointed, and went to gather his stuff.

"Don't worry," Francie said. "It's going to be okay."

Eddie ignored her, but she knew he heard her, and she felt good for saying it. Like, surely he heard it because it was so important and true and would help him. And she felt the warmth of the Jägermeister grow in her heart, helping her truth flourish and Eddie's truth.

Like love. Like a brother. That was it! She loved him like a brother!

And then she followed Stella out onto the balcony where Chet and everyone else were mostly smoking and talking.

Francie noticed that her head was fuzzy, like it was numb, and she assumed it meant she was pretty buzzed. But it felt really good and she didn't care.

Chet smiled all flirty again and her stomach flipped. Which was when she went and stood next to him and leaned back against the wall, touching his arm and melting right into him.

Stella offered Francie one of her fancy organic cigarettes, the yellow American Spirits. This time, Francie took one. Chet teased her, and Hugh lit it for her. She coughed, and everyone laughed, and she tried again and felt a new buzz in her head and gave the cigarette back to Stella.

"Perfect," Francie said.

Stella hugged her. "I'm so glad you're here."

That's when Francie smiled at Chet and he took her hand and led her inside and to his room. And they sat on the bed and he leaned in and kissed her. His lips soft and shooting electricity into her. Gathering in her belly. Then radiating out.

And then, he smiled. And she felt it again. And they laid back on the bed and kissed more, and he put his hand on her stomach and it was like an explosion right there, with excitement beaming out. All over.

She couldn't believe this was happening. It was so surreal. She was enjoying it and watching herself at the same time.

And then the fuzziness in her head started to swirl and there was a sick feeling in her stomach that rose into her throat. And she sat bolt upright.

"You okay?" Chet asked.

No.

She shook her head and made a disoriented, wobbling beeline for the bathroom. She slammed the door shut and threw up in the sink. *Oh my god.* She felt so weak and awful. She had to lie down. She washed her mouth and stumbled out. Chet was waiting outside the door.

"You okay?" he asked again, concerned.

She nodded. "Better." And glanced at everyone looking at her, but it was blurry. "I'm gonna lie down for a second."

Stella gave Francie the thumbs up, and Chet led her back to his bed, and she grabbed the pillow and lay down on her stomach.

"Francie?" she heard Stella say and saw Stella peer over Chet's shoulder.

"I can't move," Francie slurred. "I just need to sleep."

"Is she okay?" Hugh asked, peering over, too.

"She just needs to sleep," Chet said.

"Yeah, c'mon, just leave her alone," Stella said.

Francie went to say something but decided just to rest a little before trying. Everything was spinning unless she kept her head down with her face pressed on the cool pillow, listening to the buzzsaw coming from the next room, which was weirdly comforting and gave her something to focus on. Because even with her fuzzy brain, she knew it was Uncle Pete.

30

Francie woke up to banging on a door and a booming voice outside, "Check out's at eleven. I'm going to iHop if anyone wants breakfast." It had to be Uncle Pete.

But wait, where was she? What happened? She turned and felt a body next to her. Chet! His bed. His motel room. It came back. She got sick and must've slept there all night!

She sat up. Head foggy. Throbbing. Super tired. There was someone sleeping in the other bed and someone on the floor by their feet.

"FM, you're alive," Chet mumbled without moving at all.

"Sort of."

"Omigod," said a raspy girl voice from the other bed. "Why did we stay up so late?" It had to be Matilda. There was Easter-egg hair escaping from the covers.

"I'm just gonna sleep until he kicks us out," Chet grumbled and rolled away on his side.

Francie wondered where Stella and Eddie were. She also wondered if anyone would notice if she got up to pee. She had to go so bad. But didn't want to draw attention to herself.

She got up anyway. Head throbbing more. Super thirsty. And her stomach had a twinge of that barfy sharp pain. But it seemed not enough to make her throw up again.

She stepped over the person on the floor that was Trevor. Then she saw her backpack and purse by the door. Why wasn't her backpack in Eddie's car? Her phone was still in her purse and in airplane mode. *Weird.* She couldn't remember why and was too tired to think.

She continued to the bathroom in a daze and just sat on the toilet and spaced out at the wall. She started remembering kissing Chet and that made her feel dizzy and barf-sick again.

Disgusting. Jägermeister. Why?

She couldn't even think about it and got up and washed her face and drank from the sink. It was gross but she was thirsty. Plus, she always drank from water fountains. And *that* was fine!

But she had to lie down. She went back to the bed and lay on her stomach next to Chet. Better. But drowsy. She closed her eyes and dozed off.

Again, banging on the door. "Five minutes to check out," Uncle Pete yelled from outside.

"Oh, shit!" Chet sat bolt upright. "Get up! Trevor, Francie, Matilda!" He jumped up, still half asleep, and nudged Trevor with his foot on the way to the bathroom.

Trevor groaned. Chet was wearing only boxers but didn't seem to care.

Francie forced herself to sit up and looked at Matilda doing the same. Francie's head was still foggy but the throbbing was better. Matilda must've felt the same. They laughed.

Chet came out of the bathroom still a zombie and opened the door to the other room. Billy, Stu, Memphis, Jezebel and the Mohawk guys were just waking up. "Yo," said Chet. Someone launched a pillow at him. He laughed maniacally and shut the door and went to pack.

Oh my god. Where were Stella and Eddie?! Adrenaline coursed through Francie's veins. She wasn't sure if it was excitement or fear. She felt cold. And shaky.

Chet must've noticed. "Hey, don't worry," he said. "We'll get you home. I'm pretty sure I promised Stella last night. Or this morning."

"This morning," said Matilda.

"This morning," Chet said to Francie with a smile, then to Matilda, "What the hell?"

Matilda laughed and covered her face. They must've stayed up all night!

And where was Eddie? "Where's Eddie?" Francie asked.

Matilda shrugged, and Chet somehow didn't hear.

That's when Francie remembered Eddie being pissed off at her. For not going along. She immediately felt bad. He was mad. Or disappointed. *But last night it felt so okay.* He must've left and gone to Carpinteria. Confusion.

"Seriously, just come with us," Chet assured. "We'll figure it out." And he grabbed her backpack and carried it out to the minivan.

Should she tell him Eddie was in Carpinteria? That they could drop her there? Should she call Eddie? *No.*

Francie's heart started to race. She felt so fuzzy and weird and thirsty and totally like she didn't belong there. Like an imposter. Not a musician or artist. Or friend. Or from their school.

But last night it was so okay.

But last night, Stella and Eddie were there. And now Chet seemed so different.

He's the same!

But the Jägermeister was gone. And the freedom. Freedom from her mind and all the mean judges in her head.

And she really didn't want to go home. Or with Eddie. She just wanted to stay with Chet.

"Let's do it," Chet said, coming back in. "Uncle Pete's leaving."

And everyone said good-bye, hurrying to get out the door—the band, Jezebel, Matilda, the Mohawk dudes and Trevor—and it was all going too fast, and Francie knew this super fun time was over and she had to go back. They would all see each other again, and she would be alone. In her house. In her room. With the homeless man on the couch.

The dread was all-consuming. She had to stop it, but then the sharp stabbing in her stomach started.

That's when Billy plopped her Stetson on her head and said, "Don't leave without this."

And for a split-second, it was better. Maybe she could wear the hat forever.

Chet let Francie get in first so she could sit near the window. He got in next and then Stu. The back was filled with instruments and Memphis, and Billy sat shotgun.

"So what's the deal with Huberto?" Uncle Pete asked before starting the famvan.

"He went with Jeff and those other kids from Burbank, last night," said Billy.

"And your friends?" Uncle Pete asked Francie, looking at her in the rearview mirror.

"Stella's with Hughbie," said Billy. "And I don't know about Eddie."

"So you're good to go with us?" Uncle Pete said to Francie.

She nodded and smiled, "Thank you."

"And where's your final destination?"

"The Conejo Rabbit Valley," Chet teased.

"Thousand Oaks." She elbowed him.

"Right, then," Uncle Pete said and drove off. He truly was a madman behind the wheel. Normally, Francie would have been nervous but now she didn't care. She felt so miserable about going home. At this point, even if they crashed, it'd be fine. Almost better.

The guys didn't seem fazed either. They all just put in their earbuds and zoned out.

Francie rolled her jacket into a ball like a pillow on the window and closed her eyes. She couldn't sleep and just listened to Chet singing to his playlist.

It was funny and cute, and she got to hear what he liked, which was mostly old-school stuff, but all great. And his singing sounded great too; he truly had an amazing voice.

Then this one song came on and he really went nuts, doing all the instruments with his voice too and singing about being heroes for the day.

And then Uncle Pete joined in and the guys too and they were all singing this "Heroes" song. And then Uncle Pete yelled back to Chet, "Wouldya gimme that already?!" and took the phone from Chet, and Billy plugged it in, and they started the song from the beginning and all sang along, and Francie recognized it was David Bowie by the deep voice.

And they all sang and "played" their "instruments," Stu hand drumming on his legs and all over the car and Memphis making base sounds and Billy guitar sounds and Uncle Pete alternating between guitar and tambourine, and Chet just sang. And they kept doing it over and over, building more energy each time, dancing, and Francie felt the pure joy of it, like it was going to lift her out of her seat as the rhythm filled her whole being.

It kept going until they started up the giant hill between Camarillo and Newbury Park and the song ended for the millionth time. Stu started in on the drums again, but Uncle Pete stopped it. "So, where to, Miss FM?" he asked.

Francie's heart sank immediately. Both Uncle Pete and Chet noticed.

"FM, that's not a good look," said Uncle Pete, concerned. "What's up?"

Chet immediately started singing their feel-better tune: "Pair-air-air-air-rents, pair, pair parents," and Billy and Stu joined in, "Every time she's...," and waited for Chet again...

"Bumming on her parents," Chet sang.

"Pair-air-air-air-rents..." And they all continued singing as Francie just laughed.

"Did it help?" asked Billy.

"Yes, thank you." Francie instantly blushed and felt the knot in her stomach squeeze tighter. She had to look out the window because she thought she might cry.

"Come with us," Chet whispered. "Go home later."

"What?" Billy said, surprised.

Francie looked at Chet's smile. Warm. Comforting. *He means it.* And she just loved him so much. And maybe he felt the same. Maybe this was actually going to be something.

"Yeah?" Uncle Pete said. "You want to come with us to Encino for a while?"

Yes. It was all she wanted.

"How's she gonna get back?" Billy asked.

"We'll figure it out," Uncle Pete assured him with a "let it go" look. Billy flopped back.

Francie had no idea how she'd get home either but she didn't care. They were so inviting. Like a traveling band of gypsies. A family. That included her.

"Uh, yeah, sure," Francie managed. "Thank you."

"Of course," said Chet, and he gently elbowed her. Playful. Flirting.

Saved.

And Stu started up his "drums" again.

"Okay, but something else," said Billy, annoyed. "It's getting old."

But then, they all got back into it and sang the Bowie "Heroes" song at least five more times, at least all the way to Calabasas, and Francie even sang along and Chet loved that, and then Uncle Pete turned it off and they all put their ear buds in and rode quietly down the 101 Freeway, getting off at White Oak in Encino and going south towards Ventura Boulevard.

"Do we need anything?" asked Uncle Pete. "I'm gonna take a shower and do some work and make us an early dinner and then head out."

No one really responded except Billy with a slight shake of the head.

"Good, cuz I've got fresh Cornish hens waiting," said Uncle Pete. "Cornish hens suit you, Miss FM? Cuz if so, we're all set. I got those puppies thawing since yesterday."

"Uh, sure?" she laughed. "I don't think I've ever had a Cornish hen."

"Uncle Pete was a royal Parisian chef in another life," said Billy.

"You can't go wrong with Uncle Pete's cooking," said Stu.

"Cornish hens it is," Uncle Pete said jovially and accelerated across Ventura Boulevard into the hills of Encino and up to the Jones house.

It was a ranch-style suburban home, with a lawn and a tree out front, just like all the others. The guys piled out and unloaded the instruments, and Francie felt super awkward with nothing to do and pretended she was checking out the place, looking around, but was really just watching Chet, trying to come up with something to do or say but constantly thinking it was too stupid. Stu set up his drum kit in the carport then went inside and lay down on the couch and turned on the TV. The other guys brought their stuff in.

Francie just stood in the entry. "This okay?" Chet asked her. She nodded but had no idea what he meant or what she was supposed to do. "Help yourself in the kitchen and watch whatever you want," he continued. "There's Python in the DVD. I'll be back."

Back from where? "Okay," she said, feeling totally unsure and insecure.

Chet smiled and disappeared down the hall and into a bedroom.

This was so awkward, but she didn't want to leave. She wanted to hang out with Chet. And maybe that's what he wanted too. But why didn't he invite her into his room?

She didn't know and looked at Stu. He was falling asleep on the couch but made room for her, and she sat down and turned on Monty Python.

31

Francie woke to Uncle Pete singing a Puccini opera in the kitchen. Stu was out cold and so was Chet, in the chair, and she was sleeping on the couch armrest in a puddle of drool. She quickly wiped it off.

"Morning! Just in time for dinner!" Uncle Pete boomed. "Grab the menus and help me set the table. Then we'll wake the guys. You were all out cold."

Uncle Pete nodded to the printer in the living room, and Francie went over and pulled out five menus. The restaurant was "Uncle Pete's." At the top was "Tonight's Special." And below, meal choices.

"I usually order for everyone," he joked.

She read on. Tonight, they were having "Gwen's Cornish Hen Delight," "Stu's Potatoes Au Gratin," "Al's Saucy Asparagus" and "Francie's Ice Cream Framboise."

"What?" she laughed.

"That's right, you got your own dish here now. And it's a sweet one."

Wow! This was so fun! Every dish had a person, like "Chet's Fettuccini Alfredo" and "Billy's Halibut Crepes." And everything was really gourmet.

Francie beamed. She couldn't help it. Uncle Pete laughed. "We need you around more often, FM."

Francie set the table, and the guys came over, and Chet sat next to her and kissed her cheek and played footsie with her. And she played footsie back. And could feel his breath on her face. Warm. Sweet. And she remembered him kissing her the night before. And blushed. And was sure everyone saw. And was embarrassed and happy at the same time.

And they all started eating and talking about Uncle Pete's bands touring Europe, and he told funny stories. And Chet kept touching her leg. And they laughed at Uncle Pete's adventures.

And Francie was so happy to be part of something.

Special.

That seemed like it could go on forever.

Through time.

But then, the meal ended, the amazing food eaten, and everyone started checking phones, spacing out. And time slowed. Because the moment was over. And Francie knew they were all about to leave the table.

Please don't go.

But they did.

Chet looked at his watch. "Shoot, I gotta make a call." And kissed her cheek. "Be right back." And ran off back down the hall.

And Uncle Pete groaned, "I gotta go too," like he really didn't want to. Like he wanted to stay and take a nap or do the "Dead Parrot" sketch or something.

And then it got extremely awkward when Stu got up and she was just there with Billy and Uncle Pete and caught Billy making a face at Uncle Pete while gesturing to her.

"So, what's your plan?" Billy said to her, smiling and with a bit of strain in his voice.

Francie immediately got flustered, and Uncle Pete saw it. "Whatever it is, first she's gonna do my dishes," he said. "Right?"

"Yeah, yes, of course," she said and got up to clear the table. Billy helped too, whistling along, and so did Uncle Pete, until all the dishes were in the kitchen and the leftovers put away.

"Alright, you good here?" Uncle Pete asked.

"Yeah, I got it," Francie said, finishing up the rest of the dishes.

"Awesome," Uncle Pete said. "I hope to see you soon." He did a funny little bow and hurried out, yelling to Chet. "I'm leaving, guys. Come out and say goodbye, will ya?"

Chet ran out, grinning at Francie, and he and Billy grabbed Uncle Pete's bags and headed out to say goodbye at the van. Stu came out of the bathroom and followed them outside.

"I'm out," she heard Stu yell, "See ya manyana," and saw him walk off up the sidewalk. He must still be their neighbor.

Francie finished the last dish and wiped the counter and then stood there totally not knowing what to do. She looked at her stuff. Eventually she'd have to turn on her phone. But she wanted to spend more time with Chet. He really seemed to want her there. Maybe she was just paranoid and Billy was just being weird.

She edged her way to the front door to peek and see what they were doing. She heard Uncle Pete's van start up and screech off. She heard Chet and Billy laughing in front of the door.

"Oh my god," Chet said.

"Too funny," said Billy.

"Yep. And that's why we love 'im."

"So what's with...?" Billy said, suddenly lowering his voice to a whisper. "Is this a thing now? Cuz I thought you were into what's her name. Violet."

Francie froze. Were they talking about her? And *Violet*?!

"I dunno, yeah, she's hot, I like her," Chet said. "She gets it."

"Well, then you better figure something out. Cuz we're going to Fitzi's. And Violet's gonna be there. And she's not gonna *get it* if FM's there. Or want to help us. So what the hell're you gonna do?"

Francie caught her breath. It was her for sure.

"Oh, right, Fitzi's. Well, uh...V's not that into me anymore anyway, so we're good."

"Of course she's into you. She's just serious. And doesn't put up with your poetic bullshit ass that can't follow through. Or think it through. Or show up!"

"I show up."

"Because I make you!"

"Like dad?"

"Fuck you."

"Fine, we'll stay *here*. Relax," Chet said.

"It's your friggin' song! You have to be there."

"Then *she'll* stay here."

"When mom comes home?! I am not letting you hurt mom! With her just sitting here looking 'hot' because you didn't think it through. Again!"

"How is this hurting mom?!"

"I don't know!" Billy's voice cracked with frustration. "I just want to finish the fucking song. And not think about mom. Or Violet. Or how you're a complete moron about this. You're like, you can't even think about anyone else. Unless they're in your face!"

"You mean like Dad? Like, are you talking about Dad here? Cuz if you are, you need to just call it."

Silence. And then she heard a bang against the door, like a punch or a kick.

"I'm sorry," Chet said. "I shouldn't have said that. I'm an idiot. You're right."

"I just want to do the song. Okay? You and me. That's it."

"Fine. What do you want me to do?"

"I don't know, get her a Lyft?"

"You're an asshole," Chet said.

And then, without thinking, Francie just burst out the door. "Hey, guys, sorry to interrupt, but I'm gonna have to get going pretty soon." And she put on the biggest fake smile ever. Inside her heart was hurting almost more than it did for her dad. But she was channeling Stella and it was gonna work.

Chet smiled, and she couldn't believe this was happening. She couldn't believe she was this stupid. She actually believed he loved her. And wanted to be with her. And would go out of his way to be with her. And that they could be together. And that she could be part of his world.

But he can't. Not now.

"Oh, cool, right, you okay?" Chet asked.

Genuine. Concern. *I see it on his face!*

"Yeah, yeah, I called my mom, and she's gonna pick me up in like a half hour."

"Oh, perfect," Chet said, looking honestly relieved. "Did she say anything about your dad? I mean, I told Billy, I hope that's okay."

Billy smiled.

"Yeah, totally," Francie said, knowing he hadn't mentioned it to Billy at all, which hurt even more. "Yeah, I mean, not really, she said he was okay, which you know, means nothing. But at least, she can come and not him." She fake laughed. "In fact, I need to call her back and give her the address."

Francie bolted inside and grabbed her phone, "I'm just gonna take this outside and call where I won't bother you, if that's okay."

"Sure, yeah, no problem," Chet said, moving out of the door for her to pass, looking confused by her sudden change in behavior. "The address is right there on the curb," he yelled as she walked into the quiet street in front of the house where they couldn't hear her or her phone.

She took her phone off airplane mode. A bunch of texts came in and two calls. All from her dad except one text and photo from Stella from that morning asking how she was and saying they'd be home later and asking how she was getting home.

Francie felt like she was going to cry and felt the panic coming on. She was completely overwhelmed by all the messages from her dad even though she wasn't reading them or listening. She knew there was no solution. None. At all. She was completely alone in this. Her stomach gripped tighter and tighter, and her heart raced. Her throat was closing, and she was having a hard time getting air.

She deleted the texts from her dad and then the calls. She was going to channel Stella again. Which helped for like two seconds and then the relief vanished.

She had to do something else. Her mom was working. She'd gotten another film costume job that she was super excited about and that her dad hated. It meant a twelve-hour day. There was no way she could get Francie. And it was north of L.A. so there was no way for Francie to get there either.

Francie took a deep breath. She'd have to try her dad. Maybe, maybe, she'd get lucky, and her mom would be right and it was just a couple beers yesterday. She dialed.

Her dad answered, "Hello?! Is this Francine?"

She knew he was drunk immediately. "Yeah," she said and looked up and saw Chet and Billy watching her. She gave them a thumb up and turned so they couldn't see her face.

"I love you and am watching *CSI*," he slurred. "Excellent series."

"Okay, Dad, you can tell me when I come home. Bye." She hung up without letting him speak. It didn't matter.

He wouldn't remember and if she let him say anything, he wouldn't stop. She took a deep breath and smiled and walked back to the front porch.

"Okay," Francie said with as much fake cheer as she muster could. "She's coming."

"Awesome," said Chet.

"But she wants to meet me down on Ventura 'cuz she's in a rush."

"Oh, bummer. And the van's gone."

"No, it's fine. If I go now, I can get there easy. It's, what, like, a ten-minute walk?"

"With the limp, maybe fifteen," Chet said, playfully and with his most charming smile.

She felt the tears coming, "Exactly." She forced another smile, "Okay," and walked in and got her stuff. "Thank you guys. This was so awesome. And I'm sure, we'll get the video to you soon." Her voice cracked. She hoped they didn't notice.

Chet gave her a really big hug, and the tears welled. "Thanks," she said. "You're a really good friend."

"You too, FM," he said, smiling, seeing her tears. "It's all gonna be okay for you, remember that. And keep writing."

She couldn't even speak because otherwise she would cry more. At least Chet thought it was about her dad. She nodded and started to go.

"Don't forget this," said Billy, putting her Stetson on her head, smiling charmingly. "And you better come see us in two weeks, right here in The Valley."

She forced a smile, glanced at Chet one more time and just left. They definitely saw her crying, but there was nothing she could do, so she just kept walking and crying and crying.

Finally, at some point, she looked up and found herself at Ventura Boulevard. With no idea what to do and all cried out. She sat on a brick planter wall outside some office building. And stared at the ground and then watched people and cars go by.

Then she saw Chet and Billy walking down the street on the other side, chit-chatting and laughing. Like normal. Happy. Like she didn't exist. She turned away and hoped they wouldn't see her.

Finally, she peeked back and they'd turned onto Ventura, heading the other direction. Again, that awful gripping in her stomach, and she felt so alone. More alone than ever before in her life. If that was possible.

And she hated herself and felt like her life was over. And she had no idea how she was going to get home. It was getting late. She grabbed her phone and started to search for a bus schedule but her brain was like cotton from so much crying that she couldn't focus.

She looked at Stella's text and the photo she'd sent. It was her and Hugh being silly. And it made Francie laugh. Stella was so weird. Francie texted: *You are so weird.*

Five seconds later, Stella texted back: *Where are you? How's Chet?*

Francie couldn't reply and went back to the bus schedule. Facetime rang: Stella. Francie didn't want to but felt so desperate that she answered.

"Hey, FM," Stella yelled. "You're still wearing your hat!"

Francie just started crying.

"Omigod, what's happening?"

Francie tried to talk but couldn't.

"Okay, take a breath, please."

Francie did her best to calm down.

"Where are you?" Stella asked.

"Ventura Boulevard," she managed.

"Where are the guys?"

"They went to some music thing," Francie said, sniffling and catching her breath.

"So you're there alone?!"

Francie nodded.

"So, what are you doing? Why aren't you home? Why are you crying?"

Francie tried to keep a straight face but then burst into tears, "He doesn't love me." And covered her face with her hand so Stella wouldn't see her.

"Okay, okay, you're going to be okay," Stella said. "We're gonna come get you."

"No, I'll take the bus," Francie cried.

"You can't take the bus! It's L.A.! Eddie?!" she yelled back into the room.

"No, please. I'm too embarrassed."

"I don't care!" Stella yelled. "You're gonna text me the address and someone is coming!"

32

Francie stared out the passenger window at the rolling hills as they headed up the 101 Freeway. Eddie hadn't said much at all since he picked her up, just "Hi" when she got in, and then it was totally awkward when their eyes met for a split second. And she said "Hi" back and knew he was totally pissed off, and she turned to the window and said, "Thank you," barely audibly and with utter humiliation, and then tried to sit as still as possible.

Eddie pulled out and just listened to the stupid hip-hop song he was blasting, totally ignoring her, and she could practically feel the anger coming off him. And felt terrible.

They kept going onto the freeway, and the further they drove, the more angry he seemed. And then he started adjusting the air vent and got totally frustrated and swore at it.

Francie glanced over quickly and then back out the window.

He yelled at the back of her head, "Fine! Yeah. Okay. I'm totally pissed. Okay?!"

And she looked back at him for a split second and then away, which seemed to make it worse.

"Yeah. Because of Jägermeister. I am pissed because of Jägermeister! And you! I mean, really? Jägermeister? Until you barf? Because of some stupid guy?!"

Then she heard him say "Idiot" under his breath. And knew he meant Chet.

She felt the stabbing in her heart. And pressed her knees against the passenger door. Because she knew she still loved Chet.

Then Eddie said, "I'm sorry," to the back of her head again, like he was still angry but felt stupid and didn't want to hurt her. "I guess I got worried. Because I left you there. And shouldn't have."

And suddenly, out of nowhere, anger rose inside her. *Worried?!* That she was having the best time ever? And was happy and free? And *he* wanted to take that away?!!! "You don't have to worry about me!" she exploded.

And he looked over with his super-kind eyes. And she saw his heart sink. From her anger.

She turned away. And her anger squeezed her heart. Why? Why did he have to worry about *her*?! Like her mom. And make her feel like she was carrying a mountain. That was squashing her. And she couldn't breathe. And wanted to get out. And away. Why?!

Please help me.

She tried to focus. To remember. *He came and got you anyway. In spite of the mountain. And he let go. He knew how to let go! Last night he let go. He didn't squeeze you.*

Choke you. He let it be. He told you how he felt. How he was angry. And he didn't turn into a ball of pain.

Pain, pain, go away, come again...*never!* And she fought it. Because she knew Eddie had hope.

And she turned to him and said, "I'm sorry. You're right." And forced a smile, even though it was nearly impossible to make her face go that way and it made her feel sick. Because she really wanted him to believe her. And feel better. And somehow it worked.

He nodded, like he kind of accepted it, even though she saw him squeeze the steering wheel for a second. But only a second. And then he exhaled. And it seemed okay.

She exhaled too. And smiled again. And this time it was easier. "So, did we get anything good?" she asked.

He brightened and said, "We did!"

She immediately felt tears coming but pushed them back down.

And he softened and started to tell her about the awesome video they got, like the dancing at Elliston's and that whole song with Jezebel Crane, with her incredible voice. And the duet in the kitchen. And the radio station. And then he said, "Great call there, Scream Queen." And in that moment, she knew things were back to normal. And she was grateful that he didn't hold a grudge long. And that he was sweet. And kind. And a good friend.

And as he went on, she looked out the window at the hills going by and thought about the night before. And the thing Eddie was worried about. The thing that set her free. Even if it was just for a moment. The drinking and the jumping on the bed and the music and Chet. And being her. That girl that was free. And home.

Home. I was home.

The house was dark when they pulled up. "You got the key?" Eddie asked.

"Yup," she said, smiling and knowing her dad was in there "sleeping," even though Eddie thought no one was there.

"Cool, well, come over. We'll do the video," he said. "Even though you keep saying you don't want to."

"Sounds great. And thanks," she said, sincerely. And looked at him. And there were all these feelings filling the space between them still. And it felt weird. So she turned to go, grabbing the car door handle to open it.

"Hey," he said.

She stopped, still gripping the door handle.

"I'm sorry about before, if that was harsh. I'm sure you know what you're doing. And it's none of my business." He looked totally uncomfortable. But still kind. And sincere.

And she was so grateful for him in that moment. And the mountain vanished.

And there he was.

Solid.

She could see him clear as day.

Not going away.

And she knew it meant something. But she didn't know what.

She nodded and got out. And went up to the house.

He waited for her to go in and smiled as they waved good-bye. She wondered if he had any clue about her dad.

Like she had about his mom. *Maybe.* Or maybe he just tried to block it all out. In that way, she was more like him than Chet.

But that was too much to think about now, and she went in.

33

The TV was on and her dad was sprawled out on the couch asleep, mouth open and snoring. There were half-eaten nachos and empty plates and beer bottles all over the coffee table. His shirt front was covered in salsa. And his fly was open. The homeless man was back on the couch.

Francie just walked past. She put her stuff in her room and stared at her bed and her desk. Everything was the same. But she wasn't. She was sad, and she couldn't bear it. And she couldn't be there so she went into her dad's study and just sat in his chair and stared.

Then she looked at his vinyl collection and wondered if he had the David Bowie album. The one with "Heroes" on it. She was sure he had something of David Bowie's because she'd recognized the voice.

The vinyl was perfectly alphabetized by artist, and sure enough, there was David Bowie with an album called

Heroes. It had the song "Heroes," and she realized she'd seen this cover before. Maybe she'd even heard it.

She flipped up the lid of the old-school stereo and put the record on. Her dad must've shown her how to use it because she remembered, like riding a bike. She put the needle on and started from the beginning, looking at the album sleeve as she listened.

She didn't like the first song or the second, but then "Heroes" came on, and it was amazing. And gave her the chills.

She looked through more of her dad's collection and found *Hunky Dory*, another David Bowie album. And suddenly, somehow, tears started to well up. She didn't know why. But then she played it and knew all the songs. And remembered dancing with her dad to that song "Kooks," about the weird family.

She went on his computer to the "Francie" file, and there it was, a video titled "Kooks." She clicked play, and there was her dad dancing with her. She was about four years old and so happy. And so was her dad. And she remembered loving him so much, and then she thought of him lying downstairs drunk. And suddenly, she understood how she could feel so sad about him being like that.

It was because she used to love him so much. When he wasn't like that. When she was like three. And four. And five. Like, she loved him beyond anything. And then, something happened and either she became aware of it or he just disappeared. Like he used to be there and loved her and then he wasn't.

She came back to the music. It was still there. It was the only thing still there. And still loved by everyone. And it connected them all.

Power. Love. In me.

Chills.

And she and her dad and Chet and all the people she spent the day with were connected by it. By the music. It was special to them all.

Francie shut the video and her dad's computer and took the album off and went to her bedroom. She sat down at her laptop and thought about writing Chet. No, that was over. At least for now.

Instead, she grabbed her old diary that she hadn't written in for years and opened to some blank page halfway to the end. She hated writing in this diary because she didn't see the point. Her dad had convinced her to start it when she was fourteen. It was good to write stuff down, he said. But it only lasted for two seconds. She knew her own thoughts and was never going to let anyone else read them, so there was no purpose. It was just her thoughts existing in two places: her mind and the book.

But today, it was better than writing Chet and she had to connect with something, even if it was herself and her thoughts alone, in two places. But she had to get them out so she knew they were real. She needed to see the words outside of her head.

Dear weird diary that I hate to write in,

I may hate you but I'm glad you're here listening to me. Here's my thought:

Sometimes you meet someone and they just touch your poetic memory. That's a thing I read in this book they made a movie out of that my parents wouldn't let me watch that they watched called The Unbearable Lightness of Being. So I snuck the book and it had lots of sex in it, which is, I'm sure, why they wouldn't let me read it. But the thing I remember most was this poetic memory thing cuz it was something that just sounded so amazing. And it's just that. Sometimes you meet someone. And they look at you and it's a thing. Like somewhere inside you that is touched. Like your soul. That poetic memory thing. And it's like you were always connected. You've always known each other. Now. And before. And forever in the future. And it's like you were always traveling together through the galaxy and different universes. And then sometimes it's like you hang out with that person and then you don't. They've gone away. But you know they're there. And your souls are connected always without time. And you love that person. And they love you. And sometimes they just make you happy for a minute. And then they're gone. In this now. This life. But just that knowing of the connection makes you know everything will be okay.

Chet touched my poetic memory. A few weeks ago when I met him now.

Maybe my dad did too. I saw it in my eyes when I was four. And how happy we both were. He's sad now. But maybe if I know our souls are connected, I will feel better.

Francie shut the diary. Yeah, that was weird. And kind of pathetic. And that's why she didn't write stuff down usually. She grabbed Uncle Pete's menu out of her back-pack and folded it carefully and put it in the diary and threw the diary on the bookshelf. She put her Stetson on top of that.

Then, she grabbed her phone and texted Ricky to see if he wanted to play the next day. Or the day after that or any time in the coming week. She was going to get back on schedule and focus on tennis again and had to line up as many games as possible. She could do this. She had to. It was the only way she would ever be happy. It was the only way her family would be okay.

She thought about Stella and Eddie. She wondered if her soul was connected to them too. *Maybe.* But it was different. Not crazy. Just kind of real. And not going away, like her dad or Chet. It didn't make her feel nearly as safe or deeply comforted but it made her feel calm. Like she had roots. And was herself. And okay.

She grabbed her phone and texted Eddie: *Hey. Thanks again for the ride. And everything. Am psyched about the video. When can I come over to help? What do you think about the Bowie song Heroes? Maybe we can use it in the video.*

She hit send. That felt good. And easy. And she felt a little bit of hope.

ACKNOWLEDGEMENTS

Many, many thanks to:

The fabulous Noelle English, my friend and editor, whose encouragement and brilliant insight forced me to go deeper and bring to the page the heart and soul of the relationships in this story. Without her editing skills, they may have remained hidden beneath the surface.

The friends and *Yes And-ers* who listened to my writing babble and threw pivotal lightning bolts that got me to take the leap to write an actual book: James Potts, Monica Johnson, Sean Casey (and that one-off Westside Comedy creative support day), Zvezdana Popovic, in lightning-bolt order.

Screenwriter Al Brenner for encouragement and teaching me the craft of storytelling. Author Joanne Rocklin for helping me find my voice in her writing class.

Illustrator and designer Annie DiFiore for her intuition and gorgeous work.

Everyone at Earnest Parc Press, especially Jacqui Worthing for believing in this book and taking a chance on it. The awesome creative team: copywriter Kate Mazur, graphic/cover designer and marketing whiz Max Friedlander, photographers Matt Block, Holly Nakamura.

Elaine Chu, Inessa Manevich, Kate Mazur, Sarah Samuel, Jenny Shutak, Solveig Singleton, Iris Tate for enthusiastically reading the manuscript, cheering it on and giving indispensable notes.

LHMS for patience while I was glued to my laptop and my mom, Elli, for her kind heart and believing in me with unwavering support.

A few gems of inspiration in my junior tiara of life experience: Kathy Nolan, friend, rock, ally, able to leap past tall bouncers in a single bound and get in everywhere. T.O. Racquet Club and friends, especially Dee, Jess, Tom. Sopot music festival, with Polish cowboy hats and the band from Sarajevo, Plavi Orkestar, with their funny plane song. Ian Copeland's homespun gourmet menu. That movie job in Austin.

Nicole Schubert is a first-time novelist and award-winning screenwriter with a soft spot for comedy and romance. She also dabbles in other behind-the-scenes activities, like producing *Improv Diary Show* at Santa Monica's Westside Comedy Theater. She produced a music awards TV show and European-wide photo exhibition out of Brussels and enjoyed another side of storytelling working in the editing rooms of numerous Hollywood feature films. Nicole lives with her family—including The Kid and pirate cat Biddy—in Los Angeles, by way of Brussels and New Orleans, where she was born during a hurricane. Visit her online at **nicoleschubertwrites.com**.